W9-CVA-319

DIAMOND wasn't always a star. Born to penniless parents who longed for a strong, healthy son, she was a dainty, delicate daughter – and a bitter disappointment.

Discovering an extraordinary gift for acrobatics, Diamond tries to use her talent to earn a few pennies, but brings shame on her family. Then a cruel-eyed stranger spots her performing, and makes a deal with her father. Diamond is sold for five guineas, and is taken, alone and frightened, to become an acrobat at Tanglefield's Travelling Circus.

The crowds adore Diamond, but life behind the red velvet curtains is far from glamorous. Her master is wicked and greedy, forcing Diamond to attempt ever more daring and dangerous tricks. But there are friends to be found at the circus, too: gentle Mister Marvel; kindly Madame Adeline; and Emerald Star, Tanglefield's brand-new ringmaster, and Diamond's heroine.

When life at the circus becomes too dangerous to bear any longer, what will the future hold for Diamond? And will her beloved Emerald be a part of it?

www.**randomhousechildrens**.co.uk

ALSO AVAILABLE BY JACQUELINE WILSON

Join the Jacqueline Wilson fan club at
www.jacquelinewilson.co.uk

Jacqueline Wilson

From the world of Hetty Feather

DIAMOND

ILLUSTRATED BY
NICK SHARRATT

A new
star,
a new
story

CORGI YEARLING

DIAMOND
A CORGI YEARLING BOOK 978 0 440 87195 8

First published in Great Britain by Doubleday,
an imprint of Random House Children's Publishers UK
A Random House Group Company

Doubleday edition published 2013
This edition published 2014

1 3 5 7 9 10 8 6 4 2

Text copyright © Jacqueline Wilson, 2013
Illustrations copyright © Nick Sharratt, 2013

The right of Jacqueline Wilson to be identified as the author
of this work has been asserted in accordance with the
Copyright, Designs and Patents Act 1988.

All rights reserved. No part of this publication may be reproduced,
stored in a retrieval system, or transmitted in any form or by any means,
electronic, mechanical, photocopying, recording or otherwise,
without the prior permission of the publishers.

Penguin Random House is committed to a sustainable future for
our business, our readers and our planet. This book is made from
Forest Stewardship Council® certified paper.

MIX
Paper from
responsible sources
FSC® C018179

Printed and bound in Great Britain by Clays Ltd, Elcograf S.p.A.

Set in New Century Schoolbook

Random House Children's Publishers UK,
61–63 Uxbridge Road, London W5 5SA

www.randomhousechildrens.co.uk
www.totallyrandombooks.co.uk
www.randomhouse.co.uk

Addresses for companies within The Random House Group Limited
can be found at: www.randomhouse.co.uk/offices.htm

THE RANDOM HOUSE GROUP Limited Reg. No. 954009

A CIP catalogue record for this book is available from the British Library.

In memory of Joan Beswick,
who was like a second mother to me

My name is Diamond. I used to be called Ellen-Jane Potts, but my dear friend Hetty says it doesn't matter a jot if you change your name. *She* has changed her name three times. She calls herself Emerald Star for all the shows – and now she has fashioned herself an emerald-green riding jacket and has shiny swashbuckling boots to stride about in. Oh, she looks such a picture! No wonder she has 'Star' for a name: she is the true star of the show. She is the cleverest girl in all the world.

1

She is smiling now as I say this, going as red as her hair. She is writing down my story for me. I am a fool when it comes to printing and spelling because I have never been to school. Hetty has laboured hard teaching me, but without any real success. I can only write about a *c-a-t* sitting on a *m-a-t*, and so my life-story would be very limited without Hetty's help.

There *was* a cat that lived in Willoughby Buildings, along with us and all the other families – a big black creature of the night called Mouser. I don't know about mice, but he certainly dined well on rats, of which there were plenty. Mouser was the only creature in Willoughby who went to sleep with a full stomach. Sometimes we were so hungry we almost considered dining on rats ourselves.

But that was in the bad old days. Shall I get started on them? No, Hetty says I should simply tell it straight. She forgets that I am a bendy girl, so I can walk bent over like a crab and turn a back flic-flac on command! But I shall try to do my best to please her, because she is my dearest friend in all the world – and she is holding the pen.

I was born in 1883, the fifth child of my mother, Lizzie Potts, and my father, Samuel. I was the second girl, and I'm afraid I was a bitter disappointment to my parents. I have a feeling my mother had been brought up to be a bad girl. Whenever we complained about our own lot, she would not speak of her childhood but shook her head at us and said, 'You don't know you're born.' This always struck me as a little odd, because of course I knew I'd been born, and my mother – and doubtless several of my siblings – had been a witness to the fact. Not my pa though. He always made himself scarce at such times.

He stayed out all night while Ma was labouring, and sometimes the next night as well. He'd be down at the King's Arms, celebrating the new baby – or drowning his sorrows, whichever way you want to look at it. Not that he needed an excuse to go to those establishments, or any other public house, for that matter. He was famous for his love of the drink – which is strange considering he was a patterer by profession and specialized in selling religious tracts and homilies against the demon drink.

You don't know what a patterer is, Hetty? There! You don't know everything, for all your wonderful education. A patterer is like a pedlar, but he doesn't sell toys and gimcracks, he sells cards and pamphlets and papers. He wanders from village to village, setting up in the middle of the street on market days and crying out his wares. I reckon you'd be good at that job, Hetty, seeing as you can come out with all the spiel and sweet-talk whenever you fancy.

My pa specialized in little gelatine cards with gilt

edges – ever so pretty, decorated with bluebirds and rosebuds and little angels. He bought them penny plain, and Ma coloured in the drawings: blue for the birds, red for the roses, pink for the cheeks and gold for the hair – dab dab dab, and there was another one done. It's easy enough. Mary-Martha and I learned to do thirty an hour or thereabouts – you could say we were dab hands at it!

As a single man, Pa had travelled up and down England calling out his wares. *'Take the Lord Jesus into your heart and lead your life accordingly,'* he'd bellow. *'Don't forget the Sabbath. Bow your head in worship'* – though Pa himself spent Sunday lying in his lodging house till dinner time before crawling out of bed with a sore head, because even in those days, before all the troubles, he haunted all the alehouses and gin palaces his tracts warned against.

One Sunday he met up with my mother. She'd been staying overnight in the same lodging house and I don't doubt she had a sore head too. I always thought of Ma as old because she had such a careworn face and her tiny body was all skin and bone, but Pa said she was a beautiful, fresh young girl when he met her, with cheeks as rosy as the cherubs on his tracts, and long fair hair curling to her waist.

Perhaps Pa would never have had the nerve to approach her if she'd been dressed up in all her finery, because he was a plain man with a great red nose like Punch, and he was a good fifteen years older than Ma to boot. But she was sitting hunched in a corner in her nightgown and shawl, weeping bitterly because some young man had treated her badly.

Pa took pity on her, and it wasn't long before she'd buried that fine head of hair in his shoulder. He patted her back with awkward tenderness. 'There now, my girl. Old Sam will look after you and see you're all right,' he said, or something to that effect – and he was as good as his word at first.

They made an odd couple, but Pa said they were as happy as two little lambs frisking in the meadow. That was his pet name for Ma. 'Where's my little lamb?' he called when he came back from his pattering travels, and Ma would go flying into his arms.

They rented their own little home: just two rooms in a big converted house, but Ma kept them spotlessly clean and stuck Pa's tracts on one wall like a mosaic picture, making it look ever so pretty. She read the tracts each day too, pointing along with one finger and muttering aloud because she struggled with her reading like me.

'Repent and praise the Lord,' she said – and she did just that. Every Sunday she went along to the church at the end of the road and stood self-consciously at the back, not sure where to go or what to do, worried that the good churchgoers would point at her and the vicar cast her out – but instead they welcomed her eagerly. They gave her a hymn book, and as she had a good ear and a light, tuneful voice, she could soon praise the Lord for all she was worth.

She begged Pa to go with her to church, but he always shook his head.

'It's not for me, little lamb. I don't take the old tracts too serious, I just sells them to put food in our bellies. Beats me why you should want to run out on a Sunday morning, my one free day, when you could stay warm and cosy in bed with me – but if that's what you want to do, I'll not stop you. I just want you to be happy.'

That's what he said to her, and that's what she told us, over and over.

'He might not be the church-going type, but he's a dear good Christian-minded man all the same. He's always treated me so sweet and tender,' Ma said, eyes brimming.

It was true enough. Pa worshipped our ma. He worried dreadfully when she started growing big with her first baby. She was very sick every morning, often fainting dead away whenever she tried to sweep the floor or throw coals on the fire. Pa did his best to help her. He got up extra early and set the stew simmering for the day. He lit the fire to keep Ma warm and tucked her up in a blanket on the sofa.

He still went out drinking on a Saturday night, but no matter how he was feeling he hauled himself out of bed on Sunday morning to help her along the road to church. He wouldn't go in himself, but he waited and waited for her outside in the cold until the sermon was over so he could help her back home.

Ma was so little they were expecting a difficult birth. I think she laboured long and hard. I don't know, I wasn't there. Pa wasn't there either. The moment Ma started screaming he left her with the midwife and scurried away out of earshot, straight to the alehouse. He said he couldn't bear to hear her suffering. He drank himself insensible, and then wouldn't come home till morning, sure he'd find himself a widower – but when he eventually crawled back, sobbing and cursing, he found Ma in bed, still breathing, with a big blond baby boy bawling his head off in her arms.

'He's my little miracle,' said Ma. 'Oh, Sam, we're a true family at last.'

I think Pa would have been happier if they'd stayed just the two of them. He was never cut out to be a family man. But now he knew that Ma had survived the birth, he was proud to call himself the father of a fine son. He went out again that very night in celebration. Ma tried hard not to mind. She held her baby tight and murmured all the good words from the tracts as if they were magical spells to keep her precious boy on the straight and narrow.

She called him Matthew, after the first book of the Holy Gospels. A year later, little Mark was born, and two years after that, baby Luke. Ma was fair worn out coping with all three of them, and Pa was hard pressed to earn enough to keep them all fed and happy. He had to leave Ma on her own with the boys while he travelled the length and breadth of the country – and find new gimcracks to sell when folk lost interest in his tracts.

He was at a great goose fair in a northern city when he spotted some plaster fairings on a Lucky Chance stall. They were the usual sort of fancy figures: twin dogs with long ears to sit on either side of a mantel clock, or comical little husbands and wives getting into bed, or shepherdesses with woolly lambs. It was one of these that caught Pa's eye. He wondered whether to try and win one for his little lamb at home – but then he spied an angel with wings and a very holy expression.

This gave him a whole new idea. He spoke to the stallholder about suppliers, bought a rubber angel mould and ordered in a sack of plaster of Paris when he got back home. Our house became like one of his own tracts: *And lo, a host of angels descended in a holy throng*. The mould was in labour night and day, producing angel after angel. There were disasters at first. The wings snapped off – or, even worse, the heads – but Pa soon mastered the knack of easing out a perfect white angel every time.

Then it was Ma's job to paint them. She varied the colours of the wings and robes, and gave the angels dark hair to contrast splendidly with their gold paint haloes.

Pa couldn't cram more than twenty newspaper-wrapped angels into his bag at any one time, but he charged a shilling per figure and made a good profit out of them. He'd stand in the street and sing a hymn to get everyone's attention. *Hark the Herald Angels* was his favourite, and he sang it all year round, even though it was a Christmas carol. Then he'd shout out, 'Come and buy my beautiful angels. See them and marvel! Change your luck for ever. Stand one of these holy beauties on your mantelpiece and it'll watch over you and your loved ones, guarding you from all troubles, great or small.'

Folk couldn't resist them, and Pa's pockets clinked with coins at the end of each day. His patter now was so convincing, even Ma believed it, and had a flock of five angels lined up along her own mantel, one for each member of the family: Ma, Pa, Matthew, Mark and Luke. She had another white plaster angel in reserve, ready to be painted for little John, for she was going to have another baby and couldn't wait to have a complete quartet of Gospel children.

She took it for granted that her baby would be another fine blond boy. She was bewildered when she gave birth to a dark little girl. When Pa recovered from his celebrations, he declared himself tickled pink to have a daughter for a change. 'Dark, like me! Let's hope she hasn't inherited my features as well as my colouring, poor little mite!'

Ma called the baby girl Mary-Martha, the holiest female names she could think of. She was a docile baby and a sweet little girl, but sadly, as predicted, she took after Pa, even developing her own unfortunate beak nose.

Ma was a while recovering after Mary-Martha's birth, and the midwife warned her she shouldn't risk another child, but Ma took no notice. She loved Mary-Martha but still hankered after a little John. She lost two babies before their time and cried bitterly for weeks.

'What did I tell you?' said the midwife – but Ma wouldn't be told. She started all over again, and this time cried with happiness when she knew she was carrying another child. She thumbed her way through all Pa's tracts to select quotes from the Gospel of St John, highlighting them all with expensive gold paint, and then stuck them up above her bed. She asked Pa to fashion a little shelf there too, and stood the first of all the plaster angels on it, to flap his wings protectively above her all night long, keeping her little John safe.

She laboured for two whole days when her time came. The midwife was sure she would not survive the birth. But at long last the baby appeared – a small scrap of a child to have caused so much pain. It wasn't the longed-for John. It was me.

Poor Ma. She didn't want a daughter. She already had Mary-Martha. She took one look at me and turned her face to the wall. She nursed me every few hours but showed no other interest in me whatsoever. She couldn't even be bothered to give me a name.

So Pa chose Ellen-Jane, after his mother and Ma's. Both these grandmothers were already dead.

'And I shouldn't think this poor puny mite's long for this world either,' he said.

I stayed poor, I stayed puny – but I thrived.

My brothers had holy names, and they were indeed holy terrors. They tormented me royally. Matthew, the eldest, wasn't quite so bad. He would snatch and strike a blow if I ever had anything he wanted, but if I fell, he'd always pick me up and run around with me until I stopped crying.

Mark was the sneaky one, the master of sly pinches and whispered insults. Luke was the whinger, always complaining, bursting into tears if he couldn't get his own way. Pa clouted them all on a regular basis whenever he was home, but it didn't make a blind bit of difference to their behaviour.

Mary-Martha was a good child – almost *too* good. I'd cram a stolen fingerful of sugar into my mouth or blotch one of the tracts and tear it into scraps, but Mary-Martha would say, 'Ma and Pa might not know, but the *angels* do!'

I started to be terribly aware of all those plaster angels staring at me, their painted mouths 'o's of shock and horror. Once when I was very little, I tipped them all over, even the special one above Ma's side of the bed.

Ma was speechless when she saw, her mouth working but no sound coming out. She went to bed and cried because she thought it such terrible bad luck. Pa didn't care about luck – he was simply angry that so many of the angels had got chipped, losing their noses and fingers and wing-tips.

'Which of you little varmints did it?' he bellowed.

We all stared at him, trembling.

'Right then, you shall *all* suffer, even the baby,' he said, reaching for the cane in the corner of the room.

'Don't, Pa! It wasn't me! It was the baby what did it all!' Mark cried.

Pa shook his head, unwilling to believe I could be so bad. I wasn't yet five at this time and looked a deal younger.

'It wasn't you, was it, Ellen-Jane?' he asked.

He probably expected me to lie, and then he would have pretended to believe me, because he wasn't really a cruel father, not *then*. But those angels were crowding in on me, ready to tip *me* over, straight down to Hell. I didn't dare tell a lie, not in front of all of them.

'Yes, it was me, Pa,' I said.

Pa always declared he was a man of his word, so he seized his cane and beat me on my bottom. He did it lightly, but I screamed my head off.

'That'll learn you,' he said breathlessly – but all it did was teach me to fear the wrath of those angels, and to hate my telltale brother Mark.

The angels seemed determined to punish poor Ma, even though *I* was to blame. She was still hoping for a little John, though the midwife said this was madness. Ma wouldn't give up hope, though as the years passed, there were no more babies.

Pa was mightily relieved. He feared for Ma's life – and he was also finding it hard to cope with filling seven empty bellies every day. Folk within fifty miles had no more interest in his tracts and his plaster angels, and he hated to travel further afield now because Ma was in such a fragile state. She'd grown paper-pale and very thin, and drifted around our home in her nightgown like a little ghost. Her beautiful blonde hair grew thin and limp, straggling unbrushed down her back. She could barely attend to us, and the boys weren't much help about the house, but Mary-Martha tied a big apron round her waist and became a second little mother to all of us.

I was still the baby, and acted accordingly, because it meant that sometimes Ma held me close or nursed me on her knee. She had no real interest in me. She adored her three harem-scarem boys and she needed Mary-Martha. She used me like a doll, cuddling me when her arms felt unbearably empty.

Pa favoured me though. I was little and lithe like Ma, my nose was small and snub, and my hair was fair and soon grew long. When Pa was in a good mood from the drink, he'd dance me round and round till we were both dizzy. He'd call me his very little Lizzie, making a song of it. Sometimes he brought me trinkets when he came back from his travels – a blue ribbon for my hair, a set of Indian baby bangles for my tiny wrist. I don't know how poor Mary-Martha must have felt. Pa never brought *her* bright baubles.

I tried to tie my ribbon in her hair, but it would never stay in her straggly brown locks and my bangles wouldn't fit over her fat little fists.

'It's all right, Baby. I don't mind one bit,' she said cheerily – but once or twice I came upon her peering anxiously into our cracked looking glass, sighing at herself.

Ma sighed too, seldom able to shrug off her melancholy. Pa brought home a pile of fairytale books, mainly bound in leather, and set Ma to colouring in the pictures. It was intricate work painting the gossamer wings of the fairies, the coils of the serpent, the alarming genie half in and half out of his bottle. It was far harder to keep the paint within the fine lines. The boys were too impatient and Mary-Martha and I not yet skilled enough, but Pa knew Ma had a careful, steady hand. If she tried hard and did her best, he could sell the volumes at twice the price.

Sometimes she managed perfectly – but then she would start daydreaming and went over the lines. She painted a picture of a fairytale christening superbly, putting in an extraordinary amount of detail, mixing her paint so cleverly that the child looked almost real, his soft pearly flesh carefully contrasted with the shaded folds of his christening robe.

'That's my girl, Lizzie! My, it's a little masterpiece,' said Pa. 'I don't think we'll sell that book. We'll cut out that colour plate and pin it to the wall.'

Ma smiled weakly, but she seemed troubled by the picture even so. She looked at it every day, the tip of her finger stroking the fairy baby, but then she realized that her hopes of another son were vain, and she seized the pot of black paint and obliterated the whole glowing picture in five frantic strokes of her paintbrush.

'What's wrong with you, Lizzie?' Pa cried in despair. 'Why hanker after yet another child when you have three fine sons and two dear daughters? Compared with many other women, you are so blessed! And you have your own snug little house and a husband who thinks the world of you. Why aren't we good enough for you?'

'You *are* good enough. You are too good to me, Sam. But I cannot help it. I am so frightened of losing you. If only I could have my little John, then I would feel that the angels were smiling at me and I would be in Heaven on Earth,' Ma wept.

Mary-Martha and I cried too, because we hated to see her so unhappy, but the boys were restless and embarrassed by all her tears, and reared away from her like frightened ponies when she tried to embrace them.

'Ma's mad, Pa,' said Matthew bluntly. 'All this weeping and moaning! She's sick in the head. Why can't she be like other mothers?'

Pa whacked him hard about the head. 'Don't you dare talk about your poor mother in such a way! How dare you call her mad! She's simply *sad*, boy. Don't you see the difference?'

Ma didn't have any real women friends because she'd always kept herself to herself, but she'd been close to the midwife. Pa invited the woman round to

17

see if she could talk some sense into her. But Ma cried worse than ever when she saw the midwife with her white apron and her big black bag. It reminded her so painfully that she didn't have the fourth baby boy she longed for. The midwife spoke to her softly, and then ferreted in her bag and brought out a little checked-cloth bag containing crushed seeds and herbs. It looked like the lavender 'tea' Mary-Martha and I made for our dolls, but it did not smell anywhere near as sweet.

'Try my herbal tisane. It will lift your spirits, dearie – and you never know, it might just do the trick, though I shouldn't be encouraging you to have another child. You're in no fit condition.' The midwife looked at Pa. 'That will be five shillings, please.'

'Five *shillings* for a bag of tea?' he said. 'Are you mad, woman?'

'*I'm* not the one who's mad, but if you don't want to help your poor wife, then I'll save it for those who are more grateful,' she replied, snatching her bundle back.

Ma groaned – and Pa hesitated. 'Can't she have half the herbs for half the price?' he asked.

'She must take them all for them to have any effect,' said the midwife. She dropped the bundle back into her bag.

Ma did not groan again, but she sank down, her chin on her chest, her face hidden by her long hair.

'All right, all right, I'll find you your five shillings,' said Pa, sighing heavily.

It took him two days to sell enough tracts and angels to gather the money together. Then we had to endure two whole weeks of turnip stew and stale bread – but Ma got her herbal tisane and swallowed a cupful at every meal time. It was so bitter it made her shudder, but she gulped it down eagerly all the same. It acted just like a magic potion. She dressed with care, she braided her hair and pinned it into place, she joked with the boys and she taught Mary-Martha and me to sew. I was too small to do more than stitch fancy purses in bright wools, but Mary-Martha had nimble fingers and Ma taught her how to make nightcaps for Pa to sell to old-fashioned folk. Plenty of pedlars sold caps, plain or lace, but Ma stitched a tiny angel on each of ours to watch over the sleeper at night, and these proved very popular.

Soon she was sewing other clothes too: very tiny gowns, with lace and embroidery.

'That's beautiful, Lizzie dear, but I'll have to charge dearly for all the fancy work and my customers are never going to fork out a fortune,' said Pa.

'These aren't for sale,' said Ma. A radiant smile lit up her face. 'These are for our baby.'

Perhaps it was the herbal tisane, perhaps it was all those prayers to the angels, perhaps it was sheer chance – but Ma was going to have the child she longed for.

Pa was terrified she might lose the baby before her time, but she stayed strong and fit, and her stomach swelled until there was hardly room for me to climb on her lap.

I patted her big belly and pretended to talk to the baby inside.

'That's right, Ellen-Jane, say hello to little John,' said Ma, laughing. 'My sixth child, and my most blessed.'

Most sixth children in poor families like ours have to put up with cut-down nightgowns and old shawls, and sleep in drawers padded with an old pillow. But Ma prepared for the new baby as if he were a little princeling. She sewed his elaborate layette, and spent a mint of money getting an old woodcarver to make a special rocking crib.

Pa sighed at the sight of it. 'The baby will grow out of it in six months, Lizzie!'

'Don't you think it's beautiful though, Sam? Look at the shine on the wood! And the way the hearts have been carved. It's a work of art!'

'It's fine enough, but it's madness. What else are you going to order for him? A silver dish and spoon? A gold chamber pot?' said Pa. 'Do you think I'm made of money? Do you want your other children to starve?'

Ma bit her lip and looked as if she would crumple. She stroked the wooden crib, her hand trembling. 'I'm sorry,' she murmured. 'Perhaps . . . perhaps the wood-carver will take it back?'

'Oh, come now, you can keep your little crib. I can see how much you like it,' said Pa. 'Just don't go in for any further nonsense.'

'Oh, I won't, Sam, I promise! Thank you, thank you! You're the dearest, kindest husband in all the world. You're so understanding. It's just I'm so happy to be having my little John at last,' said Ma, tenderly rocking the cradle as if the baby were already lying there.

Pa took a deep breath. 'Lizzie, what if the baby is another girl? You won't be too disappointed?'

Ma stared at Pa as if he'd said something truly ridiculous. 'Of course it won't be a girl!' she said, with utter conviction. 'I *know* I'm having a boy.'

'Let us hope you are right,' said Pa fervently, and he glanced at all the angels, plain and painted, as if he were praying to them too.

Ma stayed strong and lively throughout her term. She kept the house immaculate, singing as she dusted and swept. She made sure she had a tasty stew bubbling on the stove every day, and made us children special jammy bread for our tea, smearing each slice with our initials in plum preserve. For once Mary-Martha and I did better than the boys, for M-M and E-J meant we had twice as much jam.

I knew that Ma had a baby in her tummy, of course, but I had no idea how it got *out*. I believe I had a notion that Ma might open some secret door in her stomach and let the baby out when it was big enough. I did not know that having a baby *hurt*, though I'd heard that Ma had been increasingly ill when she gave birth to each of us.

When she started her pains, I was terribly frightened. I had experienced bad stomach aches myself when we'd bought cheap meat on the turn from the butcher's – but I could see by the way Ma was groaning, doubled-up, that this was far worse.

Pa seemed terrified. He ran for the midwife and then went off in a flurry, his hands over his ears to block out the moans. Matthew, Mark and Luke were frightened too, and went off to swing from the lamp-post, their current favourite game.

Mary-Martha made bread and cheese for lunch, but the boys had all disappeared from the street, playing further afield.

'Boys are useless,' I said. 'I don't know why Ma wants another one.'

I secretly wanted to run away too, because it was so dreadful having to listen to Ma upstairs, but it didn't seem right to abandon her. Mary-Martha busied herself running for hot water and clean linen at the midwife's request. She was allowed into the bedroom with Ma and the midwife.

I couldn't help being glad that I was shut outside.

The midwife was a fierce-looking woman with a great pointed nose and chin, very much like the picture of a wicked witch in a fairy story. Her tisane *was* like a magic potion after all. I was very wary of her – and now that she was moaning like a wounded animal, I was scared of Ma too.

I stayed hunched up downstairs under the baleful eyes of the angels. I could not read, but I looked at the brightly coloured tracts on the walls and tried to take courage from them. My hands kept fidgeting, so I found a length of string and tried to play cat's cradle by myself, but I ended up knotting my hands together, and when I needed to go to the privy I had to call out for Mary-Martha to help me.

'Really, Ellen-Jane!' she said, clipping me free with Ma's big scissors. 'Why do you have to be such a baby? You must try to be a big girl like me now Ma's having a baby.'

'Why is it taking so *long*?' I asked, shivering at the sound of Ma's groans up above us.

'You took two *days* to get born,' said Mary-Martha. 'Now hurry up and use the privy. Then you must go to the alehouse and buy a pint of beer.' She pressed a few coins into my hand and gave me the tankard from the dresser.

'For Ma?' I said.

'No, silly. For the midwife. She says she needs a bit

of sustenance – and I know she means drink.' Mary-Martha tutted primly and quoted one of the tracts in a whisper: *'Beware the demon drink!'*

'I don't want to go to the alehouse. It smells funny and I don't like the men there,' I said.

'Don't be silly,' said Mary-Martha. 'One of those men will be our pa. Now *go*.'

'*You* go. You're bigger than me.'

'I have to stay and help Ma.'

I hesitated, wondering which would be worse. Then Ma groaned again, and I decided I'd sooner trail to the King's Arms than go upstairs to my poor mother.

I went to the privy and then set off, clutching the halfpennies so tightly that they embedded themselves in my palms. It was the first time I'd even been out in the street by myself. I wasn't used to going anywhere without Ma or Mary-Martha holding my hand. It felt so strange I very nearly started crying.

I ran along the gutter, one foot on the pavement so that I stumped along lopsided. I imagined being lame like Limpy Dan with his wooden leg who lived nearby. I was scared of Limpy Dan too. He disliked all children and brandished his crutch if you got near. I looked around hopefully for my brothers, but there was no sign of them.

I waited a full five minutes outside the King's Head, trying to pluck up courage to go in. The King himself grinned down at me from his sign, his face very red and leering under his crown. It looked as if he'd supped a barrel of ale himself. I didn't know why he hung there. I might not have been to school, but every child in England knew we didn't *have* a king, just a very old queen.

An old woman came hobbling up the road in broken boots, clutching her own tankard to her chest. She frowned at me. 'What are you doing hanging around outside?' she said sternly. 'This is no place for a little girl.'

'Please, missus, I've come for a pint of ale for the midwife,' I gabbled.

'Well, in you go then,' she said gruffly, and gave me an impatient push.

I staggered through the open door into the dark ale-house. The smell made my nose wrinkle. It was so dark inside I could barely see, but I was horribly aware of the men – their bleary eyes in the dim gaslight, teeth gleaming as they quaffed their beer, big red noses shining in the powerful heat. And there was the biggest, reddest, shiniest nose of all right in front of me!

'Ellen-Jane!' he said, banging his pint pot down on the table top.

'Hello, Pa,' I whispered.

'Saints alive, is it born? Is your ma all right? Tell me, child – don't just stand there dithering.'

'She's not finished yet, Pa. She's still groaning,' I said.

'Oh my Lord,' said Pa miserably, and gulped his beer. 'Then why are you here? I thought you'd been sent to tell me the good news.'

'No, Mary-Martha sent me to get a pint of ale for the midwife,' I told him.

'She sent a little tot like you?'

'I have the pennies safe, see . . .' I showed Pa my clenched hand. 'And I won't spill a drop on the way back, I promise.'

'My, did you all hear that?' Pa roared. 'This baby scarcely out of long dresses is trotting around the town running messages, God bless her. See my little maid? Isn't she a darling? The dead spit of her mother – who is right now giving birth to my sixth child. Raise your glasses and drink to my baby!'

Folk didn't seem sure whether he meant me or his coming child, but they raised their glasses all the same. Pa downed his beer in great gulps, seemingly incredibly thirsty, though he'd already been drinking there for hours. He scrabbled his fingers in my hot palm and seized the coppers.

'And another one, if you please,' he said, reeling over to the barmaid at the counter.

She poured him a full pint, and he raised it to his lips.

'No, Pa! That's for the midwife,' I said, thinking he'd simply made a mistake.

Pa bent down until his head was next to mine. His huge nose seemed to grow even larger, like a vast parrot's beak. I was sure he was going to peck me with it any second.

'Now listen here, Ellen-Jane. I'm not letting you take any ale back to that midwife. She needs to be stone-cold sober. I love your dear mother more than life itself. I'm not having some drunken old biddy in charge of her. The very idea! I don't want to come home and find your ma in hysterics and the midwife passed out on the floor!'

The only one who seemed in danger of passing out was Pa himself, but I knew better than to argue with him in his present state.

'Do you understand?' he said, poking me in the chest.

'Yes, Pa,' I said hurriedly.

'That's my baby.' Pa subsided back onto a chair. He drank deeply again, and then wiped his wet mouth with the back of his hand. 'The spitting image of your mother, that's what you are, Ellen-Jane,' he said, suddenly jovial again. He lifted me up so that I found myself standing on the table, my white kid shoes in a puddle of spilled beer.

I was very fond of those shoes. Ma had found them at the bottom of a basket in a rag shop and had wrangled to buy them for tuppence. She'd intended them for Mary-Martha, but the shoes were made for rich folk with fine, dainty feet. Mary-Martha could barely squash her toes in. So *I* got the new shoes, though I had to stuff each with a handkerchief because they were still too long. I didn't care. My new shoes looked beautiful even so. But now brown beer was seeping upwards and staining the kid.

'Set me down, please, Pa,' I said, standing on one foot like a stork.

'No, no, I want to show you off, my little maid. My, you're the very spit of your poor ma, even down to your long hair.' He ran his fingers through my curls like a comb, fluffing it up. 'See my little baby wife!' he shouted, so loud that all the other men stopped sipping and spitting and stared at me.

'She's like a fairy girl,' said one. 'Will you grant me a wish, little lass?'

'Yes, grant me a wish too, little fairy,' said another.

I'd never been told any fairy stories and I couldn't read them for myself, but I'd seen Ma painting the illustrations.

'I can't grant you any wishes. I haven't got a magic wand with a star on the end,' I said.

I was being serious, but the men guffawed with laughter. Pa roared so much, he nearly spilled his precious beer.

'She's a card, my little lass. No fairy wand indeed!'

'You could do us a fairy dance though,' said another old man.

'Yes, give them a dance, Baby. You're forever skipping about the house, so dainty. Give them a little dance!'

I tried to clamber down, but Pa held me firm.

'No, no, stay on your little stage where we can all see you,' he said.

'I want to whisper, Pa,' I said, clutching his head. 'I *can't* dance, Pa,' I hissed into his large ear. 'I don't know how, not really.'

'Well, do us a turn then! All these gentlemen want to see you perform. Go on, and I'm sure one of them will give you a penny.'

'Go on! Go on, go on, go on!' they chorused, though the barmaid tried to hush them.

'Leave the little maid alone!' She turned to me. 'I should run off home to your mother, dearie.'

But I couldn't run with Pa holding me fast, and I was scared of returning with an empty tankard. Mary-Martha would be cross with me. She might hit me over the head – and if she happened to be wearing her sewing thimble, this hurt a great deal.

So I stayed. I started to sing them a song, because there wasn't much else I could do standing so precariously in a pool of beer, but Pa wrinkled his nose as soon as I'd lisped the first line of *Praise My Soul, the King of Heaven*.

'No, we want none of that holy stuff. This isn't a preaching house!' he said. 'Sing another song!'

I didn't *know* any songs that weren't holy. Ma was the only one who sang in our house. I couldn't sing, I couldn't dance, so I did the only trick I could think of. I arched my back and lowered myself right over until my hands touched the ground and I was bent over backwards like a crab. Then I took the weight on my hands and stood upside down, hoping the ends of my long hair wouldn't dangle in the spilled beer.

There was an astonished silence. I hoped they weren't too shocked. I'd tried to tuck my skirts between my knees so I wouldn't show off my drawers. I started trembling, scared that Pa would think I was being immodest. Ma had always shouted at me when she caught me doing handstands. Mary-Martha had been very prim with me too, though Matthew, Mark and Luke had always egged me on and begged me to teach them how to do it.

I didn't know how to teach them. No one had taught me. I was just born like that. As soon as I'd learned to stagger about on my feet when I was one, I was forever rolling and tumbling. In a couple of years I could stand steady on my hands for a minute or more.

Nowadays I could stand on my hands just as easily

as on my feet, but when one of the men saw me trembling, he cried, 'Set her the right way up, for pity's sake, or she'll tumble. Look, she's shaking! She's about to fall!'

Pa seized hold of me and whisked me upright again. The men were all staring at me, jaws gaping. Then they started clapping and cheering with gusto.

Pa poked me. 'Give them a bow then!'

So I bowed, and bobbed them a curtsy for good measure. This made them laugh and clap more. Even the barmaid clapped and told me I was a little wonder.

'She should be a circus girl with a talent like that!' she said.

She really did say it, Hetty. And I was such a silly fool that I took it as a great compliment. I turned cartwheels around the room, till Pa grew impatient and the men went back to their beer.

'Settle down now, Baby. No more pretty little turns. That's enough now,' he told me.

But he still didn't let me go. He held me tight while another hour or two ticked by. I had not learned to tell the time properly, but I watched the large grandfather clock in the alehouse with alarm even so, knowing it was getting later and later.

Pa was watching it too, all the while drinking steadily. He'd long run out of money for his own beer, but the men in the alehouse treated him to wet the new baby's head.

'Will it be here yet, do you think?' Pa asked me, ridiculously, because how would I know? 'And your ma – she will be all right, won't she?'

'Yes, Pa,' I said, because I was too small and foolish to know otherwise. I wasn't really bothering about poor Ma, though I certainly hoped she'd stopped groaning. I was more worried about the witchy midwife, deprived of her pint of ale – and Mary-Martha and that thimble.

'You'd think one of those pesky boys would have come running to tell me the good news,' said Pa. 'Useless lummocks, the lot of them. Beats me why your ma was so desperate to have another.'

Here was something I was sure I understood. 'She wants to have a John to have her full set of Holy Gospels, Pa,' I said brightly.

'Oh, don't you start that madness too. Why my Lizzie had to get all holy in the head is still a puzzle to me, especially when I think of where she came from and what she was a-doing of then,' said Pa.

I didn't know what he was talking about – I still don't – but I stroked Pa's coarse shirtsleeve in silent sympathy. When I saw the tears gathering in his eyes and rolling down his ruddy cheeks, I tried to dab them away with my sleeve.

I was bewildered by his quick changes of mood and uncertain how to cope. I was feeling miserable too: worried about the situation at home – and, if I'm honest, even more concerned about my white kid shoes, which were clearly ruined now. I was close to weeping myself.

'Look at the pair of you!' said the barmaid. 'Why don't you take the little lass *home*, Samuel?'

'Because I'm a-feared,' he wept. 'I'm not sure the baby will be borned yet.'

'Well, there's only one way to find out,' she said. 'Away with you!'

So we shambled out of the alehouse, Pa swaying, clinging to me. He was tall and I was particularly small, so he staggered, bent over, all the way home. He fell twice, and I had to take a tumble with him, getting my pinafore covered in mud, which made me even more anxious about my reception at home.

But when we turned the corner of our lane, we saw Matthew, Mark and Luke sitting on the wall outside our house kicking their heels, and Mary-Martha standing there too, with a white woollen bundle in her arms.

'Oh, Pa! It's all right! The baby's here!' I cried, and I started tugging him along.

The white parcel contained a tiny baby bawling its head off. Its face was an extraordinary shade of tomato and I thought it very ugly.

34

'Is it . . . John?' I asked breathlessly.

Mary-Martha nodded.

'Oh, thank goodness!' I said. But Mary-Martha was as white as the infant's shawl, and my three big brothers all looked as if they'd just had a whipping.

'How's your ma?' Pa asked.

They looked at each other fearfully. Pa gave an extraordinary howl and blundered into the house. I followed him, terrified. I could hear him upstairs, groaning and crying. But Ma wasn't making a sound.

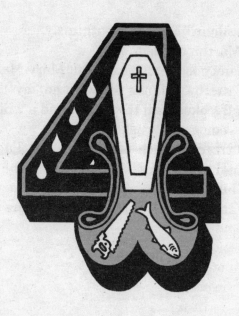

Ma was dead. Somehow I felt it was all my fault. If I'd hurried back home with a full tankard of ale, then the midwife might have felt so refreshed she'd have figured out a way of saving Ma instead of letting her bleed to death. It was my fault for behaving like a little circus monkey when my poor ma was sinking fast. It was my fault because I hadn't been brave enough to hold Ma's hand and help her, like Mary-Martha. It was my fault because I'd been such a disappointing baby that Ma had been desperate to have another child. Oh, it was my fault, my fault, my fault.

You're very kind to tell me otherwise, Hetty, but whatever the truth is, I still felt dreadfully to blame. I'm afraid Pa blamed me too.

I did not quite understand at first. I was kept busy running errands and helping Mary-Martha tend the new baby. He cried a great deal of the time, as if he were missing Ma too. A neighbour woman with a new babe of her own offered him a few feeds during the daytime and showed Mary-Martha how to give him a drink out of a bottle, but he was ailing and fretful in spite of all our efforts.

Pa borrowed money for the funeral, sending Ma off in style and kitting us all out in black, even giving the newborn baby a black shawl and a little black bonnet for his head. The baby cried all through the ceremony, and I cried too, wishing I could climb inside the hard wooden coffin and beg Ma's forgiveness. Mary-Martha didn't cry tears but her nose went very red and she frowned excessively. Matthew and Mark blubbed a little in an awkward, furtive way, knuckling their eyes and wiping their noses with their fists, but Luke cried more decorously, tears rolling gently down his pale cheeks. He dabbed at them in a dainty fashion with a lace handkerchief – Ma's best one, which he'd stolen for himself.

All the mourners patted him on the head and cooed over him. Even the undertakers admired him.

'That's a lovely little lad you've got there, sir. He's crying very decoratively indeed, bless him,' said the man in charge. He was very thin and tall, and his black top hat with trailing ribbon was the thinnest, tallest hat I'd even seen. He was like an animated lamppost. He didn't bend when he patted Luke's head, he simply loomed above him.

'You're a dear little chap, aren't you?' he said. 'Terrible tragedy for this little lad and all his brothers and sisters to lose their dear mother.' He turned to Pa. 'Please accept my sincere condolences, sir.'

Pa barely nodded. He was crying hard himself, but he'd drunk so much beer the night before, he reeked like an alehouse. You expected his very tears to trickle golden-brown.

'It's going to be very hard on you, sir, with all these little ones to feed and clothe and care for. How exactly are you going to manage?'

Pa gave a heartfelt groan and shook his head.

'I'm not meaning to twist the knife, sir, especially at such a moment, but if you should see fit to farm out any of your young folk as apprentices, to give them a fine start in life and ease the burden on your good self, then might I be first in line for the services of that little lad there – the one crying so piteously in such a pretty manner? How does he manage it? His little eyes are still so blue instead of red, and his tiny pink nose is free of slime! I can see you've done your very best to clothe him decent for the funeral, but imagine him in a fine black suit of well-cut worsted, with a fancy white collar and a black satin bow at his throat. Imagine a tiny top hat on those curls as a finishing touch. What a picture he'd look! In short, he'd make a marvellous miniature mute.' He emphasized each 'm' of these last three words so that it sounded as if he were humming.

Pa was barely listening, naturally concentrating on the ordeal of Ma's funeral. I found the ceremony bleak, but I was sure that Ma, inside her wooden coffin, would be appreciating all the hymn singing and holy words. I was horrified when we all trooped out into the churchyard and I realized that all these men were intent on lowering Ma into a big hole in the ground.

'No! No, please stop! You can't put Ma in all that mud and dirt!' I cried out.

'Hold your tongue and stop shaming us,' Pa hissed at me.

I tried to take his hand, but he pulled away from me as if he couldn't bear my touch. I nuzzled close to Mary-Martha instead, but she had her arms full of baby John and could not pick me up to comfort me.

I felt so lonely standing there, though I had my

family all around me. I wanted *Ma*. I stared at her coffin, willing her to lift the lid and climb out and wipe my tears away. But she stayed inside, and soon her coffin was covered in ugly clods of earth. I realized there was going to be no more Ma ever.

I seemed to have lost my pa too. He would have nothing to do with me, covering his eyes with his hand as if the very sight of me offended him. He used to take pride in my long fair hair, but now he said to Mary-Martha, 'Tell your sister to tie up that hair and cover her head with a scarf.' He would not speak to me directly, even when I stood in front of him.

'Pa!' I shouted, wondering if he simply couldn't hear me.

He pushed me away roughly. 'Tell your sister I want none of her fancy tricks,' he said to Mary-Martha. 'Hasn't she done enough harm, cavorting with me inside an alehouse when her own dear mother was gasping her last breath?'

'But Pa, that's not really fair,' said Mary-Martha, because she was a kind sister, and brave too: since Ma died Pa had been terrifyingly easy to upset. One word out of place and he'd seize you and smack you. All the boys except baby John had suffered Pa's belt in a matter of days.

Mary-Martha's soft entreaty was in vain. Pa had made up his mind about me and there was nothing I could do but keep out of his way. Mary-Martha was his favourite child now. She couldn't help looking proud whenever he beckoned her and called her his little darling and his special helpmeet.

He certainly couldn't have managed without her. She looked after baby John, she did the cooking, she did the washing, she did the cleaning. I helped, of course, and the boys could sometimes be persuaded to scrub the floor or go on errands, but mostly they ran wild, especially when Pa was away selling his tracts.

He stopped making angels. He swept Ma's collection to the floor one drunken night and stamped them all into powder. I was terrified, but I was glad they were gone. They had all started staring at me accusingly with their Prussian-blue painted eyes.

Pa did not make as much money now, and he drank nearly all of it away each night in the alehouse. We could not pay the rent on our dear little house, so we had to move to Willoughby Buildings, on the other side of town by the gasworks and the tannery, where all the really poor folk lived.

If Ma had known, she'd have flooded her coffin with her tears. We were now living in a den of drunks and thieves. But now Pa was a drunk himself and the boys were becoming thieves. At first they pilfered childish stuff – apples from the market stalls, sugary confections from the sweet shop, marbles from the toy shop, just dashing in and grabbing what they fancied – but soon Matthew and Mark and Luke joined up with a gang of big boys from the buildings and embarked on more organized crime, snatching purses and stealing cash.

Mary-Martha and I knew what they were up to, of course. They didn't have enough sense to keep things quiet, openly boasting about their exploits and showing off their newly acquired possessions.

'You're bad, wicked boys,' said Mary-Martha. 'What does the Good Book say? *Thou shalt not steal!*' She took after Ma and was very pious.

I wasn't pious at all, but I was fearful. 'You'll go to H-e-l-l, boys,' I said. 'And you'll burn in flames for all eternity.'

'Then at least we'll be warm,' said Matthew.

It was winter now, but we had no fuel for a fire and big Matthew had no warm clothes, though Mark and Luke could wear his cast-offs. Mary-Martha and I had to make do with shawls over our summer dresses. Mary-Martha did fetch Ma's best Sunday velvet from the trunk and ponder cutting it up to make a dress each for us, but she couldn't bear to snip into the soft material. When we buried our faces in it, we could still faintly smell our ma.

Mary-Martha did cut down a petticoat and an old grey singlet and fashioned them into a lumpy rag doll with a lacy dress. 'This can be your baby, Ellen-Jane,' she said kindly, because she was feeling sorry for me.

'Thank you so much, Mary-Martha,' I said, and clutched the doll to my chest. 'I shall call her Maybelle.'

She had no features on her poor grey face, and therefore didn't seem to have much personality at all, but she was stitched with love – and I was starved of that now. I took her to bed with me each night and carried her around everywhere, like a baby's comforter.

Of course the boys' luck couldn't last. All three of my brothers were caught red-handed burgling an old gentleman's house. The other boys in the gang had legged it out of the window before the constable caught them. My brothers had fought to get free, but he had coshed them into submission.

Pa went white with fury when he was told that they were in a prison cell, branded common criminals, with our Matthew up on an added charge of assault and battery. 'Your poor dear mother must be turning in her grave,' he said when he went to visit them.

They all cried with shame, even Matthew. Little Luke cried so piteously that the police sergeant softened.

'I can tell they're not truly bad lads,' he said. 'If you're willing to pay a shilling fine for each of them, we'll let them go with a caution, Mr Potts.'

I don't know how Pa got the money together – maybe he had to steal himself – but he managed to pay for all three boys to be released.

'I'm teaching you a lesson here and now, boys,' he told them. 'I'm not having you grow up to be thieving varmints. I'm going to get you trained up to be good God-fearing lads for the sake of your mother. She named you after the Gospels because she revered Jesus and his disciples. What does the holy tract say? *Go ye and do likewise!* So that's what you're going to do. Matthew, step forward!'

Matthew shambled up to Pa, hanging his head, his long arms dangling awkwardly.

'You're a strong boy – and those hands clearly throw a fierce punch already. I want to turn you into a *proper* man. What profession was our dear Lord raised in, Matthew?'

Matthew stared at Pa blankly. He hadn't attended Sunday school for years.

'He was a *carpenter* – a fine, skilled profession, and a way of channelling all that strength of yours. I'm apprenticing you to my old friend Micky Chip the carpenter. You're to go and live with him and learn off him, you hear me?'

Matthew heard and dared not argue, though he didn't look happy.

'Now you, Mark,' said Pa.

'I don't want to be a carpenter, Pa! I'm nowhere near as strong as Matthew,' said Mark, showing Pa his puny arms.

'Yes, you need building up, son. Do some honest work to grow some muscles. What did our Lord's friends do for a living, boy?'

Mark looked astonished. 'Do you want me to be a *disciple*, Pa?'

Pa struck him hard about the head for his stupidity. 'Where did Jesus find his first disciples, dolthead? On the shores of Lake Galilee. He was a fisherman, a fine, honest profession.'

'Is there a lake in London, Pa?'

'Not that I know of, you fool. You're not going *out* to fish, you're going to *work* with them. I've apprenticed you to Sammy Barton down the market. You'll go to Billingsgate with him every morning and help him run his wet-fish stall, do you hear me?'

Mark heard – and shook his head in horror. 'I don't like fish, Pa. Nasty slimy things!'

'And I don't like nasty slimy boys who bring shame on the family. You'll do as I say and work hard for a living or *you'll* be the one who's gutted and has his head chopped off. Now, Luke!'

Luke burst into tears in terror.

'That's it! That's my boy! The very picture! You cry hard, son, and learn to do it professional, because

45

you're going to that undertaker to get yourself trained up to be a mourner.'

'But I'm feared of dead people, Pa!'

'Nonsense, nonsense, they can't hurt you. You can *stop* the crying now because there's no call for it. You've got a nice, easy, clean profession compared with your brothers.'

Mary-Martha held baby John tightly, swaying a little. 'What about me, Pa?' she whispered.

'You've done nothing wrong, my little lass. You've done your level best, I know that. You've cared for us all *and* nursed that poor little babe. You shall stay.'

We waited. Pa did not even look in my direction, but of course he knew I was there.

'And – and what about our Ellen-Jane?' Mary-Martha asked.

Pa grunted as if in sudden pain, but kept staring resolutely at the boys.

'Ellen-Jane can stay too, can't she, Pa?' Mary-Martha continued bravely. 'She helps too. She tries her best, even though she's only little.'

Pa threw back his head and gave me one glance with his bloodshot eyes. 'No one in their right mind would take on a little minx like that one,' he said, and then he stomped out of the room.

I didn't know whether to be glad or sorry. I didn't want to be sent to be a carpenter or a fishmonger or a mourning mute. I wanted to stay at home – but I couldn't bear home any more either. I'd lost my mother, and my father now hated me.

I pressed close to Mary-Martha for some comfort, for she was all I had left now.

I had been small for my age before, but now I couldn't seem to grow at all. It wasn't just because I didn't have enough food. I had the same greasy soups and stale bread as my sister, and yet Mary-Martha grew tall, and her arms were strong too, because she was forever carrying our little brother, John. I stayed tiny – as if Pa's new contempt for me had withered something deep within me.

I tried hard to please him still, doing my fair share of the household tasks and painting all the endless tracts without once going over the lines. I nursed the baby too, though when Johnnie got to be a toddler it was a struggle to carry him properly and I had to walk with a bent back to balance him.

I was a supple girl even then. I'd naturally bend right over and scuttle like a crab, or walk upside down on my hands. This always made Johnnie go into peals of laughter, so it was a useful ploy when he was grizzly – but I took care never to perform any acrobatics when Pa was around.

He barely *was* around. He took to travelling far and wide to do his pattering. Sometimes he didn't come home for a week or more. We were often left very short of food. Once we could only beg a crust for the baby, while we ourselves starved for two whole days – and then even pious Mary-Martha wished our brothers were home to steal for us.

When, on the third day, Pa still wasn't home, I decided I had to find *some* way of earning enough pennies for food. I left Mary-Martha and Johnnie, and set out from Willoughby Buildings, clutching my rag doll, Maybelle, for companionship. I walked all the way to the market, though I was faint from lack of food. I knew there was always a big crowd there, and that was what I needed.

There were beggars a-plenty at the edge of the stalls, desperately eyeing the hot pies, the sugary cakes, the pyramids of red and yellow fruit – but the market men were fierce and very protective of their wares. There were all sorts of novelties too: a hurdy-gurdy man, with his mechanical organ and his live monkey in a little red velvet jacket, an escapologist trying to bust out of his chains, and a Punch and Judy stall. Punch looked like a miniature Pa and gave me the shivers, especially when he wielded his stick.

There were less elaborate buskers too: two girls holding hands and singing together, and a blind man reciting an endless poem about a Red Indian. They all had caps in front of them so that people could throw pennies in if they appreciated their performance. The poor blind man had a cap full of dud counters and pebbles, and every time a mean-spirited lad threw in another worthless stone, he heard the clink, paused in his recital, and murmured, 'Thank you kindly,' which made the boys laugh.

I could not sing and I did not know any poems. I had only one talent. I propped Maybelle against a lamp-post and stood up to perform.

I bent over backwards and started my crab-walk, and then tipped my weight onto my hands and walked about with my legs waving in the air. My hair fell about my face so I could not see the reaction of the crowd, but I could hear murmurings. There were raucous comments from the boys, but plenty of approval from the general crowd.

'Oh, the little lamb, just look at her!'

'She's such a tiny creature too, a little half-pint.'

'How old do you reckon she is? She must be barely out of baby robes. My, but she's nimble!'

I continued to cavort, doing my limited repertoire of tricks, until I sensed I had a big audience, and then I righted myself with a flourish and dropped a curtsy, while everyone clapped.

'Where's your cap, dear?' someone shouted.

I hadn't brought one with me because the only cap in the household belonged on Pa's head. I took off my shawl instead and laid it on the pavement. Within a minute all the wool was covered in coppers, and I heard cries of: 'Bravo, little girl!'

I barely stopped to acknowledge the praise and collect floppy Maybelle. I gathered up my money, tied a knot in my shawl, and ran off with it. I bought a pie for Mary-Martha and a pie for me, a candy cane for us to share, and a loaf of fresh bread, still warm from the oven, plus milk and porridge for the baby.

My shawl was stretched to bursting point and it was a struggle to carry it home, but Mary-Martha was so pleased to see me with my special feast. She was even hungrier than me, for she was naturally a big girl, and when she starved she had terrible pains in her stomach that bent her double, so at first she simply ate ravenously. She was so eager, she didn't even pause to cut the bread – simply broke off great chunks and sank her teeth into the soft dough – but when she'd eaten her fill and fed little Johnnie, she turned to me.

'How did you pay for all this food, Ellen-Jane?' she asked. Her voice was low, because she was rocking Johnnie to sleep, but she was looking at me intently, her eyes fearful.

'I didn't steal it,' I said quickly. 'I earned it.'

'What did you do?'

'I went to the market and put on a little show,' I said, licking the candy cane.

'*What?*'

'I pretended I was a turn at the music hall,' I said.

We'd never been to a music hall, but the older lasses at the buildings often sang music-hall numbers as they scrubbed the floors or staggered home with bags of coal, and we'd picked up some of the jolly tunes – though we didn't dare sing them when Pa was around because the words were saucy.

'You sound like a scalded cat when you sing. You can't hold a tune at all,' said Mary-Martha.

'I didn't sing. I did my upsy-daisies,' I said, using my baby word for acrobatics.

'Oh, Ellen-Jane! You're too big now to do that in front of everyone!'

'Everyone thought I was too *little* – and they *marvelled*,' I said proudly. 'They gave me so many pennies. Look, I haven't spent half of them yet!'

'I'm sure it's a sin,' said Mary-Martha worriedly. 'It's begging – and it's also very wanton, turning upside down and showing your drawers.'

'Jesus was always very kind to beggar people – and I wore my petticoats so they could only see a *little* bit of my drawers,' I said defiantly. I marched up to the wall of tracts. '*God helps those who help themselves!*' I declared.

I had her there. She fed Johnnie his bowl of milky porridge and sucked at her share of the candy cane without further comment.

So now, whenever we were desperate, I took myself off to market and did my little turn. The beggars tried to elbow me out of the way because it meant fewer pennies for them. The escapologist threatened to tie me up in his chains, and the singing girls stuck their tongues out at me, but the hurdy-gurdy man took a fancy to me and suggested I have a pitch in front of his organ.

'You can do all your little tricks in time to the music. That way they'll be more of a novelty. And I have an even better idea: I'll get Jacko, my monkey, to take his hat off and collect extra coins for you inside it, and then we'll split the takings – fair's fair,' he said.

It didn't sound exactly fair as I was the one doing most of the work, with little Jacko coming second. The hurdy-gurdy man did nothing but turn the handle of his machine, but he was big and fierce and it seemed better to have him on my side.

I soon knew all five of his tinkly tunes by heart, and could cavort and cartwheel pleasingly to the rhythm. I tried to make friends with Jacko, who looked such a sweet little creature, but when I went to pet him, he nipped me hard so I was frightened to try again. He didn't care for Maybelle at all and came near to tearing her limb from limb, so I had to keep a watchful eye on them both.

Mary-Martha came to see me one day, hugging Johnnie all the way. She seized hold of me halfway through my act, telling me that I was shaming her – but she shut her mouth when she saw all the coins showering into Jacko's cap like brass hailstones.

'You see!' I said triumphantly. Though I had to give Fred, the hurdy-gurdy man, his unfair share, I still had a fortune left to spend. 'I can buy you new shoes, Mary-Martha,' I offered.

She couldn't squeeze her feet into her old ones any more. She was making do with a pair of Luke's boots, but they were so worn down at the heel, she lurched sideways as she walked.

'I'd sooner go barefoot than have my sister doing a devil's dance,' she said.

'What about the baby then?' I said. 'When he starts running about outside, do you want *him* to go barefoot too?'

Mary-Martha looked as if she were wavering. She clutched Johnnie tight, her hands automatically fondling his tiny feet.

'No I don't,' she said, tears starting up in her eyes. 'I'm sorry, Ellen-Jane. I know you're doing this for all of us. Maybe that's why I take it so badly. *I'm* the eldest sister. *I* should be earning for you. Maybe I just feel envious seeing you dancing around looking so pretty, with all the folk admiring you so – and envy is a sin – it's forbidden in the ten commandments.' She took a deep breath and started, *'Thou shalt not—'*

'I know, I know – and it says honour thy father and mother – but Ma's dead and Pa's turned so fierce and angry with me, I can't honour him at all,' I said. 'So I'm going to carry on performing, no matter what you say.'

'I do hope Pa doesn't find out! Folk are talking about you. What if he fetches up here at the market to do his pattering? He'll whip you within an inch of your life.'

I shivered, because I was sure she was right. 'He *won't* find out,' I said fiercely.

Pa mostly wasn't there – and when he did come back, he spent very little time under his own roof. For endless hours he would pickle his brain in the ale-house. Sometimes he drank away all his week's earnings in one long evening before staggering home. Mary-Martha would try to help him get his boots off and lie down, but sometimes he was so angry he yelled at her incoherently. I always hid in the cupboard because I set Pa off worse. But frightening though these times were, we both hated it when Pa grew sad instead of bad.

'What would my lovely Lizzie think of me now?' he'd cry, his red eyes watering with tears. 'She never liked it when I'd had a drink inside me. *Beware the demon drink*, she'd mutter, quoting my own damned tracts at me. If she could see me now, it'd break her heart. What sort of a father am I to her little lambs? Where are my fine boys? Come here, Mary-Martha, and bring the little lad who was so precious to your mother.'

Mary-Martha would carry little Johnnie over to Pa. She'd let him hold him, but her arms were always out-stretched, ready to catch the baby if Pa fumbled and dropped him.

I'd watch through a crack in the door, remembering the times Pa dandled *me* on his knee. I felt so bad that I'd spoiled it all. It's all right, Hetty. I know now that it wasn't really my fault. Pa was just blaming me because I reminded him of Ma and it was too painful for him to look at me – but I was still very young, and somehow it seemed my fault all the same. One time I even tried smearing my bright hair with coal dust to make it dark and plain, but the sight of me still seemed to turn Pa's stomach.

He was cruel to me, though he was tender with the baby, rocking him clumsily and trying to croon lullabies. Once, when he was tickling Johnnie's toes, he sat holding his new kid shoes, squinting at them thoughtfully.

'These little baby boots – are they hand-me-downs from *her*?' he asked Mary-Martha. He couldn't even say my name now.

I froze inside my cupboard, so scared Mary-Martha would tell him how we had the money to buy new clothes.

'No, Pa, they're not hand-me-downs,' she said calmly. 'They're brand new for our little Johnnie.'

'So where did you get the money then? Heaven knows, I don't pass on enough,' said Pa, suddenly sounding agonized.

Mary-Martha didn't miss a beat. 'The boys like to buy things for their baby brother,' she said. 'Matthew and Mark have only stopped by once, because their masters keep a close eye on them, but Luke often comes calling when he's not needed for a service. He's very generous. Folk pay him little tips, see, because he cries so hard and prettily at all the funerals.'

My mouth was open in the dark cupboard. Mary-

Martha was such an excellent liar she almost had *me* convinced, let alone Pa.

I congratulated her fervently when Pa was fast asleep, snoring his head off, but with the baby still tucked tenderly under his arm.

'You were *wonderful*, Mary-Martha,' I whispered.

She turned a painful shade of red. 'Lying is a sin, especially to your parent. I expect I will end up in Hell,' she said miserably. 'But I couldn't let Pa know the truth, not when he's so set against you.'

'I'm sure God knows the difference between good lies and bad lies – and if he doesn't, don't worry. I've told *many* bad lies, so I will hold your hand in Hell – and at least it will be warm,' I said.

I meant it sincerely, but Mary-Martha burst out laughing. I hugged her hard and she hugged me back. I never used to be especially fond of my sister, but now I realized what a dear sweet soul she was – and the only member of my family who still loved me.

I learned to develop my acrobatic routine. I realized it was good to engage with my audience. I'd crab-walk in and out of the crowd or conduct a conversation upside down. It made folk laugh and they marvelled even more. I wasn't doing any complicated tricks. I think all three of my elder brothers could turn a neat cartwheel and I'd simply copied them. It was only a novelty because I was a girl – and I still looked years younger than my real age.

The hurdy-gurdy man still took half my money. He

made sure wizened little Jacko scampered around the crowd collecting coins in his upturned fez and then making a show of emptying them into a great pot marked MONKEY MONEY, which got another laugh and made folk even more generous.

I started to get a regular audience. Folk came specially to see me before they did their marketing. Sometimes they came back two days in a row, so I did not find it odd or unusual one week when a small man with a bald head and very narrow eyes came day after day. He watched me intently, his eyes just little slits, squinting as if he were staring into full sunlight. I could barely see the colour of his eyes, just a flash of steely grey. There was something about the intensity of his stare that made goose pimples prickle my arms.

I carried on performing in front of him, acting gay and carefree, tossing my long hair and smiling hard, even when upside down, but inside I was starting to get scared. Who was he? Could he be a friend of Pa's from the alehouse, ready to tell tales on me? I was sure I'd never seen him before.

Was he a policeman, ready to march me off to prison for performing in public? But he had no uniform and I didn't think standing on my hands was breaking any law.

Was he some sinister soul with evil desires? This seemed more likely. Mary-Martha had given me whispered warnings about such men. She had told me to beware. If such a man approached me, I shouldn't stop to talk to him, but must run away quick.

When he was there again on the third day, he waited till I was the right way up, bobbing curtsies. And then his hand came out and he suddenly grabbed me by the wrist. His grip was astonishingly strong. I'd learned to twist my hand and wriggle out of reach if any of my brothers caught hold of me in a similar fashion – but this time I was held like a handcuff.

'Let me go, Mister,' I piped in the baby voice I used when performing.

'I just need a moment of your time, little fairy,' he said. 'And what would your name be then, precious child?'

Oh, he used such pretty names for me, and he spoke softly enough, but there was something about his voice that was truly menacing.

'My name's Ellen-Jane, Mister. Now let me go, please. I've finished my performance for today,' I told him.

'Your performance! Oh, the pet!' he said, his tight mouth stretching into a grin that showed his yellow teeth.

I thought of the book of fairy tales I'd painted, with the little girl looking at the great fierce wolf, tucked up in bed, his jaws wide open, ready to eat her up.

'I'll let you go in a moment, my sweetheart. Just one or two more questions. How old are you, little one?'

'I'm five,' I lisped, because everyone thought me such a tiny tot.

'Five! Oh, bless her!' he said. Then he jerked my arm hard, pulling me right up close so that he was almost embracing me. He stared closely at my face, held my arm up and looked down at my legs. 'You're as little as five and as light as five, and you can wheedle and whisper like five – but I have my doubts, very serious doubts. I reckon you're at least seven – maybe eight . . .'

I shivered again, because I had just had my eighth birthday (a sad affair, with no presents, though Mary-Martha sang me a song and bought me a bun with pink icing). I had managed to fool everyone else. Even my own family forgot my real age at times. But this man's grey eyes seemed able to look into my soul. There was no hiding the truth from him.

I hung my head, letting my hair fall over my face to hide it.

'Ah, it's such a pretty little fairy too, with those golden tresses,' he said, running his free hand through my locks. He did it gently, so I could barely feel it, but I'd rather he'd struck me. I wriggled desperately, but he still had me tight by the wrist. My whole arm was starting to throb now.

'Please, Mister, I want my dolly!' I said, pointing to Maybelle, lolling on the ground.

'Oh, it wants its little dolly-wolly!' said Mister mockingly. I thought he might just let me go for a moment so that I could pick up Maybelle – and then make a run for it. But he wasn't prepared to release me for a second. He reached out and gave Maybelle a nimble kick. She flew up into the air and hit me on the chest. I was so startled I couldn't catch her with my free hand.

'Butterfingers!' said Mister, doing his footballing trick again. He was muddying poor Maybelle's dress. I clutched her to me this time, desperate to save her from further damage.

The crowd had ebbed away, off to jostle their way around the busy market. The hurdy-gurdy man was squatting with his back to us, counting the pennies in his bowl. Jacko jerked his head and capered towards me, chattering curiously. I held out my free hand to him and cried, 'Jacko, Jacko – here, Jacko.' I had a wild hope that he would sense danger from this man and attack him. I'd seen the monkey jump right up on a man's head and tug his hair viciously, and he frequently bit little children if they tried to pet him.

Jacko looked as if he meant business now, his teeth bared – but my captor stood his ground. He clicked his tongue in an odd way and pointed straight at Jacko.

The animal suddenly cowered away, very still in his little velvet jacket, and then scampered back to his perch by the hurdy-gurdy, whining.

'What's up with you, you little brute?' said the hurdy-gurdy man, hauling himself up.

'Oh, please help me!' I called weakly. I did not care for him and I knew he cheated me out of half my takings – but I wasn't afraid of him the way I feared this sinister man.

'Is he your pa?' the man asked as he came lumbering over.

'I'm her employer,' said the hurdy-gurdy man. 'And I'll thank you to take your hands off her.'

'I'm simply admiring the little sweetheart,' he said, not at all perturbed.

'You like her, do you?' The hurdy-gurdy man scratched the top of his head thoughtfully. 'How's about you pays an extra shilling and I'm sure she'll put on another performance.'

'No, I don't want to,' I said, struggling.

'You'll do as I say,' said the hurdy-gurdy man.

'So you're her employer, are you?' said Mister. 'She's signed up to you?'

'In a manner of speaking.'

'Mmm – speaking isn't *binding*, sir. So this little fairy's as free as a bird and can fly away wherever she wants.'

'I don't want to be with *you*,' I told Mister.

'Hark at her! Funny, wilful little creature! She'll be stamping her foot next,' he said, and laughed at me, showing his yellow teeth. 'I like a little soul with spirit.'

Then he suddenly lifted me up, tipping me, helpless and humiliated, over his shoulder. 'Come along with me, little girl. Old Beppo has great plans for you!'

'No, no, I don't want to go with you! Oh, please, Mister, set me down. I haven't got my share of my earnings!' I cried.

'Ah, a tiny businesswoman, bless her! Well, we'll let this gentleman and his monkey pocket the pennies for today. You'll earn us far more in the future, my dear,' said the man, striding along as easily as if he had a little knapsack on his back instead of a wriggling child.

'No, no, I *won't* go!' I said.

When he only chuckled, I opened my mouth wide and screamed as loud as I could. Folk stared at me, startled.

'What are you doing with that little lass?' a tall man asked anxiously.

'He's a wicked stranger and he's running off with me!' I gasped.

Mister heaved with laughter. 'Hark at her, the naughty little minx! I'm a friend of the family and I'm

65

taking her off the streets where she's been running wild.'

'Don't listen to him – he's lying! Oh, help me, help me!' I screamed.

'Is that *you*, Ellen-Jane?'

Oh dear Heavens, it was Pa! He stood there with his tray of tracts round his neck, here in the market.

'Pa! Oh, Pa, save me!' I screamed. 'This wicked man is trying to steal me away.'

Pa set his tray down. He was a little stooped now, but he was still a tall man. His nose was red to start with, but now a fierce flush spread over his whole face, even his neck. 'Put my child down,' he said, his fists clenched.

My heart started thudding violently. Pa was calling me *his child*. He was about to snatch me back. It must mean he still cared about me a bit. Maybe he was ready to forgive me. I might even get to be his own baby darling again.

'Certainly, sir,' said Mister. He took me off his shoulder and set me down in front of Pa, though he kept a firm hold of my wrist.

'So you're this little angel's father,' he said. 'Well, I'll be blowed! You're the very man I've been looking for.' He was staring intently at Pa. I saw him taking in Pa's dishevelled clothes, the sole flapping on his boots, his unshaven chin, his bloodshot eyes. I saw his nostrils quiver at the stale smell of ale that clung to his clothes.

'You were looking for *me*?' said Pa. 'Unhand that child now.' He made an ineffective grab for me, but Mister had a grip of iron.

'I need to keep hold of her or the lovely little pet will make a bolt for it. She's nervous now, but oh my goodness, sir, you should have seen her scarce ten minutes ago, prancing about like a little fairy – standing on her head and waggling her legs as bold as brass, bless her!'

I started trembling. 'He's lying, Pa! I tell you, he's lying,' I blurted, but I could not quite look Pa in the eye.

'You've been cavorting again?' he said very slowly, swaying slightly.

'No! No, I swear!'

'Oh, bless her! No need to be modest, little angel,' said Mister. 'Cavorting's the very word, sir. Quite a little act, she has. A crowd of thirty or forty gathered round immediately. She attracted a great deal of attention. She's a regular at the market now, and I reckon she earns as many pennies as the costers with their stalls – *and* she saves herself a dawn trip to Covent Garden.'

'You've been cavorting for *money*, Ellen-Jane?' said Pa, moving closer, bending his head down to mine.

'No, Pa!'

'Don't you lie to me!' he thundered.

'Oh, the bad little angel! But don't get angry, sir. You should be proud of the little pet. She's very talented, you know. With a little training I reckon she could polish up into a fine circus act.'

'A circus act!' said Pa, whispering as if the very words burned his tongue.

'I'm not a circus act, Pa! Please don't look at me like that! I haven't been a bad girl on purpose. I just did it to earn some money. We didn't have anything to eat,' I gabbled.

'I'd sooner a girl of mine starved to death than tip herself upside down in public,' said Pa. 'What would your poor ma say, Ellen-Jane? Oh, she's turning in her grave now, poor dear soul, in total agony.'

I saw Ma twisting about in her grim earthy bed, her mouth open wide in a silent scream. It was such a terrifying picture, the tears spurted down my cheeks.

'So her mother's dead, poor little lamb,' said Mister. His grey eyes were gleaming now. 'And you have the burden of bringing this moppet up, sir, feeding and clothing her and trying to keep her on the paths of righteousness?'

'Her and her elder sister and a little babe too. I have boys who went to the bad too, but I've apprenticed them out in the hope they'll grow up God-fearing gentlemen to make their mother proud,' said Pa.

Mister's eyes shone like beacons now, burning in his

pale face. 'Why not apprentice this little lass then, my good sir? I can train her up good and proper, make a real showgirl of her. She'll start earning pounds instead of pennies – and I dare say she'll send half her earnings home to her dear old pa.'

'Tainted money,' said Pa, and he spat on the ground.

'That's your opinion, sir, and you're entitled to it, but I'm sure the food and firewood it'll buy will still warm you, body and soul,' said Mister. 'Did you not say you have another daughter and a babby to care for? Well, ease your burden, sir! Let me take charge of the little fairy here and she need never trouble you again.'

'I'll not let a wastrel like you ruin her – though I fear she's already gone to the bad,' Pa sighed.

'Then let her go, sir, let her go.' The man drew a notebook and a pencil out of his jacket pocket and scribbled a sentence. He spoke the words as he did so. '*I* – what is your name, sir . . . ? Samuel Potts, I thank you! *I, Samuel Potts, do agree to give full guardianship and care over my daughter* . . . The little fairy's name is Ellen-Jane, I believe? *My daughter Ellen-Jane to Mr Silas Bernhardt*. That's yours truly, though my stage name is Beppo.'

'You can stop this fooling. I'm not signing my daughter away,' said Pa.

'For the sum of . . . Now, what would be a fair sum? How about five pounds? That's almost a year's wages for a full grown woman, a tidy amount. Think what you might buy with it.' Mister lowered his voice. 'You look careworn, sir, down on your luck. Think what tempting pleasures you could buy, all the while knowing that this little darling is safe and happy and earning her keep, all the better to keep you into a ripe old age.'

'Five pounds in cash?' said Pa.

'No, Pa! Oh, please, no, I don't want to go with him. He frightens me,' I cried.

Pa hesitated. His hand went out, as if he might stroke my hair, the golden locks he used to love.

'Make it five guineas, not five pounds,' Mister whispered.

'Show me your money.'

The man reached inside his greatcoat and drew out a leather bag with a tight cord, greasy from much handling. 'Cup your hands!' he told Pa.

I watched, scarcely able to breathe, while he counted out five gold sovereigns and five silver shillings into Pa's shaking hands. Pa thrust the money deep into his pockets and then hid his eyes with one hand so that he should not see me.

'Take her,' he muttered.

'No! Oh, Pa, please, I want to stay home with you and Mary-Martha and little Johnnie.' I was gulping tears now. I would not miss my father now he was so cruel to me, but I had become fond of my baby brother, and Mary-Martha had done her best to be a little mother to me.

'I'll take her, sir, and gladly, but I need you to sign my paper here, giving your permission. I'll not have you regretting things in a more sober light and accusing me of child-stealing. Let me write in the sum – five whole guineas. My, that's more than you'd pay for a thoroughbred horse – and this child's such a stunted little filly. There, sir, sign at the bottom. One flourish of the pen and then we'll cease bothering you. You can toss away your tray of tracts and go to the tavern and celebrate your good fortune. I see you licking your lips! You've a fierce thirst on you, sir, and it needs to be slaked.'

So Pa signed his name and then staggered off without a backward glance. My own father had sold me to a stranger.

I could not believe it. I kept poking at my eyes, trying to open them wider, wondering if I was having some terrible nightmare – but I knew I was not imagining the iron grip on my wrist.

'Come along, my little fairy,' the man said. 'Don't pull away from me like a naughty child. You have to do as I say now – and woe betide you if you don't.'

'Oh, but please, mayn't I say goodbye to my dear sister and my little brother? They will be so anxious if

I don't go home, and they'll be needing me to earn money for a bite to eat,' I begged.

'All your money is *my* money now. You're all mine, little fairy. Your pa's signed you away. You ain't *got* no pa or sister or baby brother now. You've just got me,' said Mister. 'Now stop your grizzling and walk along nicely. Stop hanging back. *Walk*, I say.' He gave my arm such a sudden vicious tug I thought he'd yank it right out of its socket.

I clamped my lips shut because I didn't want my sobs to make him even angrier, and did my best to scurry along at his pace. He might be old and wizened and his legs bent, but he was extraordinarily lithe and strong. I was soon very out of breath.

I looked all around me desperately, wondering where he was taking me. I didn't know this part of town beyond the market very well. We passed the town hall, and its clock boomed out the time – twelve noon. I shuddered at every chime. Even now, when I am so happy, Hetty, if I hear any clock striking and I count along to twelve, my heart starts thudding again, remembering that hour.

I saw an undertaker's funeral parlour and wondered if it was the one where Luke worked. I tried calling his name, but my throat was so dry with fear I could barely make a cheep. Then the long street of shops petered out. We passed several rows of new houses, big red-brick villas with gardens. There was a nursemaid trying to pull a perambulator up a flight of steps. The baby stayed safe inside the covers, but the little boy perching on the end of the pram tumbled off and bumped his head, starting up a fearful screaming.

'Oh dear, poor little lad,' said Mister, and went to pull the child to his feet with his free hand.

'You keep away from our Charlie!' the nursemaid said fiercely. 'You're from the circus, I dare say. We don't want the likes of you hanging around here.'

'Suit yourself, missus. I'll let the little lad tumble down all over again and crack his head open into the bargain, and I'll not raise a finger to help,' said Mister, swiping the boy back to the ground with one quick cuff.

The child started screaming anew and the nursemaid shrieked. Mister just laughed and tugged at me to get me moving again.

I was more fearful than ever now. What *was* this circus? The nursemaid had spat the word out. Was it even more tumbledown and filthy than Willoughby Buildings? Yet Mister seemed clean enough and his clothes were respectable, if a bit odd. He wore a worn worsted coat and checked trousers, and a flowing paisley silk scarf about his thin neck – the clothes of a silly young toff, yet Mister was old and spoke just like ordinary folk.

He saw me staring and suddenly pulled an extraordinary face, crossing his eyes and pushing his lips into a terrifying pout. I gasped, and he cackled with laughter.

'You're a timid little fairy, ain't you, my pretty one? No prancing and prinking now. Well, droop away while you can. I'll soon perk you up for the ring.'

'The ring?' I quavered.

'In the big top.'

I stared at him. He seemed to be talking in riddles.

'You'll see, you'll see. What a sweet ignoramus you are. But I'll learn you. Oh yes, I'll learn you good and proper,' said Mister. 'Come along, step up smartly. We're nearly there.'

I looked around fearfully for some dark looming building, but could only see green fields at the edge of the town. Folk seemed to have set up home in one of the fields. I saw a semicircle of brightly painted wagons, and an enormous red and white construction like the preaching tent Ma had taken us to when we were little. Then I saw a vast wild beast with a long, long nose like a wriggling eel, and I stood stock-still.

Mister laughed at me. 'Aha! What do you think of Elijah then, little fairy?'

'It's a monster!' I gasped. 'Will it eat me?'

'Yes, it'll eat you all up in one gollop if you're a bad little minx and don't do as I say,' Mister told me, chuckling. 'Come along and say how do – and if you say it respectful like, he'll shake your hand with his trunk.'

I wasn't going to shake hands with that heathen monster, even if Mister beat me black and blue. There were other exotic animals here too. As we drew nearer, I heard a roaring that set me trembling.

'What's that, Mister? Is it a dog, a giant dog? I'm a-feared of fierce dogs,' I said.

'It's not a big dog, my silly little fairy. It's a big *cat*. Ain't you heard of Tanglefield's lions? The wildest beasts in all Christendom, and yet we train them to jump through hoops of fire.'

This wasn't reassuring. I heard other alarming animal sounds – wild, high-pitched barking – coming from one of the bigger wagons.

'There's big dogs in there, Mister, I can hear them,' I said.

'They're not dogs either – they're sea lions swimming about their tank. It sounds as if it's feeding time. You watch yourself, pretty missy, or I'll chop you into little pieces and feed you to the sea lions too.' He made little chewing motions with his lips and wheezed with laughter at my horror.

This circus seemed the most terrifying place in the world, full of ravenous beasts and men like Mister, but then I saw an animal I recognized. It was a beautiful black horse, a prince of ponies compared to all the sad knock-kneed nags I saw dragging carts and drays all over town, but clearly a horse nevertheless, with an arched neck and a long silky mane and tail. On his back sat the most amazing woman I had ever seen, like a princess in a fairy tale.

She had long, wavy red hair tumbling down her back and wore a pair of bizarre baggy trousers that clung to her shapely white legs. Her horse was unbridled and she rode bareback, not even holding onto his flowing mane. He was stepping out swiftly, but she stayed erect and upright, a smile on her face.

Then she saw me and stopped the horse in his tracks. 'Who have you stolen now, Beppo?' she said, her voice sharp.

'Not stolen, Addie! What harsh words! How quick you are to jump to conclusions. I bought this little fairy child. I paid five whole guineas for her too, so I hope she'll work very hard and repay my generosity.' He gave me a little shake.

'Don't, Beppo, you're frightening her. Poor little creature, you look scared to death.' She leaped gracefully from her horse and knelt down beside me. Her face was even prettier close up, her cheeks so pink, her lips very red. I breathed in deeply because she smelled beautifully of fresh roses. I felt the tears trickling down my face.

She reached out and gently mopped them away

with a lace handkerchief. Her hand was so white and smooth and delicate. I realized how grimy I'd become since living in Willoughby Buildings, where there was just one cold water tap outside for goodness knows how many families. But even if I scrubbed all day in a hot tub, I knew I could never get my skin as white and perfect as hers.

'There now, my dear. My name is Madame Adeline – and this is my dear horse, Midnight. Would you like to pat him?'

I nodded timidly. She took me by the hand. Mister was reluctant to let go of me, but Madame Adeline pulled his fingers away from my wrist.

'Let her be, Beppo. Poor little girl! You're pinching her. She'll get a horrid bruise. There now.' Madame Adeline rubbed my sore wrist tenderly. 'What's your name, dear?'

'I'm Ellen-Jane Potts, ma'am,' I whispered.

'Not any more you're not,' said Mister. 'That's no name for a little circus star.'

'Little Star . . .' murmured Madame Adeline, sounding sad.

'Think of a name for her, Addie – you've got the knack for it,' said Mister, suddenly wheedling.

'*Twinkle, Twinkle, Little Star,*' said Madame Adeline, tucking my hair behind my ears. 'My, you have lovely bright hair. I shall wash it for you with my special shampoo and then it will sparkle in the sunlight. What shall we call you? *Like a diamond in the sky* . . . Diamond! There's your name, little one – Diamond.'

'I like it! Little Diamond, the Child Wonder!' said Beppo. 'Oh, Addie, I *knew* you'd come up trumps. That's your name now, Miss Fairy. Little Diamond. Say it now.'

'Little Diamond,' I lisped obediently.

Mister chuckled and rubbed his hands together. 'Yeth, lickle Di-mond,' he said, imitating me.

'Twinkle then, little Diamond,' said Madame Adeline, and she lifted me up, her graceful arms surprisingly strong, and sat me on top of Midnight. I gave a little shriek to be up so high, and slipped sideways the moment the horse moved a hoof.

'Whoopsie,' she said, swinging me down again. 'Well, she's not a natural horsewoman, I'll tell you that for sure.'

'Hands off! I'm not having you training her up. She's going to be a little acrobat,' said Mister.

'She's too old to start,' said Madame Adeline, which surprised me utterly.

'I'm eight years old, ma'am,' I said. 'Though most folk think I'm only about five.'

'See! Out of the mouths of babes . . . We'll bill her as an infant phenomenon,' said Mister. 'She'll do a turn with my boys.'

'No, you can't do that to her! She's a light little thing and will look as pretty as a picture once she's had a good scrub, but if you try cricking her bones bendy at this stage, you'll just break them,' said Madame Adeline.

'I'll hardly need to touch her!' said Mister. 'Right, little Diamond, show Madame Addie here what you can do. Go on then! Turn a cartwheel and walk around on those hands like a crab.'

'I don't want to,' I said shyly, ducking my head to hide behind my hair.

Mister drew my hair aside like curtains and stared straight into my eyes. 'Now listen to me, little fairy,' he whispered. His voice was so soft I could hardly hear him, but so sinister it was like the hissing of a serpent. 'It's not what *you* want any more, oh dear me, no. I'm your master now and you'll do exactly what *I* want, understand?'

I swallowed and then nodded.

'Then put on a show for Madame Addie here, pronto!'

I stepped away, trembling so that I could barely stand, but when I obediently stood on my hands, I felt steadier. Madame Adeline clapped enthusiastically at once, calling 'Bravo!' which encouraged me further. I cartwheeled in a circle, I capered backwards like a crab, I sprang up and did a back-flip and landed lightly the right way up, arms outstretched.

'Oh my, she has it all off pat!' Madame Adeline declared. 'Bless the little sweetheart. You're right, Beppo, she's a natural.'

'Wait till I've trained her up a little. I reckon she'll be better than all my boys put together. My five guineas are a very sound investment, you'll see. Right, my twinkly little Diamond, come and meet your brothers.'

'My brothers, Mister?' I thought for one moment that he'd purchased Matthew, Mark, Luke and baby John too – but when he led me over to a red wagon there was no sign of my own kin.

There were three young men there, stripped to the waist, wearing tight breeches. The eldest looked the strongest, with broad shoulders and arms like great hams, though his waist was small and his stomach flat as a board.

The middle one was slighter, but his wiry arms were taut with muscle too. He was in the middle of a wrestling match with his older brother, managing to shove and heave with almost as much strength.

The youngest was just a boy, only a few years older than me. He was watching his brothers upside down, standing on his hands. He pulled a face when he saw me and stuck out his tongue, waggling it rudely. I did likewise. I wasn't frightened of silly boys, and I could do a handstand too. But then he shifted his weight until he was standing on only *one* hand. He waved the other at me insolently. I tried not to look impressed.

'Boys, boys! Do you call this nonsense practising?' said Mister, clapping his hands. 'Pay attention now.'

The two young men stopped wrestling and the boy whipped through the air and landed lightly on his toes. All three stood to attention. It was clear Mister expected to be obeyed instantly.

'That's more like it,' he said. 'Now, I'd like to introduce you all to this little fairy here. She's Diamond, Acrobatic Child Wonder, my new shining star.'

All three glared at me. The youngest looked positively outraged, his eyebrows wrinkled and his mouth gaped, showing his missing teeth.

'Ain't *I* your child wonder?' he said.

'You're all my little wonders,' said Mister. 'This here's Tag, Diamond. You're to pay particular attention to him. He'll learn you all his tricks. Regular little crowd-pleaser, he is.'

The youngest looked slightly appeased, but he still frowned fiercely at me.

'And this is Julip, my middle lad,' said Mister. 'He flies through the air like a bird, don't you, boy?'

'Flipperty-flap,' said Julip, waving his arms.

'And this here is Marvo, my eldest. Strong as an ox, aren't you, son? Show off your muscles to little Diamond here.'

The big lad flexed his great arms until his veins looked as if they'd burst through his taut skin. Then he stepped forward, picked me up with one vast hand and thrust me high in the air. I waggled my legs in protest and he threw me free. I landed in an undignified heap on the grass. Mister and the three boys all laughed at me. Tag actually spat contemptuously.

'Pick *me* up, Marvo,' he said.

Marvo lifted him effortlessly in one hand and then threw him too. Tag tucked himself into a tiny ball and turned two somersaults in the air before landing neatly on his feet, his arms outstretched in acknowledgement. He nodded at me triumphantly.

'That's it, you show her, Tag,' said Mister. 'Give her a quick routine, boys, so she can see what we do.'

The three all instantly straightened, shoulders back, chins in the air, stepping out like little princes, though they were still barefoot boys. Marvo stood still, muscles flexed. Julip ran up to him and flew through the air, landing lightly with his feet on Marvo's shoulders. Then Tag stepped on a springboard and flew upwards too, twice the height, landing on top of Julip with barely a wobble. They stood before me, a giant man made out of three boys. Then, with a grunt, Marvo took a few steps, both boys still balanced high above him before they teetered forward. Julip and Tag somersaulted through the air before landing neatly, then all three started cartwheeling in a ring, round and round. When Mister shouted a command, they all upended themselves and swooped so far back their heads poked cheekily between their legs. They capered about like misformed monsters, pulling crazy faces. Tag pretended to bite Mister on the behind, and Mister waved his fist at him – and then, astonishingly, *he* stood on his hands and ran at Tag upside down.

I had not realized that *he* was part of the act too. I figured he was about the same age as my own pa, maybe even older, yet he was now proving as spry as his sons. I'd never been so scared of anyone before, and yet now, watching him hobble about in pursuit of the boys, pulling the drollest faces, I could not help doubling up with laughter.

I still did not understand what his act was until I saw him in full costume for that afternoon's performance. I was in the cramped quarters of the boys' wagon, trying to hitch a hammock from post to post.

Mister suddenly thrust his head through the door, and I screamed. His face was painted a deathly white, and he had a new big bulbous nose and vast red lips that smiled in a sinister way to the very edges of his ears.

'I am Beppo the clown!' he said, and then he cackled with laughter.

All afternoon I watched the circus performance. I was soon to know each routine in dreary detail, but I remember I was utterly dazzled by that first show.

I know you felt the same way too, Hetty! I loved Madame Adeline and thought her very beautiful as she rode around the ring in her pink sparkly dress. I was astonished to see Mister transformed into capering Beppo, throwing water at the other clown, Chino, and tripping over his great shoes. I laughed along with all the other children, but I squirmed in my seat too.

I was utterly transfixed by the Silver Tumblers and their acrobatic antics. Marvo, Julip and Tag looked so different in their silver costumes in the circus ring. They'd painted their faces too, shading their eyelids blue and rubbing rouge on their cheeks so that they looked robust and glowing. They'd oiled their hair so that it gleamed in the spotlight, and the sequins sewn onto their costumes dazzled the eye.

They did their handstand trick, and then many others, leaping and tumbling around the ring, shouting as they did so. I forgot that they were rude boys who larked around. They were amazing aerial beings, as magical as fairies, and I was entranced.

I clapped so hard my hands stung. I watched the monkeys and the lions, and the performing seals and the astonishingly huge elephant, marvelling at them all, but I was still seeing silver sparkles before my eyes. I stood up and cheered as all the performers paraded around the ring at the end, and then hovered uncertainly as everyone scrambled for the exit flap of the tent. Should I try to walk away too? Maybe I could find some kind lady and beg her help to get home. I knew Pa had been glad to be rid of me, but I could hide when he was around. Mary-Martha would be glad to see me – and oh, I wanted to see *her* so very much. She could be vexingly pious at times, but she was the only one in the world who had tender feelings for me now and I loved her dearly.

What was I waiting for? I had only to run! Beppo might be lurking somewhere close, but I was just one small girl amid hundreds. I spotted an old shawl someone had left behind on her seat. I snatched it up and wound it over my head, covering my long bright hair. Then I joined up with a whole gaggle of children – they were with a flustered old dame who couldn't keep control of them. Several stared at me in surprise, but I just ducked my head and pressed close to them.

All I had to do was get out of the big tent and run. I didn't know this part of town, but the field was only streets away from the big shops. I could be home in half an hour.

The crowd jostled all about me. I shut my eyes and prayed to my poor dead mother: *Dear Ma, please watch over me and keep me safe, and don't let Mister snatch me back!*

I could almost feel her long hair brushing my head, her gentle hands on my shoulders. She seemed to steer me through the crowd, right out of the tent, across the grass – she was truly helping me—

'Hey, you! Diamond, come here!'

It was Tag, a wrapper over his silver sequins, his slicked-back hair making him look like one of the performing seals. He was gesturing at me impatiently. I turned my back on him and started running. I prided myself on being speedy. Mary-Martha could never catch me, even though her legs were longer than mine, but Tag was a different proposition. He was after me in a blink. He didn't waste time telling me to stop. He threw himself at me, wrestling me to the ground and pinioning me in my stolen shawl, nearly choking the life out of me.

I had fought with my brothers often enough, but they usually played fair with me. They'd never used their whole strength and they'd never actually hit me with their fists. Tag sat down hard on my chest, beating a tattoo on my head.

'Get off me, you brute!' I gasped. I tried to spit in his face but I didn't have the strength. My spittle dribbled down my own chin.

'Ha ha, dirty little cat,' said Tag. 'You come quietly now.'

'Please let me go! You don't want me here, so why are you keeping me?' I said, struggling.

'Of course we don't want you, you useless baby – but Beppo does,' said Tag. 'He's the boss.'

'He's not *my* boss! He's not *my* pa!' I said.

'He's not mine either,' said Tag.

'But he said you were his boys.'

'Marvo and Julip – not me. Beppo got me even

younger than you and trained me up,' said Tag. He didn't let me go, but at least he'd stopped hitting me now.

'Did your pa sell you too?' I whispered.

'Didn't have no pa. No ma neither,' said Tag.

'But you must have had them once. Did they both die? My poor ma died,' I said, suddenly welling up with tears.

'Crying, eh? *Baby!*' said Tag. 'No, there was just me. I lived with some other boys, but I didn't like it and I ran away. And then Beppo got hold of me.'

'I'm not crying because of *you* – but get off my chest, I can't *breathe*,' I gasped.

He did roll off me then. I sat up, knuckling my eyes.

'You could run away from Beppo too. We both could,' I said.

'I did at first. And he caught me and beat me until I couldn't stand up. He'll do the same to you – and he'll wallop me too for not looking out for you, so think on, Diamond.'

'I'm not *called* Diamond. It's just his silly name for me,' I said. 'I'm Ellen-Jane.'

'Not any more, you're not. You're everything that Beppo says. Now come *on*, or we won't get any grub between shows.' He took hold of my hand and yanked me to my feet.

I might still have run, but I knew he'd catch me.

I didn't think then that Mister would really give us a beating – not *me* – but I certainly didn't want to make him angry. And I was hungry. Very hungry.

I let Tag pull me along to the big blue wagon beside the boys' ramshackle home. Marvo was squatting on the ground stirring a big cauldron over a fire. Julip was tearing chunks of bread off a loaf. Mister himself was sitting on the steps, a robe over his under vest and trousers. He'd taken off his great clown's shoes, displaying very holey striped socks, but he was still wearing full greasepaint, and a little bowler hat on the back of a mad grey wig. He should have looked ridiculous but there was nothing comical about his suspicious glare.

'Where have you two been? She didn't try to do a runner, did she?' he said.

I held my breath.

'No, boss!' said Tag. 'She just tumbled over a guy rope, that's all.'

'Tumbled, did you, little fairy?' said Mister. 'Oh, we'll teach you tumbling soon enough.'

'You'll never teach that one, Beppo. She's not got the pluck,' said Tag.

'She'll learn. I'll just throw her up in the air and hope for the best. Once she's landed with a crack on that pretty little head often enough, she'll get the knack of tucking herself up tight,' said Marvo.

I wasn't sure if he was joking or not. I sat some distance away from him when Mister served the meal, just in case. It smelled good, very good indeed, a thick dark savoury stew with dumplings and large pieces of meat. I had been living on bread and scraps of cheese and bruised fruit. My mouth started watering.

Mister served me up a whole bowlful. There were no forks or spoons. I had to scoop it up with my bread. Mister and the boys slurped their stew straight out of the steaming bowl.

It tasted astonishingly good, strong and succulent, the meat so tender it scarcely needed chewing. I ate ravenously, sucking each chunk to the bone.

'That's it! Eat up, little fairy,' said Mister.

'It's very good meat,' I said. 'Is it beef, I wonder – or lamb?' I had rarely tasted either but I did not want them to think me ignorant.

They all guffawed with laughter.

'Haven't you ever had horsemeat before?' asked Marvo.

He *had* to be joking this time. I looked over the fields to where Madame Adeline's beautiful Midnight was tethered.

'It's not truly horse, is it?' I quavered, my mouth still full.

'No, it's succulent little pony,' said Beppo, and he gave a high-pitched horse's neigh.

I choked on my mouthful and had to spit it out. This made them all laugh uproariously.

'Don't you want your gee-gee then?' said Tag. 'Give it here. I'll soon polish it off.'

I was still hungry but I couldn't eat any more. I let Tag have my bowl and turned my back on them all so I wouldn't see them chewing away at the meat. Madame Adeline was sitting on her own wagon steps, eating her own meal. She beckoned me over when she saw me watching her.

I wandered towards her.

'Why did you give your bowl to Tag, dearie?' she asked gently. She gave me a little poke in the tummy. 'You're the one who's all skin and bone. You need to eat your fill, little Diamond.'

'I don't like that stew,' I said.

'Well then, have some of mine.'

I peered into her pot anxiously. 'Is it horsemeat?' I whispered.

'No, it isn't,' she said. 'I have eaten that and it tastes good, but I haven't got the stomach for it, not when my horses are just like family to me. This is chicken, dear – an old boiling bird, but still quite juicy.'

'Like you, Addie,' Mister called, chuckling.

She pulled a face at him. 'Take no notice of Beppo. *I* don't,' she said, scooping a fresh portion of chicken stew into a mug. 'Here, child, eat. And when you've finished,

I'll see if I can find you something special for afters!'

I ate the chicken stew with relish, thanking her fervently. Then she took me by the hand and led me up the steps into her wagon. I cried out in surprise and delight.

'Oh my, it's so pretty and neat and you have such lovely things,' I said, touching the lace antimacassars on her crimson sofa, the delicate fern in its polished brass pot, the china ladies dancing on top of her cabinet. 'It's just like a dear little home.'

The boys' wagon was dark chaos, just three beds and a tumble of discarded clothes – and the wagon smelled so terribly of boy too. Madame Adeline's wagon smelled of lavender bags and verbena soap and her own sweet rose perfume. I breathed in deeply.

'Do you like the smell?' she said, smiling at me. She took a cut-glass bottle from her dressing table and dabbed some rose scent behind my ears.

'Oh, it's lovely!' I said.

'Well, if you like roses so much, we'll find you a special treat for your dessert,' she said. She opened a tin and showed me two little cakes inside: fairy cakes with pink icing, each studded with a candied rose.

'One for you and one for me,' she said, offering me the tin.

'But they're yours,' I said, though I wanted one dreadfully.

'It's twice as nice to share – and I shall get twice as fat if I eat both,' said Madame Adeline, patting her stomach.

I ate my little cake happily, saving the rose till last and then sucking it slowly to savour it. I looked around Madame Adeline's beautiful home. I could see her dressing table, and a white nightgown hanging behind the door, but I couldn't see any bed. I looked up at the ceiling, but she didn't have a hammock. I stared at her velvet armchair, wondering if she curled up there at night. She was watching me, amused.

'I do have a bed, you know,' she said, as if I'd spoken aloud. 'Do you want to see it?' She tugged at a handle on the wall and pulled down an entire little bed that had been hiding inside, ready made up with fresh white linen and a patchwork quilt.

'Oh, how clever!' I said. 'May I try it out?' I flopped down on the bed and found it very comfortable indeed. It was really quite large – roomy enough for two.

'I wish *I* had a beautiful bed like this,' I said wistfully. 'I only have a hammock and I'm scared I shall tip myself out in the night.'

'Well, if you do, Marvo is an expert at catching people,' said Madame Adeline. She paused. 'I wish you could come and sleep with me, Diamond. I think you'd be much happier.'

'Oh, I would, I would!' I said.

'Well, I will talk to Beppo and do my best to persuade him.'

She tried very hard, but Mister wouldn't hear of it.

'She's *my* property, not yours, Addie! I'm not having you molly-coddling her and feeding her titbits and making her fat and soft. She needs hardening up – and quickly. She has to earn her keep,' he said.

'I will do my dance and walk on my hands as pretty as you please,' I said.

'You're not here to prink about like a child at a party, little missy. You're a professional now. We're going to have to work on your act night and day to get you up to scratch,' said Mister. 'You'd better make the most of today. Now watch the act with particular care at tonight's performance. See how sharp my boys are. And afterwards I want you to list the whole routine for me – somersaults, flic-flacs, each and every tumble. You have to learn quick. Make the brain inside that pretty little bonce work overtime.' He tapped me sharply on top of my head. It felt as if his finger had poked right through flesh and bone.

Instead of being stirred into action, my brain now seemed paralysed with fear. I sat down to the evening performance and watched tensely, waiting for the silver boys to start their act. Beppo capered about the ring with Chino, and every child in the big top laughed delightedly – but I shrank down in my seat, terribly aware of his steely grey eyes. They seemed to be staring at me even when his head was turned away.

I craned my neck until it ached to watch Flora, the Queen of the Tightrope, then slumped uncomfortably in my seat when the sea lions balanced balls and honked little trumpets with their whiskery mouths. My head started to nod when dear Madame Adeline cantered round and round the ring. It had been a long and terrible day, the tent was stiflingly hot, my stomach was very full . . . I was soon fast asleep and didn't wake up until the grand parade at the end of the show.

I sat up with a jerk, bewildered by the claps and cheers all around me. I called out for Mary-Martha, in such a daze I thought I was back at Willoughby Buildings – but then my dazzled eyes made sense of the gas-lit tent and I remembered everything. I remembered everything – except the silver boys' routine! And Mister was going to quiz me on it in detail.

I thought I'd better attempt another escape, but Tag was waiting for me again and I was too tired to tussle with him. I let him drag me over to the wagon. Marvo and Julip joined us. All three boys seemed subdued, standing apart, arms hanging limp.

'It was *your* fault, Marvo. You weren't standing straight on,' Julip muttered.

'You didn't spring high enough, you fool,' Marvo told him.

'Well, Tag messed up his cartwheels and I got distracted,' said Julip.

Their act had clearly not gone well. They kept looking anxiously over their shoulders. I saw Mister in the distance discussing something with Chino, both of them smoking cigars. Madame Adeline was busy grooming Midnight and covering his back with a blanket for the night. She waved at me and I waved back, though my arm felt leaden.

Then, at last, Mister came striding towards us. He was a small man and he walked with his shoulders hunched. Marvo was twice his weight and Julip a head taller, but they cowered visibly. Tag was sweating through his greasepaint, clenching his fists.

'Fools!' Mister muttered, and then he reached up and slapped each boy hard about the head. 'Slipshod amateurs! We're rehearsing at seven sharp tomorrow – and if you dare mess up again I'll whip you all within an inch of your lives. Understand?'

It was clear he wasn't bluffing. Marvo and Julip bent their heads. Tag shivered all over, his face screwed up to stop himself crying.

Then Mister looked at me. 'Well, little trembling fairy, I hope you paid attention to the act? Tell me how it begins, reciting each individual exercise. Woe betide you if you get any wrong!'

I stared at him. I stared at Marvo and Julip and

Tag. Marvo moved his hand minutely, twirling one finger.

'They – they somersaulted into the ring,' I stammered.

Marvo pointed downwards.

'And – and Marvo stood on his hands,' I continued, but Mister had spotted Marvo's twitching finger.

'Don't you dare help her, you sneaking lummox,' he said, and he lashed out at Marvo again, hitting him so hard his head rocked.

If he could nearly knock a young ox like Marvo off his feet, what could he do to me? I felt sick with terror.

'I'm waiting,' said Mister. 'And as my boys will confirm, I'm not a patient man.'

My mouth was so dry I could only make a little croaking sound. I did not dare look at Marvo again. I simply stood there, opening and shutting my mouth.

'I can't hear you!' Mister came towards me, bending down so that his painted face was close to mine. His crimson lips leered at me. 'Louder, little fairy. Speak up, *if* you remember. If *not* – well, you must take your punishment.'

'Oh, Mister, I can't tell you!' I blurted.

'You can't tell me?' said Mister. 'You mean you weren't *paying attention*?'

'I was, oh indeed I was, but – but when the act went a little wrong and Julip slipped, quite by accident,

I had to shut my eyes tight because I was so upset,' I said. 'I *couldn't* watch because I knew you would be vexed.'

Mister stared and then seized hold of me. But he didn't strike me. He twirled me round as if we were doing a dance.

'Oh, what an artful answer from my little fairy!' he said. 'I think you will prove worth your five guineas after all. Now, go to bed and get your beauty sleep. Go, all of you.'

I visited the unspeakable latrine and then shut myself in the wagon with the boys. I did not have any nightgown to change into. I climbed into my hammock and curled up tight. The boys below me argued in whispers, cursing and complaining, but they soon started snoring. I lay awake, aching for Mary-Martha and little Johnnie, wondering if I'd ever see them again.

I had only just gone to sleep when I was woken by one of the boys giving my hammock a violent swing so that I nearly tumbled out.

'Practice time!' Tag hissed. 'Quick!'

We had no breakfast – just a hot drink. I peered at mine suspiciously. It was the same mug in which they'd served the horsemeat stew and it smelled.

'What drink is this?' I asked.

'Horse's pee,' said Julip.

All three boys collapsed with laughter when they saw my face.

'It's tea, black tea, I promise you,' said Marvo, but I still wouldn't drink it.

'You'd better have some. You'll be thirsty soon enough. Beppo works us hard,' he told me. He held the mug to my lips. 'Come on, little Diamond, drink up.'

I managed a few reluctant sips. 'Why is he so cruel to everyone?' I asked.

'It's just his way. His father was hard on him. It's the way we learn,' said Marvo.

'But you're bigger than him now,' I said. 'You could hit him back.'

They all three looked at me as if I were raving.

'You try hitting him, Diamond. Go on, I dare you!' said Tag.

'He's got a special cane,' said Julip. He pulled his singlet up to show me his back. 'Look!'

I saw terrible weals that made my eyes water. 'Why did he do that?' I whispered.

'We fell out. He hit me night after night because I lost my nerve and wouldn't always try the flying double somersault at the end of the act. I hate performing. I never wanted to be an acrobat – still don't, but there's nothing I can do about it. I ricked my back falling clumsily and it made me even more awkward, because it hurt so—'

'He made you perform even when you were in pain?'

'Beppo's in pain all the time,' said Marvo. 'He hurt his back too – broke it. He was six months scarcely able to move, and now he has to be a clown.'

'So it makes him all the more severe with us,' said Julip. 'One night I just wouldn't try at all. I did the simplest baby routine. The crowd probably didn't even realize – they'll roar and clap at anything – but afterwards Beppo beat me. The next day I could hardly move and all the wounds were seeping, but I still had to do two performances.'

'Will he beat me?' I whispered. 'I can't do one somersault, let alone two.'

'You'll learn soon enough,' Marvo told me. 'You're a little fairy, like he says. You'll be flying through the air in no time.'

'Flying through the air from the tip of my boot unless you all get cracking,' said Mister, coming out of his wagon and pointing at us threateningly.

He looked very old in the early morning light, his face grey without his greasepaint, and I noticed how stiffly he walked, his eyes twitching at every step, though they were still steely. I saw how a man twice the size of Marvo could still fear him. He was holding a great coil of rope and I wondered if he was going to beat me with it or maybe tie me up and hang me. I shrank from him in terror.

'Easy now, little fairy,' he said, chuckling grimly, and seizing me by the wrist. 'Come along with your Uncle Beppo.'

The rest of the circus performers were still in their wagons, fast asleep. Even the animals were quiet in their cages, slumped in slumber, though Elijah the elephant stood tethered to a tree, idly plucking leaves from the branches. I shrank from him too, scared that he might trample me or knock me over with his great trunk, but the boys all called to him affectionately as if he were their friend, and Tag reached up and patted his vast wrinkled thigh.

The circus ring was empty.

'Right, boys, cricking time,' said Mister.

They seized hold of each other's legs and stretched them hard, working them round in their sockets till I thought they'd be pulled right off.

'Your turn, little fairy. Got to get those puny arms and legs supple . . .' Mister pulled me close and then yanked my legs up to my head ten or more times. I screamed with pain.

'Now now, no fussing!' said Mister, panting with the effort.

'You're breaking me in two! Please, please, stop it!' I begged.

'A little bit of cricking never hurt anyone,' said Mister, persisting. When he set me down at last

I could barely stand, but he took no notice.

'Right, let's get to work now you're warmed up. Tag, practise your somersaults. Marvo, Julip, help me with the ropes.'

He took a strange belt and tied it tightly around my waist. 'So little, my tiny girl. A true Thumbelina!'

There were rings on either side of the belt, through which he threaded ropes. Marvo stood on one side of me, Julip on the other, holding the ropes tightly.

'Now, Diamond, first you must learn the back somersault, the easiest of all. Simply spring up, tuck and turn backwards. Show her, Tag.'

Tag did a whole series of back somersaults, landing each with a jaunty flourish.

'Now, you try, Diamond,' said Mister.

I did my best, in spite of my aching back and buckled legs. It was a clumsy attempt, and I pulled heavily on the ropes and fell as I landed – but it was *almost* a back somersault.

'That was hopeless!' said Tag, sneering.

I thought Mister would be vexed with me, but he waved Tag away. 'Not bad for a first attempt, little fairy. I think you're going to be a natural,' he said.

He kept me working at it half the morning, until I was wringing wet with sweat and the blood was pounding through my body. Then he let me rest for half an hour while he made the boys repeat their act. He was especially hard on Julip, forcing him to do his double somersault again and again. Then it was my turn to do my very simple back somersault, while Marvo and Julip held my ropes. I still couldn't turn and tuck neatly enough. Tag kept sighing at me and then somersaulting exquisitely himself, showing off.

The friction of the tight belt was rubbing my waist raw and chafing terribly.

'Enough,' said Mister. 'We don't want to saw the little fairy in half.'

'Little flop, more like,' said Tag.

'We will work on your handstands instead,' Mister went on.

'I can do that!' I said eagerly, and demonstrated.

I thought I did it well enough. The crowds at the market had always clapped me – but I didn't impress Mister or the boys.

'Terrible! You must straighten your line and position those legs. There are two different postures. The first is with the legs open in the form of a Y, the second with the legs straight together like an I, toes pointed. Show her, Tag.'

Tag executed both handstands neatly in triumph. I did my level best to copy him, and must have made a fair stab at things because Mister nodded.

'Better,' he said, which was clearly the nearest he

came to praise. 'Now try bending backward, arching your body.'

'The crab-walk! Oh, I can do that too!' I said, doing so.

'Yes, yes, so now you can try the curvet. Arch your body back until your hands touch the ground and then relax all the muscles of your legs so that you rebound back onto your feet. Simple!'

It wasn't simple at all. Tag showed me several times, but I couldn't get the hang of it. I kept tumbling and hurting myself – one time so badly that I cried, tears streaming down my face.

'No, no! No grimacing, no tears, no matter how much it hurts. A true artiste always smiles through the pain so that no one knows. *Smile*, Diamond – stand up and smile and do the curvet again – properly this time,' Mister commanded.

I clenched my teeth and smiled, and managed a reasonable stab at the horrible curvet.

'Mmm . . . Well, it will become second nature to you in time.'

I did not believe him, but I practised morning after morning. When I could do a back somersault without the ropes, Mister said it was time he fitted me out with a costume.

'With a *costume*?' said Tag. 'She can't go in the ring! She still can't do anything!'

'Don't you question me, boy,' said Mister, slapping him about the head. 'She don't *need* to do anything, she just has to look sweet. She's got a lot to learn, but she has to earn her keep meanwhile. We'll work her into the act. She can run in and do her tiny tricks in turn with you boys, and then, when you start your balancing and make your human tower, she can caper about and point – look, Diamond, like this.' He bent down with a groan, contorted his mouth into a huge O of surprise and pointed his finger in exaggerated pantomime. I was forced to copy him until I could do it to his satisfaction.

Tag mimicked me cruelly behind Beppo's back. 'You don't look sweet at all,' he hissed that night in the wagon. 'You look so stupid everyone will laugh at you.'

'Take no notice. Tag's just worried they'll all look at you instead of him,' said Marvo, trying to be reassuring.

'I hope they *do* look at her instead of me,' said Julip. He had nearly slipped again that night, and Beppo had hit him savagely afterwards.

I lay trembling in my hammock, wondering if Mister would beat me too.

The next morning Beppo left the three boys training in the ring and took me to see Madame Adeline. She was still in her rose-patterned wrapper, brushing Midnight until his skin shone glossy black.

'Can you give us a helping hand, Addie? I'm putting the little fairy here into the ring today. She can wear Tag's old silver leotard, but I'd like to pretty it up a bit – make her look like a real little fairy. You don't have any frills you can lend her, do you? And maybe a ribbon for her hair.' Mister ran his hand through my bedraggled curls. 'It's not as fluffy as it was,' he said, pulling my hair.

'It looks as if she could do with a good wash,' said Madame Adeline. 'Leave her with me, Beppo.'

I hadn't washed since the day Beppo snatched me from the market. The boys never bothered much, just ducked under the communal tap and then shook themselves dry like dogs. But Madame Adeline filled a big bucketful, then heated it up over her fire and poured some of the hot water into a big shallow tin tray.

'There now, paddle your feet,' she said, swiftly undressing me. 'Let's give you a good soaping.'

Mary-Martha always used carbolic on me, but Madame Adeline had wonderful verbena soap. I loved the smell so much, I didn't even mind when it made my eyes sting. She rubbed another fragrant potion on my head, piling my hair up and rubbing with her fingertips until I was all over froth.

'This stuff is beautiful!' I said rapturously.

'It's my very special Ladies' Rainbow Shampoo,

108

dearie. Look!' Madame Adeline rubbed the foam between her thumb and forefinger, and then opened them slowly so that a web formed. She blew gently.

'Oh, rainbow bubbles!' I said.

'You do one now . . .' She let me play, entranced, for a full five minutes.

'You'll have to ask Beppo for one of his old pipes. You'll be able to blow enormous bubbles,' she said. 'Come now, you're starting to shiver. Let me sluice all the soap off you.'

'I wouldn't dare ask Mister for anything. He's far too fierce,' I said.

'Oh dear. He seems very taken with you, so I'd hoped he'd be kind, especially as you're so young. He hasn't hit you, has he?'

'No, but he hits the boys *lots*, especially Julip.'

'Poor Julip. He's struggling. He's skilled enough – Beppo is a good trainer, but Julip's heart isn't in it. It's a very hard life for a young man. It's a hard life for *all* of us.' She shook her head forlornly, suddenly looking like an old, old lady. She hadn't put on her face paint yet, and she had somehow tucked all her beautiful long red hair into a strange velvet turban.

'Are you sad, Madame Adeline?' I asked.

She made her mouth turn up into a big smile. 'No, I'm very happy, because I have a dear little new friend to keep me company,' she said. 'Is that all the soap gone? There's a few suds left in your hair. Let me give you one more rinse. Close your eyes!'

'They're tight shut,' I said. 'Madame Adeline – do you mean . . . me? Am *I* your new friend?'

'Of course I mean you, Diamond,' she said, wrapping a big soft towel around me, and then pulling me closer and hugging me.

'Oh, I love to be hugged!' I said. 'Sometimes Ma would hold me on her lap and it was the best feeling in the world.'

'How your mother must have loved you, dearie,' said Madame Adeline.

'I don't think she did – not very much, anyway,' I said. 'She loved the boys more than me – and Mary-Martha was the useful one. I was just a nuisance. I used to be Pa's favourite, but then, after Ma died, he started to hate me.'

'Oh, what a sad story! Well, listen to me, Diamond. If you'd been *my* little girl, I might have loved your brothers and your sister, but I'm certain *you* would have been my favourite. Now, are you dry, dear one? We'll find you some new clothes to wear in the ring, and I'll give your old clothes a good scrub too.'

She sat me on the velvet chair in her wagon, popped a violet chocolate in my mouth and told me to towel my hair while she did a little sewing. I was astonished to see that her *own* hair wasn't under her turban at all. It was hanging on a stand on her dressing table, the long flaming locks reaching down almost to the floor.

Madame Adeline saw me staring and raised her eyebrows ruefully. 'I'm not quite the natural beauty people think any more,' she said.

'I think you're naturally beautiful with your hair or without it,' I said stoutly.

'Bless you, child! I shall store your words up in my head and treasure them. I don't get many compliments nowadays.'

'Don't you have any gentlemen come calling, Madame Adeline?'

'No, dear, not any more, but I don't mind that in the slightest. I've seen enough gentlemen to last me a lifetime.' As she spoke, she rummaged through the lowest dressing-table drawer, bringing out a tangle of bright ribbons and embroidered scarves and lacy undergarments. 'Now then, shall we see if we can turn you into a real fairy?' she said.

She snipped the lace off a torn chemise and started sewing it around the neck of Tag's leotard. She bunched some sparkly net around my waist, fashioning a little skirt. Then she found some wire, bent it into a strange shape, and set me wrapping it round and round with silver satin ribbon.

'What is the wire for?' I asked.

'What do all fairies have?' said Madame Adeline.
'Wings!'

'Exactly. I have some white muslin. We will stretch it over the wire – and you can have a little fairy wand too, with a silver star on the end.'

We worked peacefully together making my costume. Then Madame Adeline had me sit in front of her while she brushed my damp hair. I wriggled delightedly at each firm stroke of the brush, trying to count along with her, but getting muddled after a while. I knew how to count up my pennies, but I'd never needed to know large amounts. Madame Adeline asked me to toss my hair forward over my eyes so she could sort out all the tangles. I wasn't used to my hair being so soft and silky. Sunlight poured in through the open wagon door and made little coloured lights gleam in it. It truly *was* rainbow shampoo.

Madame Adeline wound my front curls round her fingers until they sprang into place, framing my face, and then she opened a beautiful carved jewellery box and brought out . . .

'A crown!' I gasped, staring at the wonderful sparkling gems. 'A diamond crown!'

'No, dear, a tiara – and these stones are only glass. But it looks pretty in the ring and the diamonds catch the light. Perfect for little Diamond, the Acrobatic Child Wonder!'

112

'You truly don't mind my wearing your beautiful tiara?'

'You will look a picture and do us all proud,' said Madame Adeline. 'Come, let us put on your costume.'

I stepped into the sparkly leotard, now with gauzy little wings flapping at the back.

'Turn around, little fairy. Act as if you're in the spotlight,' she told me.

I pivoted around on one foot, pointing the other, my arms raised.

Madame Adeline laughed and clapped me enthusiastically. 'Bravo! Oh, wait till Beppo sees you. He will be delighted,' she said. 'Let us show you off to him.'

I hung back. 'I don't want to. I don't like him. I'd much sooner be with you. Oh, Madame Adeline, can't I be *your* little wonder?'

'I would like that very much, my dear – but Beppo wouldn't. I'm afraid he is your master now, whether you like it or not. It's the first rule of the circus. You must never steal another artiste's act.'

She took me by the hand and led me to the big top, where Beppo and Chino were working on a new clowning routine with a big penny-farthing bicycle.

'Look at your little protégée now, Beppo,' said Madame Adeline, giving me a gentle push forward.

He took one look at me, wobbled precariously, and then fell right off the tall bicycle. I thought he'd be cross with me in consequence, but his face was all smiles – even his steely eyes softened. He brought his two hands together, almost as if he were praying.

'Perfect!' he breathed. 'Oh, Addie, you've excelled yourself! It looks like I've got my five guineas worth. My, that old fool should have asked me for ten.' He turned me round and round, getting me to put my head to one side and point each toe in turn. 'Oh, you're a picture, my little fairy girl,' he said. He took my wand and waved it over me. 'You will be the star of the show and make old Beppo's wishes come true!'

I stood behind the tent flaps in a long line of artistes waiting to go into the ring. The ringmaster, Mr Tanglefield, was announcing the acts, his voice reedy and distorted as he was speaking through a megaphone. I was almost as scared of Mr Tanglefield as I was of Beppo. He was just as small and mean, and he went everywhere with a whip clamped in his hand. I'd seen him flick it at man and beast indiscriminately. I was always very careful to keep my distance. Now, I could hear the audience laughing and talking through his announcements, barely paying attention, for he sounded such a silly old man. Then the band struck up.

Mister pointed his finger at me to stay in my place with Marvo, Julip and Tag, and then pushed his way through the tent flaps with Chino, both of them waddling in their oversized clown shoes. A shriek of laughter rippled around the ring at their capers.

'Good audience tonight, by the sound of it,' said Sherzam, the elephant keeper. He was a small, slender man, strangely dark, with big brown eyes with long lashes. He smiled at me encouragingly.

'Good or bad, they'll always laugh their silly heads off at the clowns,' said Flora, the tightrope walker. She was a very large lady – by far the fattest member of Tanglefield's Travelling Circus apart from Elijah the elephant. The other acts often teased her. I'd heard Tag ask her why she didn't leave the circus and earn her living as Flora the Fat Lady in a fair, but she just cuffed him in a casual way, not bothering to take offence.

'Looking forward to your debut, Diamond?' she asked, stroking my hair admiringly. 'My, you look quite dazzling.'

Tag groaned, and staggered backwards, covering his eyes with his hands, pretending to be dazzled.

'Silly boy,' said Flora. 'How are you doing, dearie?

Addie asked me to keep a special eye on you.'

Madame Adeline herself didn't come on until almost the end of the show, so she wasn't standing in the line-up yet.

'I'm very nervous,' I whispered.

'That's a sign of a true artiste. I've been doing my act for many years now—'

'Hundreds and hundreds of years,' Tag muttered rudely.

'And always at this moment my stomach churns and I quake with fear.' Flora clutched herself and shivered dramatically. 'But when I climb my little rope ladder it's as if I am entering another world entirely. I forget all those people gawping up at me, wondering if I'm going to slip and fall. I even forget the rude boys pointing and poking fun at me.' She shook her head at Tag. 'Up on my tightrope, my hands don't tremble, my feet are sure and certain in their satin slippers, and I walk, I skip, I dance along my wire. I am Queen of my own airy world.'

'But you are talented, Miss Flora. I can't really do anything yet,' I sighed.

'I'll say,' said Tag. 'You can't even do a forward somersault. I could do that years and years ago. You're useless.'

'She'll learn soon enough,' said Marvo. 'Don't be so hard on her, Tag.'

'If she'd had any sense she'd scarper now, while she can,' Julip muttered.

He was wearing greasepaint on his face but I could see the sweat standing out on his forehead. I took his hand. It was as cold and clammy as a dead fish.

'What's the matter, Julip?' I asked.

He shook his head and pulled his hand away.

'Leave him be,' said Flora. 'He is just having a little nervous crisis, like me.'

'He's in a funk because he keeps slipping,' said Tag. 'He's *useless*.'

Julip was too miserable to respond, but Marvo seized Tag and turned him upside down.

'So Diamond's useless – and Julip too, Mr Taggle? What about me? Am I useless?' said Marvo, shaking him.

'Don't! Let me up!' Tag said indignantly, struggling.

Then Mr Tanglefield came rushing through the tent flaps to seize hold of Elijah for his grand appearance. We all saw Beppo for a moment, capering in a corner of the ring, his head turned towards us. It was enough to make Marvo set Tag on his feet and Julip stand to attention.

'No fooling while you're waiting to go on,' Mr Tanglefield muttered, taking hold of Elijah's chain from Sherzam. I pressed backwards nervously as the great elephant plodded wearily through the tent flaps, his wrinkled skin sagging off his huge bones. His trunk was swinging so that it brushed my bare arm. I craned upwards and saw the tiny eyes embedded in his vast head. He didn't look as if he enjoyed performing either.

Flora went on next. I peeped round the tent flap till I could see her dancing along the tightrope, waving her pink parasol, even pushing a perambulator, clearly enjoying herself. I hoped with all my might that I would enjoy performing too when I was actually out there in the ring. I'd quite liked doing my little tricks to earn money in the marketplace – but I hadn't had Mister lurking, ready to find fault.

Flora gave a last twirl and then clambered down her rope ladder. She spread her arms when she was back on firm ground, turning to acknowledge the cheering crowd, her face flushed with triumph.

Marvo took a deep breath. 'Right, my friends.' He clapped Julip on the back. 'You'll be fine,' he said. He chucked Tag under his chin. 'You too, Tag.' Then he gently pulled a lock of my hair. 'And you'll knock 'em dead, Diamond, just you wait and see.'

Then Flora came through the tent flaps all aglow. Beppo seized hold of me and murmured, 'Dance, little fairy!' and gave me a push right out into the ring.

I stood blinking in the bright spotlight, breathing in the strange smells of sawdust and animals and saveloys and oranges and gingerbread, in such a daze that the circle of crowded seats whirled round and round and I felt so dizzy I didn't dare move. I saw the sparkle as the silver costumes of my three new brothers caught the light, and then Marvo's hand was in mine, pulling me along so that I had to run with all three of them around the ring. I was only *running* – and yet a great murmur started. 'Oh my, look at the little one!' 'She's so tiny! What will she be, four? Five at the most? The little darling!' 'She's just a baby, bless her – and doesn't she look gorgeous: good enough to eat!'

Marvo started his routine, flexing his muscles and leaping about, doing cartwheels, flic-flacs, forward somersaults, every movement neat and precise. Then Julip began, and I felt my mouth go dry, but his routine was faultless too. Some of the girls in the audience squealed excitedly, appreciating his dark good looks. Tag's display was faster and wilder. He didn't always land as cleanly and the lines of his body weren't always perfect, but he had so much wild energy that people cheered.

Then it was my turn. I pointed my toes and twirled this way and that, and then tried a couple of cartwheels. It was the easiest exercise ever, yet everyone gawped and clapped as if I'd done something splendid. I bobbed a little curtsy to the audience, which made them laugh, and then continued my baby routine: my handstands, my crab-walk, my backward somersaults – thankfully each one perfect.

It was time for the silver boys to start serious tumbling, using the springboard, so that first Julip and then Tag spiralled through the air. I pointed and exclaimed and applauded enthusiastically, just as Mister had instructed. The audience lapped up my emphatic performance. I was so relieved when Julip landed with utter precision on Marvo's broad shoulders, and then stayed still and steady in turn after Tag spiralled upwards and landed on him that I clapped wildly – and the audience clapped with me.

The four of us stood in a line, arms out, and then we ran out into the wings, waving goodbye to everyone. Mister was standing by, smiling.

'There! I knew they'd love you, little fairy five guineas,' he said, before he had to caper on with Chino to distract everyone while the lion cages were assembled.

'Well done, little one!' said all the circus artistes waiting in the queue. Even the performing monkeys chattered and clapped their tiny paws at me. Madame Adeline was waiting at the end, glorious in her pink spangles and fleshings, with her glossy black Midnight.

'My little star!' she said, giving me a big hug, so that I breathed in her wonderful perfume.

I truly *felt* a star – happier than I had ever been in my life. I danced across the grass, throwing my hands up as if the audience were still surrounding me. Then someone pushed me violently in the back. I stumbled and very nearly fell.

'You hateful little show-off!' said Tag, punching me. 'You stole the whole act with your mincing and your prancing! They weren't even looking at us half the time.'

'I – I *had* to point and dance. Beppo *told* me to!' I stammered.

'You didn't have to do it so *much*. It was sickening,' said Tag. 'Tossing your head and fluffing your stupid hair!' He yanked at it so hard that my precious borrowed tiara was knocked sideways.

'Leave her be, Tag! Stop acting like a jealous little fool. Take no notice, Diamond. You did splendidly,' said Marvo, gently setting my tiara straight.

'So splendidly she can take over from me soon,' said Julip.

'She'll never be a real part of the act. She just does pathetic baby tumbles – and yet she steals all our applause,' said Tag.

'I'm sorry! I didn't mean to! I was just trying to do my best,' I said, and struggle as I might I couldn't stop the tears spilling down my cheeks.

'Now look what you've done, Tag. Shame on you,'

said Marvo, picking me up effortlessly and patting me on the back.

'Cry-baby! See, Julip, she's even turned Marvo against me. And did you see Beppo smarming all over her! *We* do all the work and yet all we get is blows!' Tag shouted, and he stormed off across the field.

'Oh, Tag, please, come back! Don't be cross. I promise I won't dance about next time. I won't do *anything*,' I cried.

'Leave him, Diamond. He's just cross because *he* usually gets all the attention. You did perfectly – and if you please Beppo he'll be all the sweeter to us too,' said Marvo.

'He won't ever be sweet to me,' said Julip, and he mooched off in the other direction.

'Oh dear,' I said, sniffling.

'Don't worry. They'll both be back for the grand parade at the end of the show. Come, let's go back to the wagon, little girl. You're shivering.'

I had three real older brothers, but they'd never treated me as kindly as dear Marvo. I couldn't stop shivering even back in the wagon, so he wrapped his huge greatcoat around me to warm me up. It trailed across the floor when I walked and my arms came only halfway down the sleeves, which made us both laugh.

'I think we need a little tonic,' said Marvo, and he produced a bottle of ginger beer. We shared it, sipping from the neck alternately. Marvo rummaged in his tea-chest and found an old pack of dog-eared cards.

'Here, I'll light a candle. Can you play Beggar my Neighbour, Diamond?'

I couldn't, but I learned soon enough and we had a grand game together. Marvo didn't have a pocket watch, but he knew by instinct the correct time to return to the big top for the closing parade. When we got there, Julip and Tag were already waiting. Julip gave me a little nod. Tag still glared, but when it was our turn to go into the ring he clasped my hand. We stepped out, all four in a line, and when I saw the smiles spread across the faces of all three boys, I made myself smile too, and the audience roared louder. Someone threw something at me and I ducked, startled. Another object came flying towards me, and I gasped, wondering why I was under attack.

'They're oranges,' said Marvo. 'They're throwing them at you because they like you! Gather them up. We'll share them out tonight.'

So I gathered up a great armful of oranges. Tag had a fair share too. Beppo took three and juggled with them, capering along beside us. He was still smiling when we got out of the ring.

'Well done, all four of you!' he said. 'We'll have a slap-up supper to celebrate.'

Marvo grinned, Julip squared his shoulders and

even Tag smirked. We didn't have the usual dubious stew. Beppo sent Tag running to the nearest butcher's for five fine chops. He fried them with onions and streaky bacon and mushrooms, and then we each sucked an orange for afters. I asked if I could take an orange to Madame Adeline as a present, and Beppo was in such a good mood he just nodded cheerily.

'For me, darling?' said Madame Adeline, when I shyly handed her the orange. 'But it's yours, my love. You eat it.'

'You're always giving me nice treats, Madame Adeline,' I said. 'Please take it.'

'Bless you, child . . .' She looked as if she might cry, and insisted on giving me a slice of cake and a special violet chocolate in return.

'Don't stuff yourself too much, little one,' said Beppo, seeing my full mouth. 'We don't want you sicking it all up in the second show for all to see.'

I found I was desperately nervous all over again for the evening performance – and this time I worried even when I was in the ring, though I took care to keep a big smile on my face. I knew I had to perform the way Beppo wanted or he would beat me – but I didn't want to make Tag hate me even more, so I gave a very subdued performance, trying not to prance too much. I was so anxious that I stumbled when I did my back somersault and very nearly landed with a bump on my bottom in the sawdust – but this mishap made the crowd love me even more. 'Aaah, the little pet!' they cried. 'Nearly took a tumble, and no wonder, she's so tiny.' 'Doesn't she look a real star? Such a pretty baby!'

I felt my face flushing – while Tag's was scarlet with rage. When we came running off he pushed me violently again and called me terrible names. Beppo saw and heard it all, though Tag didn't seem to care.

I thought Beppo would be angry, but he simply chuckled.

'My, the boy's jealous! What a temper!' he said.

'I'm sorry, it's all my fault,' I said.

'No, you haven't put a foot wrong. Well, you *did*, actually – that was a hopeless back somersault and you should be ashamed of yourself, little Miss Fairy – but it didn't matter a jot, did it? They loved you even more, God bless 'em.' Beppo pinched my cheek. 'Five guineas well spent!'

I couldn't help feeling proud, especially when folk lingered outside the big top and called my name excitedly, wanting another smile and wave from me. I wished Mary-Martha could see me, and Matthew and Mark and Luke and little John. I wished Pa could see me too, though it might upset him. But we'd already moved on from my home town. We moved on most Saturday nights, everyone working together the moment the show was over.

I had to help too, collecting up the cushions from

the best seats and storing them in great boxes. I helped Madame Adeline wrap all her pretty china in newspaper for the journey and helped Flora pack up her perambulator and her parasol and her long tightrope in a special trunk. All the menagerie artistes wanted to feed their own animals and secure them in their travelling cages. I certainly did not want to go near the great yellow lions who smelled so rank and devoured their meat so ferociously.

I was even a bit afraid of their water cousins – the males were too big and whiskery and they barked their heads off at the sight of a bucket of fish. I was certainly too much in awe of great Elijah to stand too close to him. But I started to help cage the troupe of performing monkeys, and loved packing up all their props and tiny costumes. I adored the monkeys – especially little Mavis, the baby.

These monkeys were much more interesting than surly little Jacko. They looked just like tiny, ugly people, but with such cute faces and lovely furry bodies. They had a special cage with real trees planted in great pots, so that the monkeys could swing amongst their branches, clinging on with their tiny hands, sometimes upside down, using their curling tails.

When I could get away from Beppo and the boys, I'd go and watch the monkeys in their cage. It took me a while to sort out all the adults, but right from the start the baby was my favourite. Most of the time she rode on her mother's back or clung upside down to her stomach, but would sometimes wander off on little forays of her own, especially if she spotted a choice nut or apple chunk that had fallen out of the feeding tray. She'd suddenly dart off, seize the morsel, scamper right up to the highest branch she could find, look around furtively to see if any of her older relatives were watching, and then nibble happily at her treat.

I don't know if the older monkeys *were* all relatives, but Mr Marvel, their trainer, got them decked out as a real family when he showed them in the ring. The oldest male was Marmaduke, and he had a tiny top hat and wore astonishing miniature boots on his hind paws. When he sat down on his little velvet armchair he kicked them off one at a time while his 'wife', Melinda, scurried to his side with a tiny pipe and a pair of diminutive carpet slippers. Their grown-up 'daughter', Marianne, went to a ball with a ribbon about her neck and waltzed round and round with a very small fiancé monkey called Michael, who kept trying to puff on a toy cigar while dancing. Marianne objected, and eventually seized the cigar and bit it in two.

Baby Mavis was by far the funniest little performer. Melinda would fetch her from the 'nursery', tenderly lifting her out of her little rocking cot and giving her a real bottle of milk. Then she made a great to-do of patting her on the back until Mavis made a rude windy noise, which made everyone laugh.

Melinda tried to get Mavis dressed in a napkin and little knitted jacket, but Mavis kept wriggling, attempting to get away, until eventually Melinda lost patience and sat on her head to keep her still. When she was dressed at last, Melinda took her for a walk in the perambulator while Mavis peeped out coyly, waving to everyone.

Mr Marvel then did a whole set piece where he was a photographer, and the entire family had to squeeze up together on the sofa to pose for their portrait. There was a great deal of pushing and shoving, and Mavis stole her father's pipe and puffed at it rakishly. When Mr Marvel had them all assembled in their positions, Michael put his paws over his face – and then they all did, even Mavis. Mr Marvel shook his finger and muttered at them, pretending to give them a talking to.

'Smile!' he commanded them – and simultaneously they all opened their mouths and gave great monkey grins.

For their finale Mr Marvel gave them each a little sparkly silver bow, as if they were tiny members of the Silver Tumblers' act! They all turned somersaults with immense agility and then stood in a line, clapping their paws. Whenever I watched them, I clapped until my hands hurt, and I took to visiting them every day in their cage.

Mr Marvel didn't seem to mind too much. Sherzam was very wary about folk pestering Elijah, and Carlos shouted angrily if anyone came too close to his lions. Even dear Madame Adeline was very protective of Midnight and scolded me gently when she caught me feeding him a piece of my cake. But Mr Marvel let me share some of my oranges with the monkey family. I cut them into segments and poked them through the bars. Soon baby Mavis chattered excitedly at the sight of me and clung to the bars, her little mouth open and shutting. She didn't mind too much if I couldn't muster an orange or a few peanuts – she just seemed happy to see me. She sniffed my fingers and gave them little approving licks.

'Watch out or she'll bite you, lass,' said Mr Marvel – but she never did.

'Reckon you've got a way with my monkeys,' he told me.

I *liked* Mr Marvel. Most of the circus men were too grand or busy to talk to me, or downright cruel and threatening like Beppo – but old Mr Marvel was a quiet, kindly gentleman. He looked a bit like his own monkey troupe. He was very brown, with so many

131

wrinkles that you'd run out of pencil if you tried to draw his face. His little brown eyes were sunk deep into his head and his mouth contained two or three teeth at most. He looked some great age – eighty or ninety at least. Tag insisted he was over a hundred years old. Madame Adeline said this was nonsense: she reckoned Mr Marvel was around seventy.

I plucked up courage and asked Mr Marvel himself. He squinted at me and said, 'As old as my eyes and a little older than my teeth,' which told me nothing.

Another time I asked him if he'd thought about retiring.

'I've thought about it, yes, missy, thought about it a lot – and concluded it's not an appealing thought. I'd be sitting in the same chair every night twiddling my thumbs, and Marmaduke, Melinda, Marianne, Michael and little Mavis would be rattling around in their cage, bored out of their skulls. They love performing in the ring and so do I, so we're not going to stop if we can help it.'

'Well, you would disappoint hundreds and hundreds of people if you did,' I said politely. 'Yours is the most popular act – well, you and Madame Adeline and Midnight.'

'Yes, dear Addie is another old trouper, bless her. She used to have six fine rosin-backed horses but that was in the old days. It's too expensive to feed so many horses on the pittance old Tanglefield pays now.'

'Well, I'll certainly help you feed all your monkeys, Mr Marvel,' I said earnestly.

'You're a good little lass. You've taken to this life like a duck to water. Anyone would think you were born to it.' He looked at me carefully. 'Beppo's not too hard on you, is he?'

'Well . . .'

Beppo was starting to be very hard indeed. I had thought my small success in the ring would be enough, but he had much bigger plans for me. He was training me up to be a proper acrobat and it was proving horribly hard. My bones ached from all the cruel cricking and I had bruises all over my body from the tumbles I took during rehearsals. Mister was threatening me with a royal beating if I didn't shape up.

I felt panicky just thinking about it. 'I wish . . . I wish I was part of a monkey act like yours, Mr Marvel,' I said wistfully.

'Do you not enjoy doing all your pretty tricks, Diamond?'

'I can't do many things,' I said, swallowing hard, scared I might start crying. 'I don't think I'm any good at acrobatics. I'm all right on the ground, when it's not too far to tumble. But now I have to try the springboard – and I haven't enough spring. And I can't even do a forward somersault yet. Mister Beppo says I'm a disgrace.'

'Oh dear, oh dear, poor little maid,' said Mr Marvel. 'Maybe Beppo's not training you right. I teach all my monkeys to do acrobatics and they love it. It's all done with kindness and encouragement – and titbits as a reward. I can't learn you any springboard tricks because that's specialist work, but I'll help you with your forward somersault – that's simple.' He leaned forward on his bowed legs, curled himself into a ball, and turned over in the air, landing neatly right way up in his carpet slippers.

'Oh my goodness!' I said, clapping him.

'You'll learn in no time, little lass,' he told me. 'It's just one simple twirly over, forwards instead of backwards.'

'But I always land on my head and it hurts,' I said.

'We'll put my old mattress on the floor, and then if you tumble it won't hurt a bit. That's what I use for my monkeys. Oh, they love a little bounce on my mattress!'

Mr Marvel encouraged me for several days. Each time I tried a forward somersault he gave me a piece of chopped date whether I landed properly or not. He clapped me no matter how clumsy I was, and consequently I lost all fear and could soon do the front somersault effortlessly.

'Bravo, Diamond! I knew you were a natural,' he said.

'Oh, wait till I show Mister Beppo!' I said gratefully.

'Don't tell him I helped you. He won't take kindly to it,' Mr Marvel warned. 'We don't interfere with each other's acts. I'm a mild man, but if I caught Beppo training my monkeys I'd be furious. Let him think *he's* taught you.' He tapped the side of his nose. 'You need some tactical common sense, dearie.'

So the next rehearsal with Mister, I deliberately made several clumsy attempts at the wretched forward somersault, with Tag jeering, Julip staring moodily into space, and Marvo smiling encouragingly.

'Dear Lord save us, it's simple enough,' Beppo said, raising his hand to hit me. 'Watch Tag one more time and then *do* it!'

'She'll never ever do it because she's useless,' said Tag, doing an effortless somersault and then thumbing his nose at me.

'Could *you* show me, Mister Beppo?' I said, lisping like a little girl.

'Stop that baby nonsense,' he said, but he turned a somersault all the same.

'Ah, *now* I see,' I said – and copied him perfectly.

They all looked astonished.

'Again!' ordered Mister.

I turned one again – and again and again.

'So we have the knack at last!' he said. 'Right! Now we'll work out a proper routine for you.'

135

I started to wish I hadn't mastered the forward somersault after all. Mister worked me extra hard for weeks, trying to make me perfect various bizarre kinds of somersault. I begged Mr Marvel to help me master the monkey's somersault and the lion's somersault and the Arab somersault, but he had never learned these himself, and couldn't help me. I was blue with bruises again, and had to paint white greasepaint on my arms so they wouldn't show in the ring.

'She'll never learn,' said Tag – but I *did* start to master each somersault, one by one. I grew thinner than ever, but now I had hard little muscles in my arms and legs, and my stomach grew so strong that I didn't flinch when Tag punched me.

He punched me a great deal, because Mister had worked out quite an elaborate little routine for me now, and it increased my popularity. I could have taken a bath in orange juice every night with all the fruit thrown by the admiring audience. Sometimes they waited outside the big top with bunches of flowers, or once, wondrously, a very large box of chocolates.

'It's not *fair*. She gets all the praise and presents while we do all the *real* work!' Tag complained bitterly.

'You got your share of her chocolates,' said Marvo. 'I don't see what you're moaning about.'

'Me neither,' said Julip. 'You carry on and take over the whole act, Diamond – and then I can escape.'

'I'm only a *little* part of the act,' I said. 'I can't use the springboard.'

'Not yet,' said Marvo kindly. 'But in a few years you might be ready. Tag was only twelve when he started springboard work.'

'I'm not twelve for years and years and years,' I said quickly. 'And even when I am, I never want to do springboard work.'

'You'll do as you're told,' said Mister, overhearing. 'In fact we might as well start training you up now. Think what a draw it would be – the little fairy who really can fly through the air! All the big circuses would be interested in such an act. We'd maybe make Askew's and have a permanent gaff in London.'

I hoped desperately that Mister wasn't serious, but at the very next rehearsal he had me try the springboard.

'Ha!' said Tag. 'You're going to come a cropper.'

'She's still too small, Beppo,' said Julip.

'If she misjudges her leap, she could break her neck,' said Marvo.

'She won't misjudge it, not if she concentrates. And we'll have her in the training harness,' said Mister.

'She can't wear the harness for performances,' Marvo persisted. 'You can't risk her doing springboard work, Beppo, it's not right.'

Mister went to stand beside Marvo, his eyes

narrowed, his mouth so set that his lips disappeared. Marvo towered above him – and yet took a step back, looking fearful.

'Are you telling me what I can or can't do?' Mister asked.

'No, Beppo. I'm just saying – in *my* opinion.'

'Well, shut your mouth. No one's interested in your opinion, you great plank of wood. You're not in charge of the act. I am. And I shall do as I please. And I didn't waste all that good money on the girl just to have her do a few baby somersaults and a prance or two. She's got natural ability. She'll learn quickly.'

I didn't seem to have any natural ability left. I couldn't learn at all. I was terrified, even wearing the safety harness. The springboard propelled me upwards, but each time I panicked, unable to tuck myself into a neat ball to turn the double somersault required. I failed to land neatly on my feet. I didn't come to too much harm as the safety harness held me upright, but it dug into me under my armpits and jarred my whole body.

I was forced to practise for hours and hours every morning, and then appear to be as fresh as a daisy for the afternoon and evening performances. I was sick one morning because I was in such a state of terror. Mister wouldn't let me have any breakfast at all after that, so I had to train on a totally empty stomach.

'That poor little child is exhausted,' said Madame Adeline, coming into the big top and taking hold of me by the shoulders. 'For shame, Beppo. Just look at her!'

'You mind your own business, Addie,' he growled.

'See the circles under her eyes. She's nothing but skin and bone. Can't you see, Beppo, you're killing the little goose who'll lay you golden eggs,' she told him.

'Do I tell you how to train that nag of yours, Addie?' he asked.

'If you saw me beating my poor Midnight to death I hope you'd step in and stop me,' said Madame Adeline. 'Because you'd realize I was losing my mind.'

'That's enough, woman. I won't have anyone talk to me like that, let alone some raddled old biddy who should have been pensioned off years ago,' said Beppo, suddenly cuttingly cruel.

Madame Adeline flushed. 'I believe you're at least five years older than me, Beppo,' she said, calmly enough. 'And at least I am still an artiste – not reduced to clowning.' She walked away, her head held high, but when I saw her later at the afternoon's performance her eyes were red.

My eyes were red too – and there were ugly scarlet weals across my back because Beppo had given me the threatened royal beating at last.

He didn't beat me again. He didn't need to. The fear of his stick made me quiver every time he looked at me. I strained even harder to learn springboard skills, but still failed miserably.

Mr Marvel spoke up for me too.

'You're wasting your time, Beppo. Try when the child is a year or two older. She hasn't got the strength or the skill just yet. It stands to reason: she's still only a baby. I know my little Mavis is the star of the act – she knows it too, bless her – but I don't try to teach her too many tricks just now because it will only confuse and frustrate her. Patience, Beppo. Be thankful. Your Diamond is a little star.'

'Hold your tongue, Monkey Man,' Mister replied. 'I know what I'm doing.'

I heard him discussing me with Chino, the other clown. I was hiding from him, under the wagon.

'You know the boys' big finale is the human column I devised. When it used to be just Marvo and Julip it didn't look anything special. But then young Tag came along and I trained him hard, and once he joined, it became a showstopper, the three of them balancing together. And if only that maddening little fairy would take flight it would look magnificent. She's so light, and Marvo's steady as a rock. Imagine it, Chino, the four of them in a column. All she has to do is somersault and land on Tag's shoulders, one simple tiny trick – and it will bring the house down. I could have posters made. She'd be like the fairy doll on top of the Christmas tree.' Mister groaned and thumped his fist against the wagon, making it shake.

I curled up into a tight ball. I wondered about running away. It would be difficult, though, to slip off undetected. Tag always knew where I was and what I was up to, and he'd tell on me. Mister would find me and drag me back and give me another whipping.

I shivered at the thought. I wasn't even sure where

I was now. We'd travelled far away from home. If I *did* somehow manage to escape, it would take me many days to walk back. I had no stout boots, only the soft slippers I wore in the ring. And how would I know which *way* to walk? I had never learned geography. I knew there were such things as maps, but I couldn't read enough to make sense of them.

And suppose I *did* manage to stumble all the way home – what would I do then? I very much doubted that Pa would take me back. My brothers had never really cared for me – and even Mary-Martha might have forgotten me. I couldn't really call Willoughby Buildings home any more.

I fell asleep on the damp grass beneath the wagon dreaming of a real home. I'd have Madame Adeline for my mother and Mr Marvel for my father and all the monkeys for my brothers and sisters. Mavis would be my special favourite, and would cuddle up with me every night in my safe, warm bed. I would eat pink cake and violet chocolates and sweet dates every day. I might perform on a little stage to earn my keep – an easy carpet act of somersaults and handstands – but my dear parents wouldn't hear of my attempting any springboard movements. It would be a solo act, no silver boys. Or perhaps it could be a double act with little Mavis.

It was Mavis herself who helped Mister's dream to

come true. One wet and stormy Saturday night we were all working hard pulling down the drenched big top and securing the animals when a bolt of lightning flashed right above us. Elijah trumpeted in alarm, nearly pulling free of his tether. The lions roared, the sea lions barked, Midnight and the wagon horses reared up on their hind legs, whinnying in fear.

Mr Marvel was in the process of cajoling his monkeys into their travelling cage. They were all chattering anxiously, baring their teeth.

'Into your cage, my lovelies, and I'll draw the curtain and then you won't see the horrid lightning,' he told them.

'Come along, little Mavis, in you go,' I said, giving her a gentle flick.

The four adult monkeys sprang into their familiar cage, cowering together in a corner, but just as baby Mavis was scrabbling in, a great boom of thunder made her squeal. She spun round and darted away, across the muddy grass, before either Mr Marvel or I could catch her.

'Mavis! Come here, baby! Come to your papa!' Mr Marvel called frantically – but she was already out of sight.

'Help!' I cried. 'Mavis is missing! Please, everyone, try to catch her!'

It was hard because everyone was busy and the

other animals were still frantic. It was pitch dark in the pouring rain, but most people came running to help all the same. Mr Marvel was crying unashamedly, hobbling backwards and forwards, calling hoarsely.

We looked amongst the cages, the wagons, the sodden folds of the great big top, but there was no sign of the little monkey.

Madame Adeline got Midnight safely into his horsebox, and then joined in the hunt, with only a shawl to protect her pink spangles. She had a chunk of her special cake in her hand. 'It's Mavis's favourite. I give her a few crumbs as a special treat,' she explained. 'Mavis? Mavis, where are you, darling? Come and have some of Madame Addie's lovely cake!'

My silver boys all helped to search too. Tag dashed everywhere, but even his quick eye could not spot Mavis. Mister mounted the clowns' penny-farthing and started trundling the whole length of the field.

'We'll have to start moving soon or we'll never get to Waynefleet by morning,' shouted Mr Tanglefield.

'I can't leave without my baby,' Mr Marvel wept.

'Then you'll have to stay here and join us later. I can't halt the whole circus for a monkey.'

'It's not *any* monkey. It's my Mavis!'

'I'll stay and help you find her, Mr Marvel,' I said, clutching his arm.

'You'll do no such thing. You're coming with us,' said

Beppo. 'Now get in the wagon. You're soaking wet. We can't have you catching your death of cold and then sneezing your head off in the ring. Do you hear me?'

I heard – but for once I didn't obey. I didn't even care if he beat me. I *had* to help Mr Marvel find Mavis. I trotted off meekly enough, but instead of jumping up the steps after Marvo, Julip and Tag, I crept off into the darkness. I called again and again for Mavis, making little clicking noises with my tongue.

'Come here, Mavis! Come, baby, come to Diamond,' I said, over and over again.

There was more lightning, zigzagging through the sky with a terrifying sizzle, and then loud thunderclaps. I could hear the animals panicking all around, with men running and shouting and cursing. I thought how scared little Mavis would be. She was so quick, she could have crossed the entire field by now. She might already be running amongst the carriages and cabs, in terrible danger of being trampled.

I was crying now as I ran around calling – and then I heard a wailing high above me. I looked up, the rain hitting my face, almost blinding me, but when the lightning flashed I saw a tiny creature darting about at the top of a very tall, thin tree, horribly buffeted by the wind and the rain.

'Mavis!' I cried.

She wailed again.

'Oh, Mavis, come down! Come down, baby. Come right down now!' I held out my arms, but Mavis was so scared she didn't even seem to recognize me. She climbed even higher, and when the lightning flashed again she screamed.

'Come *down*!' I called.

If the lightning struck the tree, poor Mavis would be burned to death. It was too terrible to contemplate. If she wouldn't come down, then *I* had to go *up*.

I'd never climbed a tree before. I was scared of heights but I didn't even think about it. I tucked my skirts into my drawers and started up. I didn't really know what I was doing. At the bottom there were not enough branches to cling to, but I'd watched the monkeys for many hours. I climbed the way they did, gripping with my hands and feet. My arms and legs were strong as steel after all the practice and the two performances every day. I went up and up.

'Diamond! Oh Lord, girl! Come down – you'll kill yourself!'

I peered down into the dark. It was Mr Marvel, calling hoarsely, beside himself. It was a huge mistake to look down. He seemed horribly far away already. I lost my rhythm, stretched up awkwardly, and slipped.

Mr Marvel gave a great wail.

I clung to the tree trunk desperately, managing to

hang on by gripping with my knees, though I felt my stockings rip on either side.

'Stay still! I'll come and rescue you!' Mr Marvel shouted, but he was too heavy and weighed down with sodden garments to get any kind of purchase on the tree.

'I don't need rescuing. *I'm* the rescuer. I'm rescuing Mavis,' I cried.

I reached up and started climbing again. The tree seemed to go on for ever. I had once hand-coloured a fairy story about a boy and a beanstalk that grew up to the sky. I remembered the ogre right at the top, with a grotesque scowl and a huge warty nose that I painted deep red, like Pa's.

But there was no ogre hovering above me, just a tiny little monkey, whimpering in terror.

'It's all right, Mavis – it's Diamond. I'm coming to get you. You'll be safe soon,' I called.

She could hear me now, but she must have thought I wanted to hurt her because she darted along a small branch right at the top of the tree. It swayed even under her small weight. I knew I couldn't possibly shin along it.

'Please come back, Mavis! I can't reach you there! Come back along the branch or you'll fall. It's Diamond – remember, I feed you oranges. I come and see you every day. I'm your friend. Oh, please come to me – please please please!'

Mavis clung to her tiny branch, not responding. But then there was another flash of lightning, so near this time that I felt its heat and power going right through me – and, with a squeak, Mavis ran back to the main trunk in three bounds . . . straight into my arms.

There was a cheer from below – a whole chorus of cheers. There must have been a proper audience by now, but I took care not to look down to check. I cradled Mavis close and she shivered, crying. Clinging to the tree with just one hand, I stuffed her down the front of my bodice, and then I began my precarious descent. It was much more difficult going down. I couldn't see what I was doing or get into any rhythm. When I tried to slide, I scraped the little skin I had left on my legs.

Then I heard Mister shouting, 'Tag's coming to get you, little fairy!'

'I don't *need* Tag,' I called back, and scrambled down as best I could, jumping the last few feet and landing in Mr Marvel's arms.

He hugged me close, tears pouring down his face, while everyone cheered.

Mr Tanglefield gave me a pat on the back. 'Well done, little 'un! Now, Marvel, keep a firm hold of that monkey, do you hear? We're setting off immediately – even if a whole cartload of monkeys escape, we'll just wave goodbye to them and be on our way, understand?'

Mr Marvel took little shivery Mavis from me and

cradled her in his arms. 'I'm in your debt for ever, young Diamond,' he said croakily. 'I don't know what I'd have done if I'd lost my little star.'

'*Diamond*'s the little star,' said Madame Adeline, putting her arm round me. 'But you must never do anything as reckless again – do you promise?'

'She'll promise no such thing!' said Mister. 'My, did you see her shin up that tree? Like a monkey herself, she was.'

'Any fool can climb a tree,' said Tag angrily. 'Watch *me* do it, Beppo.'

'You come back here, boy. We've had enough shenanigans for one night. But I tell you what – it's shown me the way forward for the finale to the act. Diamond will master the springboard in time, I dare say – but meanwhile she can *climb* up the human column and stand on Tag's shoulders.'

I hoped he might be joking, but of course he was deadly serious. On Sunday we were all exhausted after travelling through the night in the storm – but Mister had the four of us practising this new trick. First he had me scramble up Marvo and stand on his shoulders, and that wasn't too hard at all. I knew that Marvo would reach up and catch me if I should sway or stumble. It was far harder when I was forced to climb up Julip too. He was less steady, and it felt so much higher balancing on his shoulders. He had his hands gripping my calves, but it still didn't feel at all safe.

When I'd mastered this at last, Mister immediately told Tag to balance on top of Julip, and expected me to climb up all three boys in a trice. He had me on training ropes – he held one, Mr Marvel the other, so that if I fell, I wouldn't tumble on my head. I was terribly frightened even so. Marvo was very encouraging and Julip nodded at me sympathetically, but Tag jeered at me. I didn't trust him to hang onto me properly when I scrambled uncertainly to the top. Several times in succession I wobbled until Tag and Julip fell. They knew how to roll over and land neatly on their feet. I knew too, but panicked and forgot – and then I was brought up short with a judder on the end of the practice rope, flopping and gasping like a hooked fish on the end of a line.

But there was no backing out now. Mister was adamant. The fourfold human column must end our act. He announced we had to try it out the very next performance. I was sick with nerves – literally so. Marvo discovered me vomiting miserably into a clump of nettles at the edge of the field.

'Don't fret so, Diamond,' he said, wiping my face and smoothing my tangled hair.

'I'm going to have to do it without the practice rope, and I'm so scared I'll fall,' I wept.

'You won't fall – but if you *do* I shall catch you, I promise. I'll reach out and grab you,' said Marvo, demonstrating.

'And then Julip and Tag will fall down.'

'They can look after themselves – and it would do young Tag good to take a tumble. He's been behaving abominably, the cocky little pup.'

Tag had been teasing me cruelly, telling me I was a terrible acrobat and would spoil the whole show.

'I think he's right. I *will* spoil the whole show,' I mumbled.

'That's nonsense. Tag's just saying that because he sees how the crowds love you. His nose has been put out of joint. But he's not a bad lad at heart. He'll try to make it easier for you,' said Marvo.

To my great surprise, he was right. While we were waiting to go on, and I was white and shivery, wondering whether I would vomit again, Tag suddenly seized my clammy hand.

'You'll do all right,' he whispered. 'You're quite good at it really – not as good as *me*, of course, but not bad for a girl.'

But it was a Julip who was the most help.

'I know just how you feel, Diamond,' he said. 'Beppo and Marvo and Tag tell you not to worry – but you will. I do, anyway. But I try and tell myself that I won't always be here in a foolish silver costume, frightened to death. One day I'll be too old to perform . . .'

'Will you be a clown then, like Beppo?'

'Never! I'll leave the circus and find a job – any job. I'm good with animals, I'm good at fixing things, I'm strong. I'll work and save until I have my own house – not a cramped wagon, a real little house in a village. I'll have a garden and grow flowers and vegetables, and I'll find a wife and we'll have children and we'll live in the same place for the rest of our days. I think about each little detail of my new life until it starts to feel real. I might be leaping high in the air doing a double somersault in front of gaping fools, but inside I'm in my own living room, sitting before a fire, with a cat on my lap and a dog at my feet.'

'That's why you wobble and fluff, you fool. You should concentrate properly,' said Tag.

'If I concentrate it makes it worse,' said Julip. 'Try my trick, Diamond. It helps.'

So I tried hard to blot out the shouts of the crowd and the rustle and roar of the animals, and imagined jumping on a giant springboard that catapulted me years into my future. Did I want my own little house like Julip? I thought of the house where we'd once lived – Ma and Pa and the boys and Mary-Martha and me. Had I been happy there as a baby? I tried to remember what it was like to sit on Ma's lap, but she was fading in my memory now. I could only picture her pale as a ghost in her nightgown, crying sadly to herself, and it made me want to cry too.

I didn't have Ma any more, and Pa didn't want me. Perhaps I could one day share a little cottage with Mary-Martha and baby Johnnie? I tried to picture the three of us, and as I was running around the ring, cart-wheeling and capering, I chose our armchairs and embroidered our cushions. When I did my crab-walk, I filled our pantry with tins of pink cake and jars of dried dates. When I had to climb up Marvo and Julip and Tag at the end of the act, I pictured climbing the stairs to sleep in my own soft little bed – and though I still trembled, I got right to the top and stood on Tag's shoulders and kept my balance and smiled while everyone cheered.

I hoped it would get easier. After all, I could now turn neat somersaults as easily as winking. But the human column was different. It was a twice daily terror. Julip was right – the fear never went away. But there were good times too. I loved visiting Madame Adeline and eating cake and chocolates, I loved chatting to Mr Marvel and playing with little Mavis, but even then, when I was most relaxed, the fear was there in the pit of my stomach.

Mister haunted me every day and stalked my

dreams at night. I could never please him now. The more he threatened me, the worse I got, until I stumbled doing the simplest cartwheel and started whenever he said my name. I developed a nervous twitch that made him even madder. 'Stop jerking about like a little lunatic! Stop it at once, I say!' he'd hiss. I'd put my hands to my face, struggling to keep it still, but I could feel it twitching beneath my fingers.

I lost all sense of where we were and how far we had travelled. We pulled down the big top every week, rain or shine, travelled through the night, arrived at a new town or village, slept through the morning, and rehearsed and performed all the rest of the week. We could have been down in sunny Cornwall or up in chilly Inverness for all I knew. We might even have returned to my own home town without my realizing.

I never left the circus field, and they all looked alike anyway. I didn't know, I ceased to care. I took part in the circus parade through towns and villages, and barely noticed whether I was passing great stone mansions or humble cottages. All I had to do was smile until my cheeks ached, smile even when my eyes pricked with tears.

I was hiding under the wagon one evening because Mister had threatened me with a beating and I was pretty sure he meant it. I couldn't help sobbing, though

I put my hands over my face to try to stifle the sounds. Then I heard a scuffle – and someone bent right down and peered under the wagon at me.

Yes, Hetty, it was you!

I was so startled I curled up small, trying to hide.

'It's all right, I'm not going to hurt you,' the someone whispered. 'And I won't let anyone else hurt you either. See my red hair? I am so fierce that everyone is scared of me. Even the biggest, ugliest ogre quakes when he sees me coming. Evil giants tremble and whimper at my approach.'

I couldn't help giggling. I wasn't sure if this strange girl was grown up or still a child. She was very little, like me, but she was wearing a prim cotton lady's dress, though she wore her long hair loose about her shoulders, not caught up in a neat bun. I loved her voice. She didn't sound like the circus folk. She didn't sound like the Willoughby Buildings people. She didn't sound like the gentle country folk. She didn't sound like the proper ladies and gents who lived in big houses. She simply sounded like herself, warm and friendly and funny.

'But I never ever hurt little fairy girls,' she said. 'And *you're* a little fairy, aren't you?'

I shivered at the name, because that was what Mister called me, but I could tell she meant it kindly. She couldn't think I was *really* a fairy, could she?

'Please, miss, I'm the Acrobatic Child Wonder,' I explained, wiping my eyes and sniffling.

'Here, I have a handkerchief,' she said, pulling a little piece of cloth from her pocket. It had embroidery all over it.

'There's pictures and letters,' I said, stroking the little blue and yellow satin thread flowers. They were bluebells and primroses. I remembered Mary-Martha taking me to the woods long ago, where we picked great bunches of flowers and brought them home for Ma. We put them in jam jars all around the room and they looked so beautiful that we clapped our hands and laughed, and even Ma seemed happy . . . but within a few hours our beautiful flowers were drooping and dying and we had to throw them away.

I traced the letters embroidered underneath. The girl sensed I was less sure now, and told me they were her initials – SB for Sapphire Battersea – 'Although no one calls me that now. All the folk here call me Hetty.'

I said I was called Diamond and she thought it a most beautiful name, which pleased me greatly. I thought the handkerchief so pretty I didn't want to spoil it, so I wiped my nose on my petticoat instead. Hetty smiled at me and said I could keep the handkerchief if I liked it so much.

'Really? For my very own?' I said, and I tucked

it away quickly in case she changed her mind.

Hetty tried to persuade me to creep out from under the wagon.

'I'm scared to come out, because Mister will get me,' I said.

Hetty looked horrified when I said he would beat me. 'Can you tell your father?' she asked. She said the word 'father' as if she thought all fathers very special men who protected their daughters. I thought of my own pa and how he had sold me for five guineas, and I started sobbing again.

'Isn't there anyone kind who will look after you?' Hetty asked, wriggling under the wagon too so she could put her arm round me.

'Madame Addie is kind,' I said.

Hetty's whole face lit up. 'Oh, Madame Adeline! Yes, I am sure she is very kind,' she said, as if she knew her. 'I have come looking for her. Will you show me her wagon, Diamond?'

So I crawled out and she took my hand, squeezing it tightly when we went past Mister's wagon. We went to Madame Adeline's lovely green wagon right at the end. She was sitting on her steps before her fire wearing her favourite green silk gown, looking magical. She saw the tear stains on my face and held out her arms to me.

'Come here, darling,' she said, and I ran to her,

proud that Hetty should see that such a lovely exotic lady cared for me.

She cared for Hetty too. She called her Little Star, and this made Hetty burst into tears too! They talked of when they'd last met, both so tender, and then Hetty cried again when she said that she'd lost her dear mama.

'Is your mother dead too, Hetty?' I asked. 'Mine went to live with the angels.'

'My mama lives there too,' said Hetty, wiping her eyes. 'I'm sure she has wonderful white feathery wings and a dress as blue as the sky. Maybe they fly from cloud to cloud together. But my mama flies down to see me every now and then. She creeps inside my heart and speaks to me. She is a great comfort. Perhaps your mama will do the same.'

I thought this over carefully. I wasn't really sure I welcomed the thought of Ma squatting beside me, watching my every move. I was sure she'd be disappointed in me. She'd weep more than ever. I put my thumb in my mouth, and rocked myself sadly.

Madame Adeline smiled at me comfortingly. 'Now, my girls, I'm going to have a cup of tea. Would you like one too?'

I took my thumb out of my mouth. 'And cake?' I said hopefully.

Madame Adeline laughed. 'I expect we can find a cake if we search hard,' she said.

She made a delightful game of it, pretending to hunt the cake in her beautiful wagon, looking under the table and in her bed, which was so funny I cheered up enormously.

We ate our tea and each had a big slice of pink and yellow cake. I nibbled mine slowly, peeling off the marzipan and saving it till last because I liked it so much. But then I heard Mister shouting and the cake turned sour in my mouth. I thought he was after me, but it turned out he was challenging a stranger from the village who had come marching across the field and was running from wagon to wagon, calling for Hetty.

'Oh my Lord, it's Jem. He must have followed me,' said Hetty, flushing.

I peered out of Madame Adeline's wagon. This Jem looked very fierce and angry – a farm labourer with a cap and cords, so strongly built, he was almost a match for Marvo. But when Madame Adeline intervened, he doffed his cap and shook her hand.

'Pleased to meet you, ma'am,' he said, just like a gentleman.

Madame Adeline offered him tea but he politely refused.

'I'd better be getting back – and so had you, Hetty,' he said firmly, taking hold of her arm.

It was clear that Hetty didn't like this at all. 'I want

to stay here with Madame Adeline,' she said, sticking out her chin.

I wanted her to say 'and Diamond too'. I liked her so much, I wanted her to stay for ever. She made me feel I didn't need to be so frightened any more.

But Jem was intent on chivvying her out of the wagon, his arm about her.

'Perhaps you had better run along with your brother just now, Little Star. But will you come and see the show tomorrow?' asked Madame Adeline.

'I would not miss it for the world,' Hetty replied. She kissed Madame Adeline goodbye, and then turned to me. 'I shall look out for you in the ring tomorrow and give you a big cheer,' she told me.

I stood in the doorway of Madame Adeline's wagon and waved until Hetty and Jem were just two tiny dots at the very edge of the field.

'Do you think she'll really come to watch me in the show, Madame Adeline?' I asked.

'I'm sure she will, dear.'

'I wish that brother hadn't come and taken her away.' I thought of *my* brothers, Matthew and Mark and Luke, and then Marvo, Julip and Tag. 'He didn't *act* like he was Hetty's brother. He acted more like her sweetheart.'

'Maybe he is,' said Madame Adeline. 'He's not her blood brother. She was just brought up with him in the village until she was five or six, and then she was sent away to the hospital. She lived there for years.'

'In a *hospital*? Was she very, very ill?' I asked.

Hetty was almost as thin as me, but she looked extremely robust, not at all like a sickly invalid.

'No, she wasn't ill. She lived in the Foundling Hospital. It's a special institution for children.'

'Like a workhouse?' I asked, astonished.

'A little. Perhaps not quite as harsh.'

I was amazed that a girl like Hetty had been brought up in an institution. It had always been Ma's biggest fear that we would run out of money altogether and end up in the local workhouse. She said the word in a whisper, and always shuddered. When we went to the park, Mary-Martha and I sometimes walked past the great stone workhouse. We never caught a glimpse of the people shut up inside, behind the barred windows – but once we heard someone screaming, a terrible piercing wail that echoed endlessly in our dreams for weeks.

Had Hetty been locked up in a similar dark place?

'How could she bear it?' I said.

'She ran away when she was ten, and came to find me. We'd met years before that, when she first came to the circus. We seem to be meeting in five-year cycles,' said Madame Adeline.

'I can't wait another five years to see her – I like her so!' I said.

'Well, she will come to the show tomorrow. We must give our best performances,' said Madame Adeline.

'I shall try,' I said.

I still had to face Mister, and when he caught up with me at last he threatened me with the dreaded beating.

'Please don't beat me, Mister. I shall try harder, I promise. I will do every trick cleanly and won't wobble once when I'm at the top of the human column,' I said earnestly. 'And I will smile and smile and smile at the audience tomorrow – just you wait and see.'

'What's perked you up then, little fairy?' he asked.

'I – I just gave myself a good talking to,' I said, which actually made him chuckle.

I threw myself into rehearsals the next morning with unusual gusto. When it was time to get ready for the afternoon show, I was so nervous and excited I could hardly stand still.

'Do you think Hetty will really come and watch, Madame Addie?' I asked as we lined up by the tent flap.

'She might not come until this evening, dear.' Madame Adeline had painted her face very brightly, but I could still see the dark shadows under her eyes. The strange half-light made her look much older.

163

I realized that dear Madame Adeline might well be quite an elderly lady, though I still thought her very beautiful.

'Try not to worry, Diamond. Hetty will come to at least one of the performances, and I'm sure she will be enchanted with you and your act,' she said kindly.

'She will be enchanted with you too,' I said at once.

Madame Adeline laughed, but she didn't sound very happy. 'I rather think she'll find me wanting,' she said quietly. 'My act is a sad shadow of the one I used to do with my six rosin-backed horses, when I was the star of the show.'

'You're still the star now, Madame Addie,' I protested.

'I am lucky to have Midnight. He is a dear spirited creature and never lets me down, but I'm getting sadly decrepit. I can barely stand up on his back now, let alone turn my somersaults.'

'I could help you practise if you like, Madame Addie. And I would give you a date each time you did it neatly.'

'You're a sweet girl, Diamond,' said Madame Adeline. 'There now, take a deep breath. Flora's just taking her bows. It's time for you to go on.'

I gave her hand a quick squeeze, and then I went running into the ring with Marvo, Julip and Tag. I did my somersaults all around the ring, ending with a little flourish, my hand in the air – and immediately spotted Hetty right in front of me, clapping hard. I gave her a happy wave, and then rushed to start the next routine. It all went perfectly and it was a good audience, cheering the simplest little thing. I played to the crowd, adding little dance steps and curtsies, opening my eyes wide, smiling from ear to ear.

'Stop that prancing!' Tag hissed as he hurtled past me, but I wasn't going to stop for anyone now. I wanted to show off to Hetty.

I managed to scramble up Marvo and Julip and Tag at the end of the act, standing straight and tall on Tag's shoulders. I waved both hands in the air and milked the applause.

When we ran out of the ring, the audience still clapping hard, Mister caught hold of me.

'That's the ticket, little fairy! You're getting it at last. I *knew* I'd make a little performer out of you. Given time, you'll be worth all three of these boys!' he said, patting me on the back.

He did this in front of the silver boys, which made them all very put out and petulant, even kind Marvo, but I didn't care. I was just pleased I'd performed well in front of my new friend, Hetty. I wanted her to think me a real circus trouper.

I hoped that she would be waiting to congratulate me after the show, but there was no sign of her. I ran to Madame Adeline's wagon in case she'd gone there.

'No, Hetty's not here, dear. I expect she had to go home,' said Madame Adeline. 'Don't look so disappointed, Diamond. Maybe she'll come to tonight's performance too. She loves the circus.'

'I do too!' I cried. 'Oh, I do *hope* she comes back. Did you see how she clapped me? Do you suppose she thinks I'm really good?'

'I'm sure she does. You *are* good, Diamond. You've learned extraordinarily quickly – too quickly, in fact. Beppo takes too many risks with you. I get frightened when I see you.'

'*I'm* not frightened,' I lied, dancing about.

I was so excited I could not settle. I could not even eat my supper. I just wanted to be back in the ring, performing.

But somehow it all went wrong for the evening performance. I didn't fall, but I stumbled twice doing my somersault routine, and when I did my little dance, some rude lads in the audience started jeering at me. They were a rowdy lot, and inclined to throw their oranges *during* the act, thinking it funny. I tried hard to ignore them because Hetty *was* there, back in the same seat, only this time she'd brought her young man, Jem, and I wasn't sure I liked him.

I liked Hetty though. I liked her so much. When I was up on Tag's shoulders I looked down to wave at her – and suddenly everything slipped sideways. A dark dizziness came upon me and I very nearly fell. I clung on desperately, scarcely able to see, doing my best to keep smiling even so, though I was terrified.

'Watch out, you fool!' Tag hissed.

I could feel the whole column wobble. Marvo called 'Down!' and I scrabbled backwards, and Tag and Julip did their somersault and landed gracefully, and then we all four clasped hands and bowed, as if nothing had happened. The audience clapped even so. Hetty clapped too, but this time I knew she was clapping out of sympathy.

I felt my face flushing. Beppo was staring at me, his forehead creased ominously. For once I didn't care. I only cared about Hetty. I had wanted to put on another grand show for her and I'd made a mess of it all. And now I'd likely never see her again.

I was wonderfully wrong! Hetty returned the very next day. She did not even wait for the four o'clock performance. She came when we were all making lunch!

Mister saw her and tried to frighten her away, but Hetty stood her ground and then went marching past him – left, right, left, right, swinging her arms.

'Hetty! Oh, Hetty!' I cried, running to her. 'Oh, Hetty, I saw you talking to Mister! You really aren't afeared of him!'

'That's right. *He's* the one that's afeared of *me*. I told you. He'll be quaking in his bed tonight, wondering if that red-haired girl is coming to get him. Most likely he'll wet his sheets in terror,' said Hetty.

I burst out laughing and hid my face in Maybelle. Hetty asked to be introduced to her, taking her very seriously, as if she were a beautiful china doll with real curls and an outfit from Paris. She did wonder whether Maybelle might be feeling a little chilly in her drawers. I told her that I'd given Maybelle's dress to little Mavis Monkey.

'Well, never you mind. I am very good at stitching tiny dolly dresses,' said Hetty.

My heart started thumping hopefully. Would she really make Maybelle a new dress? Madame Adeline was delighted to see Hetty too, and gave us tea and cake. I wasn't sure I should have the cake as Mister was always telling me off for eating too much. He wanted to keep me as small as possible.

'He's a monster, wanting to stunt your growth,' said Madame Adeline. 'You take a slice of cake, Diamond. You need some sweetness in your life.'

'You can't do back-flips on a full stomach,' I said, though I had a big bite of cake all the same.

'And what's a back-flip?' Hetty asked.

Here was my chance to show off! I took her behind the wagon and demonstrated. I had practised so many times it was easy enough. Most folk in the circus could do a back-flip as easily and casually as blowing their noses – but Hetty marvelled.

'Oh, show *me* how to do it!' she cried, and even though she was nearly grown up, she tucked her dress into her drawers and did her best to copy me. She tried again and again, but always tumbled onto her back. I did my best to show her, but she didn't have enough spring. I wondered if she could do the crab-walk, for I could do it myself long before I joined the circus, but she couldn't manage it at all. She lay flat on her back, chuckling – yet she still seemed to have a fancy to learn circus skills.

When we were back in the wagon, she turned to Madame Adeline. 'Could I ever be an equestrian like you?' she asked.

Madame Addie must have been even fonder of Hetty than I thought, because she said she could try riding Midnight. I'd never known her let anyone else on his back. Tag had often begged for a ride but she'd always refused.

She lent Hetty a pair of her white fleshings so she wouldn't expose too much leg, and then gave her a lesson in the big top. Oh dear! Even I could tell that Hetty was never going to make a good horsewoman. She couldn't even sit straight on Midnight's bare back. She slid forward, grabbing his mane, which he didn't care for at all. He became very fidgety and Hetty fell straight off. She landed hard but she did not cry. She begged to have another go, and then another and another.

Madame Adeline gently told her that was enough.

'I was so good at riding when I was a little tot! Maybe if I practised hard every single day I might get the hang of it. Then perhaps one day I would be good enough to be part of your act?' said Hetty.

'Oh yes!' I cried, because it would be my idea of Heaven if Hetty joined the circus too.

I am sure Madame Adeline thought this as well, but it was clear she didn't think Hetty belonged on the back of a horse. She took her off to show her around the circus. I longed to go with them, but Mister caught hold of me.

'Where do you think you're going, missy?' he said. 'Back into that ring, for a practice!'

'Oh please, Mister, mayn't I go with Madame Addie and Hetty just this once?' I begged.

'You're not going anywhere near that girl! She's an insolent little chit. Addie's got no business letting her poke around here. The circus is private, no place for strangers. And you need to practise more than ever, Diamond. Last night's performance was a disaster. You deserve a good whipping for such carelessness. If you're not perfect this afternoon, I'll send you to

171

Mr Tanglefield, and he'll be so horrified you're letting the whole circus down he'll take his whip and give that bendy little back a set of stripes!'

I knew this wasn't just a grisly joke – Mr Tanglefield had marked both Tag and Julip before now. Utter fear sharpened up my steps and stopped every stumble. I gave an immaculate performance that afternoon, though I could feel my mouth stretched in a grim parody of a smile. I must have looked like a mechanical doll as I revolved round and round the ring, concentrating so hard I barely blinked. I sneaked just one look around and saw Hetty, watching and waving. She was there again at the evening performance. I hoped and hoped that she'd come and find me afterwards, but she went off with Jem. He had his arm round her protectively.

Hetty had seen four whole shows now. I hardly dared hope she'd come back yet again, but an hour or so before the next afternoon's performance she came running into our ring of wagons. I was practising my tumbles. I had trembled every time Mr Tanglefield cracked his whip during yesterday's performances.

I greeted Hetty happily, hoping she would play with me.

'I would *love* to play with you, Diamond, but I'm afraid I have other business just right now,' she said, walking on.

I scrambled to my feet. 'Are you calling on Madame Adeline? I shall come too!' I said eagerly.

'I'm not intending to visit Madame Adeline either, not just now. I am here to see Mr Tanglefield.'

I was so shocked I could scarcely draw breath. It was as if she'd announced she was going to take tea with the Devil himself.

'He is very stern!' I said. 'If Mister is very cross with me he threatens to send me to Mr Tanglefield for a good whipping.'

Hetty looked horrified. 'Does he really *whip* you, Diamond?'

'No, but I'm always afeared he might. He has a very *big* whip, Hetty, and every time he cracks it in the ring it makes me shiver.'

I pointed out his big fancy wagon, a real dazzler in red and yellow and green. No one ever dared disturb Mr Tanglefield in his wagon, especially when he was getting ready for a show.

'I don't think you had better disturb him right this minute,' I cried, trying to catch hold of Hetty, but she wouldn't be stopped. She ran up the steps and tapped on the door. Mr Tanglefield opened it, half dressed, his hair awry, looking furious – and oh, he had his terrible whip in one hand.

'Hetty! Run!' I called – but she didn't seem to hear me. She went inside Mr Tanglefield's wagon and stayed there for a long time, while I paced up and down in agitation, listening for cries.

I heard Mister calling for me to get ready for the show, but I hid beneath the wagon.

'Drat that little miss,' he muttered. 'She's starting to be more trouble than she's worth. I'll teach her a lesson she won't forget!'

I couldn't help gasping, though I covered my mouth with my hands.

'I can hear you! Where are you?' said Mister, spinning round.

I huddled into a tight ball, praying that he wouldn't look under the wagon. Then I heard Mr Tanglefield's door banging, and light footsteps.

'Hey, girl, where are you going?' Mister called. 'No strangers allowed here.'

I dared wriggle towards the light. I could just see Hetty, dancing about on the grass. She was wearing a very odd outfit. She'd hitched up her skirts and wore her borrowed fleshings and a smart scarlet coat, with a tall black hat on her head, tipped at a jaunty angle.

'I'm not a stranger here, Mr Beppo . . . *sir*,' she said, mocking him. 'I'm the new star act. Just ask Mr Tanglefield if you don't believe me.' She swept him a mocking bow, hat in hand, and then bounced off towards Madame Adeline's wagon.

I couldn't believe my ears. Surely Hetty could not

mean she was *joining the circus*? I gave a squeal of joy and rolled right out from under the wagon, ready to run to her to find out more – but Mister was too quick for me. He caught hold of me by the hair and yanked me upright.

'*There* you are! How dare you hide from me!'

'Oh, please don't be angry, Mister Beppo! Tell me, did Hetty – that girl with the red hair – did she really say she was going to be the star of the circus?'

'That chit!' he said, and he spat on the ground. 'She's talking nonsense. Ask Mr Tanglefield indeed! He'd whip her into the middle of next week if he could hear her impertinence. If she's a circus performer, then I'm Queen of the Fairies.'

Mister should have sported a wand and wings – because *it was true*!

We were up extra early the next morning because we were moving on mid-week, making for Gillford, a town only six miles away. And the moment I stumbled out of the stuffy wagon, I saw Hetty! She was dressed in her ordinary grey frock, but she had her tall hat and scarlet jacket in one hand and a suitcase in the other.

'Oh, Hetty, Hetty, is it *true*? Oh, tell me it is, please, please!' I said, rushing to her.

'Is *what* true?' said Hetty, laughing and whirling me round and round. 'Is the moon made of green cheese? Can pigs fly? Can cats bark and dogs miaow?'

'Are you joining the circus!' I shrieked.

'Yes, I am! Isn't it marvellous?'

'I can't believe it!'

'I can't quite believe it myself. I – I hope I'm doing the right thing,' said Hetty.

'Of course you are! So what are you going to do? Are you going to be an acrobat like me? Oh, Hetty, do come and be a silver girl!'

'Don't be silly, Diamond. You've seen me trying to do a somersault. I'm hopeless.'

'Then are you going to ride Midnight with Madame Addie?'

'I wish I could, but I'm no horsewoman. I'm not going to work with the monkeys or the big cats or that grand Elijah or those fishy old sea lions either.'

'Then what *are* you going to do?'

'I'm going to be the new ringmaster,' said Hetty, her cheeks flushing with excitement.

I was so astonished I didn't quite know what to say. How could Hetty possibly be a ringmaster, when this was Mr Tanglefield's job? She was only a small girl, even if she dressed up in her high hat and man's jacket. It seemed a ridiculous idea – but Hetty was Hetty. She wasn't afraid of anyone, not even Mister. If she said she was going to be the ringmaster, then I had to believe in her and trust she'd do it splendidly.

I believed it. Dear Madame Adeline believed it too. I could not help being jealous when I learned that Hetty was going to share Madame Addie's wagon.

'Oh, please, can't I come too? I won't need a bed, I can just take my hammock – or I can curl up in a corner on the floor. I won't take up any room at all, but *please* let me come and share,' I begged.

'Oh, darling, I've explained again and again why it's not possible,' said Madame Adeline, taking me on her lap. 'You know you belong to Beppo. I can't take you away from him, much as I'd like to.'

'But you're letting *Hetty* come and share your wagon.'

'I don't belong to horrible old Beppo. I don't belong to anyone,' said Hetty.

'It's not fair,' I said sadly.

'I know it's not fair – but don't fret, Diamond. When you're my age you won't have to belong to anyone either, I promise,' she told me.

I thought about this. It seemed a little too scary to be totally independent.

'Could I perhaps belong to *you*, Hetty?' I asked.

'Of course!' said Hetty, which cheered me up considerably.

We only had time for a cup of tea and a buttered muffin before we had to help out with the break-up of the show.

'I must attend to Midnight,' said Madame Adeline.

'And *I* must attend to all the monkeys to help Mr Marvel. He can't manage without me,' I said proudly.

'Well, *I* must attend to everyone and everything else,' said Hetty cheerfully, rolling up her sleeves.

She showed extremely willing, rushing up to everyone and saying, 'Hello, I'm Hetty, though my professional name is Emerald Star. I've joined the circus. How can I help you?'

At first she tried to help the hands tugging down the great big top. They barely acknowledged her, and then laughed when she couldn't take the tug of the ropes and had to wring her soft hands. She tried to help move the rows of seating, but she didn't have the strength for that either.

'Push off, little girl, and stop bothering us,' they said – or words that were even less polite.

So she tried to help all the artistes with their animals, but that didn't work either. She was a stranger. They acted skittishly while she was around and balked at going quietly into their travelling cages. She had enough sense to steer clear of the big cats and Elijah, and she shuddered at the sea lions, but she did try to pet the poor groaning bears, who always hated travelling. She poked her hands through the bars of their cage and stroked their grizzled heads.

'What on earth are you doing to my animals?' Bruno cried, running over.

'Hello, I'm Hetty, though my professional name is Emerald Star.'

'I don't care if you're the Queen of Sheba. You can't touch my bears! Are you an idiot? They're wild animals. They'll snap your hands off soon as look at you,' said Bruno.

'They're all muzzled and chained too! Can't you give them a bit of freedom within their cage? They look so restless and miserable. Their eyes are so *sad*.'

'They're beasts. They need to be chained. It's *you* that's upsetting them. Clear off or I'll fetch Mr Tanglefield,' Bruno told her.

'Hetty, Hetty, come and help me with the monkeys,' I said, tugging at her arm.

She came willingly and introduced herself to Mr Marvel. He nodded at her kindly enough, but when she told him she was going to be the ringmaster he burst out laughing.

'Is your new friend soft in the head, Diamond?' he said. 'Ringmaster! I've never heard the like!'

'You wait and see,' said Hetty loftily, though she looked a little vexed.

Very few people were willing to give her the time of day, and no one wanted her to help, but she didn't give up. She scurried across the field and back again, until

Madame Adeline tactfully asked her to wrap and store all her ornaments and china so that they wouldn't fall and chip during the journey.

It took a full two hours before the tent was in little pieces and roped neatly into place in a wagon, and all the horses buckled into their shafts. Midnight was far too grand and important to pull any wagon, of course. He rode *in* a wagon so that he didn't get tired and spattered with mud – but when we saw the spires and chimney tops of Gillford in the distance, Madame Adeline led him out and he stepped along proudly as part of the procession while she sat on his back in spangles and pink fleshings.

I had to parade in my fairy frock, skipping and smiling and turning the odd somersault. Marvo strode forward with Julip sitting on his shoulders, calling to the crowd of excited onlookers, while Tag capered crazily, expending far too much energy showing off, doing ten flic-flacs in a row and ending up in the crowd himself, nearly squashing the smallest children at the front.

We were all on show as Mr Tanglefield's Travelling Circus. Mr Tanglefield was up in front, hair blacked, moustache waxed, in a black frock coat and white silk breeches and boots so shiny you could see your face in them. He rode one of the horses, cracking his whip in the air, which made everyone jump.

Hetty was given a horse to ride too – old Sugar Poke, the oldest shuffling mare, as sweet-natured as her name. I had ridden Sugar Poke myself and it was as simple as sitting in a chair, but Hetty sat too tensely, hunched up, clearly a novice – though she still managed to wave her hat in the air and smile at the crowds. I thought she looked splendid in her scarlet coat, and her shapely legs in white fleshings made many of the lads whistle – but even so, there was a resentful muttering amongst the circus folk.

'Who *is* that silly girl? What does she look like, slumped on that horse like a sack of potatoes? It's clear she knows nothing about riding.'

'Why is she wearing that get-up – all dressed up like a showman but with no act to speak of?'

'Riding right up at the front too, only second to the boss himself. Has he taken leave of his senses?'

Oh, the mutterings got riper and ruder, and my cheeks burned on Hetty's behalf. She must have heard some of the comments, but she took no notice whatsoever. She held her head high and gestured grandly, though she had to grab frantically at Sugar Poke's mane if she quickened her pace at all.

When we got to Gillford Meadow at last, we had a great to-do setting up. There was no afternoon show, but we were booked to do an evening performance, so we had our work cut out getting the big top safely up with every seat in place, and the animals fed and watered and exercised.

Then we practised in the ring, as always. It was all confusion, for Flora could not get the tautness of her tightrope right, and a wheel was threatening to come off the lions' cage, and the handlebar of Chino's penny-farthing had got slightly knocked out of true in transit. There was a lot of swearing and shouting.

Hetty crouched in a corner, watching intently, then scribbling in a notebook.

While Mister was fixing the springboard with Marvo, I ran over to her. 'Hello, Hetty!' I said. 'What are you doing?'

'I'm making notes,' she said, frowning a little.

I watched her fill line after line with fancy squiggles. I could sometimes pick out words in print, but this fine handwriting defeated me. 'You're very clever,' I said admiringly.

She stopped writing and looked at me. 'No one else thinks so – and I'm not sure I think it either,' she said. She reached out and took hold of my hand. Her own was cold as ice. 'Oh, Diamond, what have I done! Whatever possessed me? How did I ever have the nerve to think I was equal to this? I managed to convince old Tanglefield that I could be a novelty child ringmaster with an artful way with words – but I don't know anything about the circus!'

'It's fine to be a little nervous,' I said, trying to reassure her. 'That's the mark of a true performer. Even Madame Adeline gets scared before a show. I am *always* frightened.'

'But you both do something splendid. I have nothing to offer but patter,' said Hetty despairingly.

'You can make a living out of pattering,' I said. 'My father . . .' My voice wobbled and I felt the sting of tears in my eyes, because it still hurt so much to remember that he had sold me.

'Oh, Diamond, I'm sorry. I didn't mean to upset you,' said Hetty, quickly putting her arm round me. Her notebook fell to the floor. The pages flicked over, all of them crisscrossed with her squiggly writing.

'You've made an awful lot of notes!' I said, marvelling, for my hand ached if I attempted even a few lines of *The cat sat on the mat.*

'Oh, this is my memoir book,' said Hetty. 'I'm just writing notes on the last page.'

'What's a memoir?'

'Well, I suppose it's just a grand name for a story about yourself,' she told me.

'I love stories!' I remembered the little fairy tales Mary-Martha and I had coloured. 'Does your memoir have fairies and witches and ogres and a handsome prince on a white horse?'

'Well, you can be the fairy, Diamond. There are

certainly several witches in the first volume – and one or two ogres in the second and third. And I suppose there *was* a handsome prince – but I don't want to be his princess,' said Hetty. She looked suddenly as if she might start crying. 'I don't *think* I do, anyway.'

I did not really understand, but I gave her a hug to try and comfort her.

'Diamond! Get down here and watch the boys. It's time you learned springboarding too. Leave that useless girl alone, do you hear me?' Beppo bawled from the ring.

I felt Hetty wince at the word useless. 'You're not a *bit* useless, Hetty,' I said fiercely.

'Everyone else thinks so,' she said. But then she put her chin up. 'So I shall show them.'

And she did, oh she did! I was so scared for her at that evening's performance. As we all lined up by the tent flaps, there was a great muttering, especially when we saw Mr Tanglefield stand *behind* Hetty. She looked very small and girlish, though she cut a fine enough figure in her scarlet riding coat and tall black hat.

'The boss has taken leave of his senses,' Beppo muttered. 'That girl's only got a mouse squeak. How can that silly flibbertigibbet ever hold the crowd?'

The band played a fanfare. We all stared at Hetty,

half the folk thinking she might make a break for it and run off into the night. But she marched forward into the ring. We could not see her properly once she was there, but oh my goodness, we could *hear* her.

'Ladies and gentlemen!' she cried, in a voice so rich and loud, I think the entire town of Gillford heard her. 'Ladies and gentlemen, girls and boys, little children and babes in arms – take heed! You are about to see sights that will dazzle your eyes and delight your hearts. Here is the amazing, magnificent and ultra-marvellous Tanglefield's Travelling Circus!'

A great cheer rang out around the ring. All the circus artistes stopped their mutterings and gaped. Hetty was extraordinary! She played with that audience, announcing each act in astonishing sentences that tripped off her tongue as if she'd been a ring-master all her life. Even Beppo shook his head and mumbled, 'Well, she's certainly got a way with words, I'll say that.'

The audience was so well warmed up and appreciative that it made performing easy. We were all at our best. I was so excited I very nearly dared somersault down from Tag's shoulders when we did the human column, so keyed up I felt my little wire wings might even fly me up to the top of the tent and back.

The applause at the end of the act made my ears throb. I glanced all around the cheering audience and saw one man hunched at the end, the only one not clapping. He wasn't looking at us. He only had eyes for Hetty. It was her foster brother, Jem.

I do not know if Hetty saw Jem. She didn't mention him. She was flushed with triumph at the end of the show. Mr Tanglefield was so delighted with her success, he called for two of the circus hands to fetch beer from the nearest alehouse and held an impromptu party for his new star. There were still many circus folk who resented this new girl's status, but they'd seen for themselves that she could work the crowd wonderfully, and they all drank to her success — even Beppo and my silver brothers. Madame Adeline was utterly delighted, hovering by Hetty's side, feeding her little titbits and putting her own wrapper round her when she saw her shivering in the night air – though I think it was from excitement rather than cold.

Hetty drank little beer herself. She offered me a sip, but the very smell reminded me so painfully of Pa that I pressed my lips together and shook my head violently, which made everyone laugh. The men drank their fill, happily making the most of Mr Tanglefield's rare generosity, and after an hour or so grew wild and raucous. Hetty only had half a glass, but she acted slightly drunk too, laughing and joking with everyone, slapping each man on the back and kissing Madame Adeline and Flora and me.

I did not want to risk upsetting her by talking about her foster brother. I knew it might make her sad to think that he had walked all those miles from their village to Gillford to watch her perform.

During the next few days I wondered if Hetty was thinking of him. She was still very anxious before each performance and wildly elated afterwards. She was restless between times, pacing backwards and forwards like the big cats in their cage. Sometimes she went off for long walks by herself and came back with sore eyes and a sad face, though she insisted she hadn't been crying.

'Are you missing your home and your folks?' I asked her timidly.

She did not answer – just bent her head so I couldn't see her face.

'You won't get so homesick that you leave the circus?' I asked, desperate for reassurance.

'No. No, this is what I want,' Hetty said. 'This is the life I've always longed for . . .' But she didn't sound sure. She held onto me tightly. 'Do you sometimes feel . . . torn, Diamond?'

I didn't know what she meant. I fingered my own shredded petticoat anxiously. 'Torn, like my petticoat?' I asked.

'Torn in two – one of you wanting to be here, one of you wanting to be home. Only I don't even know where my real home is.'

I tried to follow her, but it was too difficult. I had never *wanted* to be here at the circus until Hetty came along. I knew where my home was, but there was no point wanting to be there. It was like one of the riddles on the joke cards Pa sold for parties.

Hetty saw my puzzled face and gave me a hug. 'Don't look so worried, Diamond. Take no notice of my silly ramblings. Yes, your petticoat *is* torn. I'll fix it for you. In fact I'll make you a brand-new petticoat and a pretty dress to go over it. Would you like that?'

'But I have my fairy dress for the show.'

'This won't be for the show. It'll be for *you*,' said Hetty. 'What colour dress would you like?'

I blinked at her, too overcome to decide. Did she really mean it? I'd never had a new dress for myself. I'd always worn Mary-Martha's cast-offs, and they weren't even new when she got them. Ma had bought all our clothes in bundles from the rag shop.

I reached for the skirt of Hetty's dress, a soft grey cotton patterned with tiny white flowers. 'Could I – could I have a grey dress like yours?' I asked.

'You don't want *grey*,' said Hetty. 'Grey cotton is for servants and country girls. You are a special circus girl, Diamond. You can wear something really bright and beautiful. You could have primrose chiffon or rose-pink muslin or sky-blue silk. Go on, choose!' She looked at me, her blue eyes shining. Blue seemed the most wonderful colour in the world.

'Please may I have blue silk?' I whispered.

'Of course you can!' Hetty snatched up Maybelle. 'She can have a blue silk dress to match. And I'll make you each a white broderie anglaise pinafore so you can play at making mud pies whenever you fancy without spoiling your dresses.'

I still thought this might be a delightful game of make-believe – but the next morning Hetty went to the market in town and came back with great armfuls of material wrapped in brown paper. I spotted a wisp of sky-blue silk and felt a throb of happiness in my chest.

'But how can you afford such fine materials, and so many?' I said, slipping my hand in under the brown paper and stroking brocade and velvet and my own beautiful blue silk.

'I made Mr Tanglefield give me an advance on my pay so I can make costumes for the company. And I got them very cheaply. I am old friends with the market men of Gillford. I used to drum up customers for them,' said Hetty.

'You can do *everything*, Hetty,' I said.

I meant it sincerely, but she laughed at me.

'My Lord, Diamond, I am hopeless at most things. I was the worst servant girl in the world. I was dismissed without a reference!'

'When were you a servant, Hetty? Tell me more,' I said.

'One day I'll read you my memoirs,' she promised.

Hetty made my dress first. She helped herself to one of Mr Marvel's newspapers – he kept a whole stack for lining the bottom of the monkey cage. She drew a design of a frock upon the pages: the bodice, the sleeves, the wide, wide skirt.

'Isn't it too wide all the way round, Hetty?' I said doubtfully. It looked as if it would fit Flora's ample girth.

'It's going to be gathered up until it fits snugly round your weeny waist, don't worry. But I want it to be very full. I'm going to make you a very flouncy petticoat too. Then you can whirl round and round like a little spinning top.'

'Oh yes! Oh please, yes!'

Hetty pinned the pattern to the blue material and cut it out with her special sharp scissors. They made an alarming rasping sound as they sliced their way through the silk, and my throat dried with panic in case it would all be spoiled, but Hetty seemed satisfied with each segment. She pieced them all together, her mouth full of pins, and then, when they were all assembled just so, she started the stitching.

She sat cross-legged like a tailor, head bent, her hand darting up and down as her needle flashed in and out of the material. I liked to kneel nearby and watch, loving the tiny *puck-puck-puck* sound of the needle and thread. Hetty stitched all day and half the night. When the dress was finished, she went to Madame Adeline and borrowed her flat iron, heating it very carefully and then letting it cool a bit in case it sizzled the silk. Then at last she called me and slipped the magical dress over my head. The silk was so smooth and soft it made me shiver.

'Oh, Hetty, it's so lovely! Does it look nice? Do I look pretty?' I asked, dancing round and round.

'You look beautiful,' said Hetty, and she took me to peep at myself in Madame Adeline's looking glass. A different girl entirely peered back at me – a fancy girl in a splendid frock, a girl so grand I felt I should curtsy to her, yet she was *me*!

'Oh, Hetty, I love my dress more than anything,' I breathed, scarcely able to speak. 'It's so bright and so *soft*!'

'All little girls should wear soft, bright dresses,' said Hetty. 'I had to wear dreadful itchy brown frocks when I was at the hospital and I absolutely hated them. Your dress looks lovely on you, Diamond, I must admit. It will look even better with new petticoats. I will start them next.'

She was as good as her word, making me two flouncy petticoats edged with lace. I twirled round in them until I was dizzy.

'You're showing a little too much, Diamond,' said Hetty. 'I'd better make you a matching pair of drawers to keep you decent.'

I'd never worn proper drawers before and thought them delightful. Tag teased me unmercifully when I wore my finery, sometimes snatching up my skirts and laughing and pointing at my lacy legs. I was mortified, but Hetty came to my rescue.

'What's this fascination with Diamond's drawers, Tag? Do you want a pair for yourself? How many frills would you like? And would you like a set of petticoats to go with them?' she teased. He soon stopped tormenting me!

Hetty made me a crisp white pinafore to go over my dress while I was playing, and with all the leftover scraps of material she stitched a miniature set of clothes for Maybelle, lacy drawers and all.

I dressed her in her new finery and then danced her around with me. Hetty had sewn proper features on her face, and her little embroidered mouth smiled ecstatically. I ran to show Madame Adeline, and she admired us both.

I saw how worn Madame Adeline's own clothes looked in strong daylight and wondered if Hetty might make her a new outfit too.

'I'd like to, but I don't want to offend or embarrass her,' said Hetty.

'You made me my dress and pinny and I'm not one bit offended or embarrassed,' I said.

'Yes, but you're a little girl.'

Hetty thought about it hard, but decided a new frock for Madame Adeline would be too personal – and it would involve lots of complicated measuring. She couldn't just go ahead and make one as a surprise. She decided to make her a new wrapper instead. The rose-patterned one was very pretty, but faded from much washing, the roses just fuzzy blurs. Hetty chose to make the new wrapper in black silk. I thought it might be a little plain and severe, but Hetty produced a bag of bright embroidery silks and set to work stitching wonderful red and yellow tulips all around the neck and hem.

She could only work on it intermittently, crouching in my wagon or sitting under a tree at the edge of the meadow, so that Madame Adeline wouldn't see. When it was finished at last, Hetty let me be there when she gave it to her. I was a little worried at first, because when Madame Adeline held the beautiful embroidered wrapper up against herself, she burst into tears.

'Oh, Madame Addie, don't you like it?' I said. 'Hetty worked so hard to make it nice for you, but I'm sure she'll fashion you another one if you'd like it better.'

'I like *this* one,' Madame Adeline sobbed. 'It's the most beautiful wrapper in the world. It's absolutely exquisite!'

'Then why are you crying?'

'Because no one ever gave me such a wonderful present,' she said. 'Oh, Hetty, you are just like a daughter to me.'

'And you are just like a mother to me now,' said Hetty. I knew that meant a great deal, because Hetty had told me privately that she loved her dear mama more than anyone else in the world.

Hetty bought more silk – in brilliant colours this

time: scarlet and purple, colours so hot it seemed strange that the material should still feel so cool and silky.

'Are you making more wrappers, Hetty?' I asked, wondering if she might be making one for me.

'I'm making a costume for Mr Tanglefield,' said Hetty.

'For *Mr Tanglefield*?' I said. I knew Hetty disliked him just as much as I did. She did a wonderful imitation of him – pouting and issuing little whining commands while waving her arms in the air so that everyone snorted with laughter. Tag always begged her to do it again and again.

'I promised him a costume when he let me join the circus. I need to keep him on my side,' said Hetty, spreading her silk out and pinning a paper pattern to it. It seemed a very large piece of paper.

'Won't the shirt be a little too big for him?' I wondered.

'It's not a shirt, exactly. It's like a robe. Indian gentlemen wear them down to their knees.'

'Like a *dress*?' I said, looking forward to seeing Mr Tanglefield in such a ridiculous outfit.

But when Hetty had finished making the scarlet robe, with wide purple trousers for underneath, worn with a gold brocade waistcoat and a vast turban of gold and purple, I did not laugh. Mr Tanglefield was immediately transformed into an Indian rajah, and couldn't help looking utterly splendid. Hetty fashioned another tunic and turban for Sherzam, the elephant keeper, but in plain creams to make his lower status plain.

'Now we must dress Elijah up to match,' she said.

I squealed at the thought of a giant dress and trousers for the elephant – but Hetty contented herself with a brocade cloth for his great back. Then she helped herself to Chino and Beppo's greasepaint, ran up a stepladder, and painted beautiful swirly red and black and gold patterns on Elijah's head. Elijah wasn't at all sure he wanted to be made up at first, but Hetty fed him a whole big bag of penny buns while she was doing it, so he held still and let her paint while he munched.

When Mr Tanglefield, dressed in his new oriental splendour, rode the adorned Elijah into the ring, there was a great gasp from the audience, and then a huge burst of spontaneous clapping. Mr Tanglefield held his head high – possibly to keep his turban in place – and gave himself princely airs and graces. Elijah himself seemed to take a new pride in his exotic decoration. He picked up his huge feet and swung his trunk and swivelled his vast painted head so that all could admire it fully.

Hetty introduced them very imaginatively, though

she veered a little from the truth, describing a wild beast captured on the Indian plains, bought for a small fortune, and trained with great courage and difficulty, whereas we all knew Elijah had been born in captivity as part of a Hippodrome Spectacular. He'd always had a temperament as meek and mild as mother's milk, and had been sold at a bargain price to Mr Tanglefield when the Hippodrome Spectacular went bankrupt.

'You needn't think you're dressing *us* in silks and satins,' said Tag, who suffered enough in his silver spangles.

'I would quite *like* a bright silk costume,' said Julip.

'So indeed would I, Miss Hetty,' said Marvo.

I don't think he particularly wanted a new fancy costume, but he seemed very keen to please Hetty. He followed her everywhere, trying very hard to be a gentleman, opening wagon doors for her and offering to lift her over muddy patches in the meadow when it rained.

Hetty was polite to him, but I could see that his attentions irritated her.

'Can you find out if she has a sweetheart, Diamond?' Marvo asked me.

I wasn't sure if the foster brother counted as such. I thought it best not to bring him up with Hetty, but I did ask diffidently if she liked any of the circus men.

'Oh, *yes!*' she cried. 'You have found me out, Diamond. I am lovestruck! My heart goes all of a flutter whenever I am near him.'

'Oh, who is it? Is it perhaps Marvo? He will be so pleased,' I said.

'No, it certainly isn't Marvo, though he's a very sweet man.'

'Then who is it? Julip?'

'It's not Julip either. All right, I'll tell you, Diamond, but you must promise not to breathe a word. It's Mr Marvel!'

'*Mr Marvel?*' For one second I actually believed her, even though Mr Marvel was such a vast age and as wizened as his monkeys. And then I started giggling, and Hetty did too.

'You're teasing me!' I said.

'No, no, I'm absolutely serious. I shall set my cap at Mr Marvel and marry him, and all the monkeys will be my stepchildren and little Mavis will be my special baby,' said Hetty.

'No, Mavis is *my* baby!'

'Oh, very well, you can have Mavis, but you're definitely not getting my Marvel too, even though he told me *you* were his sweetheart.'

'Did he really? He is very kind to me and I love him dearly, but he's even older than my pa, and *he* is *very* elderly,' I said.

'I have quite a young pa,' Hetty told me, suddenly serious.

I was astonished. I'd thought Hetty was an orphan. I knew she'd lost her mother, but this father was total news to me. I wondered why she did not live with him.

'Did he not want you, Hetty?' I said. '*My* pa didn't want me. He sold me to Beppo for five guineas.'

'Then he was very silly, because you're worth at least five *thousand* guineas, Diamond. No, I think my pa *does* want me. He made me as welcome as he could when I went to stay with him. But his new wife did not care for me at all. She'd sell me for five pennies and think she'd got a bargain!'

'And . . . have you any other family, Hetty?' I asked tentatively, thinking of the foster brother.

Perhaps Hetty was thinking of him too, because her blue eyes looked very shiny, as if they were full of tears. But then she gave a great sniff. '*You* are my family now, Diamond,' she said. 'You and Madame Adeline.'

This time I knew she was serious and I felt wondrously joyful. But she was certainly a little fond of dear old Mr Marvel, even if she didn't quite want him for a sweetheart, because she bought new material the next time she found a clothes market, and made a whole set of clothes for the monkey family.

She stitched Melinda and Marianne wonderful tiny frocks in silk bombazine – one heliotrope with navy stripes, one brilliant peacock blue, both with bonnets to match and fur-trimmed mantles. Both girl monkeys had to mind their manners now they were dressed as elegant ladies. It took them a while to get used to their new costumes, and they wriggled and scratched and pulled off each other's bonnets in a very comical fashion. But Marmaduke and Michael adopted a dandy air as soon as Hetty kitted them out with little jackets and waistcoats and pinstripe trousers, and wore their mini bowler hats at a comical angle, crammed over their little round ears. Hetty dressed Mavis as a real baby, with a long cream gown and infant bonnet, and Mr Marvel taught her to tuck her gown up into her napkin, which always got a huge laugh from the audience.

Hetty worked on her own clothes too. She cut a very fine figure in her borrowed fleshings, but she hated it when lads in the audience shouted out that she had 'a cracking pair of pins'. She bought a length of good quality cream cotton and tried to make herself a proper pair of riding breeches. She had difficulty fashioning the legs at first, and wasted her first length of cloth, which made her swear because it was expensive. But the second time around she mastered the flair of the leg, while getting a good tight fit around the hips.

It was perhaps a little too good a fit, because the lads started shouting rude remarks about her nether regions instead. One windy day she found a fine top hat that must have bowled right off some gent's head. It was a little muddy, but after a stiff brush it came up as good as new. I thought she'd throw her stovepipe hat away, because even I knew it was old-fashioned and it had become very shabby – but she rolled it up in a length of silk and kept it stowed away in an old pillowcase as if it were as valuable as a jewelled crown.

She gazed at herself in Madame Adeline's looking glass, flourishing her top hat and striking poses in her new breeches.

'You look lovely, Hetty,' I said admiringly.

'Hmn,' said Hetty. 'I really need proper boots though. Polished riding boots.'

I was in awe of Hetty because she could make most things, but I knew even she couldn't manage a pair of leather boots. I saw her eyeing Mr Tanglefield's shiny black boots enviously.

'Perhaps he's got an old pair he doesn't wear any more,' she said thoughtfully.

'He's a small man, but his feet are still twice the size of yours,' I pointed out.

'I could stuff the toes with paper,' said Hetty. 'Oh, I *wish* I had a proper pair of boots.'

'Are they very expensive, Hetty?' I asked.

'Desperately so. I've asked at the bootmaker's in town. Their best pair is five guineas.'

'Oh my goodness, *I* cost that much,' I said.

'I suppose I can save up, but it's going to take such ages.' Hetty kicked up her legs and sighed.

But she didn't have to wait ages after all. The next day Madame Adeline went out straight after breakfast and came back with a great brown paper parcel in her arms.

'What have you got there, Madame Addie?' I asked.

'It's a little present, Diamond,' she said.

'It looks like a very *big* present.' I looked at it hopefully.

'I'm afraid it's not for you, sweetheart. But I dare say I can find you a chocolate treat, and that can be your very *little* present,' said Madame Adeline.

'Then who is it for?'

She nodded towards Hetty, who was wobbling all over the meadow on Chino and Beppo's penny-farthing cycle. She kept falling off, but she just brushed herself down and tried again, laughing.

At that moment Mister spotted her too and came hobbling towards her, spitting with fury. 'You, girl! Get off that machine immediately! What do you think you're doing? That contraption cost a small fortune. If that wheel's buckled, I'll have your guts for garters.'

Hetty jumped off the penny-farthing and untucked her skirts, laughing at him. 'Don't get so agitated, Mr Beppo. See – your penny-farthing's utterly unblemished.' She handed it over to him, dropping him a little curtsy.

'Don't put on airs and graces with me, you little trollop. You might have old Tanglefield so dazed he's practically signing his whole circus over to you – but you don't impress me one little bit,' said Beppo.

He climbed onto the penny-farthing himself to establish his rightful ownership – but he wasn't as skilled as Chino, and when he rode away he wobbled precariously, got the front wheel stuck on a tuft of grass, and fell right off, landing comically on his behind.

'You're such a funny clown!' said Hetty, and ran off to join Madame Adeline and me.

'Watch yourself, Hetty. It's not wise to tease Beppo too much. He can be a bad enemy,' said Madame Adeline.

'When you've grown up with terrible pig-faced matrons who hit you and locked you up in the attic, you don't get frightened of silly little circus men,' said Hetty.

Madame Adeline shook her head at her, but I was thrilled to hear her talking like that, even though I knew she was showing off. It helped *me* not to be so frightened of Mister.

'You're a naughty girl, Hetty, and a bad example to little Diamond,' said Madame Adeline. 'You don't really deserve a present – but here, take a look at this.' She handed Hetty the parcel.

Hetty held it, feeling the shapes under the paper, suddenly shocked into silence.

'What is it, Hetty? Oh, quick, tear the paper off!' I shouted.

Hetty gave a tiny pull at the wrapping, exploring something that gleamed conker-brown underneath. She gasped, and then suddenly tore the rest of the paper off so that it fluttered in shreds to her feet. She was left holding a pair of polished riding boots.

She cradled them as if they were two babies.

'I hope they're the right sort,' said Madame Adeline. 'They should be a reasonable fit. I took an outline of your shoes to show the bootmaker.'

'Oh, Madame Adeline, they're simply beautiful,' Hetty whispered. ' But – but I can't possibly accept them. They are far too expensive. They're the best present in the whole world, but as you say, I don't deserve them!'

'No, Hetty, you gave *me* the best present in the whole world – my wonderful tulip wrapper, made so carefully and lovingly. All *I've* done is buy a pair of boots,' said Madame Adeline.

'But they're so expensive. You must have used up all your savings!'

'It seems a little silly for me to save for my future

when I may not have one,' said Madame Adeline. 'You girls have all your lives ahead of you.'

'And so have you!' said Hetty fiercely. 'You're still the absolute star of the show.'

'I don't think so, dear, though it's sweet of you to say so. No, you are both our little stars – our tiny fairy Diamond and you, Hetty, our loved and brilliant ring-master.'

'A ringmaster who now has the best boots in the world!' said Hetty.

We settled down into a steady rhythm of setting up, practising, performing, taking down, travelling to the next village – and the next and the next and the next. I lost the tight feeling in my stomach, the squeeze of fear that made me tremble. I was still wary of Mister, but Hetty made sure she was nearby when we practised and he did not beat me in front of her. He stopped trying to teach me new tricks using the dreaded springboard. I was still anxious every time I scrambled up my silver brothers to make the human column, but it was becoming second nature now, almost as simple as running up a flight of stairs.

Every single day I played with Hetty. My doll, Maybelle, stayed neglected in my sleeping hammock. I had no need for a cloth friend now. Hetty and I ran wild races and balanced on the sea lions' rubber balls and stole the clowns' penny-farthing. At these times Hetty forgot she was practically grown up, and gloried in being bold and boisterous, charging around with her skirts tucked up.

'I never got to play when I was in the Foundling Hospital. I'm making up for lost time now!' she declared.

We had wonderful quiet times together too. She tried to teach me to read. I learned my alphabet and could figure out simple words, but I much preferred it if Hetty read to me, because she did so with such expression that it all came alive, as if the story was really happening. She read me her favourite book, *David Copperfield*. I grew a little fidgety when David became a man, but I loved hearing Hetty read the first few chapters when he was still a small boy. I wanted to play on the beach with him and little Em'ly. In the summer we had spent weeks at seaside venues and I couldn't get enough of the sands and the great swooshing sea.

Hetty had high hopes that we might visit a certain seaside town on the south coast called Bignor.

'I had such a dear friend there called Freda – a very large lady, but so gentle and refined,' she said. 'Oh, I do so hope I get to meet her again.'

But sadly we didn't go anywhere near this Bignor, with its big lady, and Hetty did not mention her again.

We turned back on ourselves and made our slow, meandering way through several counties, heading back towards London.

I was so happy living day by day that I did not realize I was in familiar territory. I performed in the first show, I had my stew, I ate cake with Madame Adeline and Hetty, and then I went into the ring for the second evening show. There was the usual laughter and applause as I did my little routine – but when I started climbing up Marvo and Julip and Tag to make the human column, someone called urgently, 'Watch out, Ellen-Jane – don't fall!'

I nearly *did* fall, I was so surprised. I couldn't see until I got right up on Tag's shoulders, and there, way down below me, was my dear sister Mary-Martha clutching a small boy, standing up in her seat, her mouth a big O of awe.

I waved at her very proudly and she waved back, and made the child wave too – my own little brother Johnnie.

I could hardly contain myself when I came out of the ring. 'My family are in the audience!' I said. 'They were watching me!'

I didn't just tell Marvo and Julip and Tag and then Madame Adeline. I told Mr Marvel and every little monkey. I even hung on Elijah's trunk and told him too.

'It's no use that pa of yours thinking he can come and fetch you back,' said Beppo. 'I bought you, fair and square, and he signed the piece of paper. You're my property now and he's not entitled to a penny of profit.'

'Was Pa there *too*?' I squeaked.

He hadn't come – of course he hadn't. But Mary-Martha was there, and she was the one I loved most. At the end of the final parade, she came rushing up to me.

'Oh, Ellen-Jane, I could scarce believe my eyes!' she cried, giving me such a fierce hug that baby Johnnie was squashed between us.

He wasn't the only brother come to see me. Luke was hanging back awkwardly, scarcely recognizable, he'd grown so pink and plump and rosy-cheeked.

'Oh, Luke!' I said, and gave him a hug too. 'You look very well!'

'I look too well for my profession. On funeral days they have to powder my cheeks so that I still look respectably pale,' he said. 'They're talking of reducing my food too. I do hope not – the missus is a marvel at cooking. You should taste her pies, Ellen-Jane! And her cake and tarts – oh my!'

'Luke fetches some home for us if he can,' said Mary-Martha. 'Oh, we should have brought you some.'

'I have cake too – pink and yellow with marzipan – and chocolates!' I boasted. 'And all the oranges I can ever eat. Did you see the folk throwing them?'

'We saw *you*, Ellen-Jane – and oh, you were grand! I couldn't believe it, my own sister got up like a little fairy queen and flying through the air! Don't you get frightened at all?'

'No, of course not,' I lied. 'Did you see my forward somersault? Shall I show you now?'

I demonstrated. Mary-Martha and Luke gasped most satisfyingly, and little Johnnie went into peals of laughter.

'I'll have to take you home with us. You'd be wonderful at diverting him when he starts one of his crying fits,' said Mary-Martha.

'Then . . . *can* I come home?' I said.

She looked stricken. 'Oh, me and my big mouth! I didn't mean it like that. Oh dear, I wish you *could* come home more than anything, Ellen-Jane, I miss you something chronic, but Pa would go mad. He won't even let us talk about you now.'

I swallowed hard. 'Perhaps I could creep home while Pa's out drinking?' I suggested.

'He doesn't drink a drop now, not since that day when you ran off with the circus man,' said Mary-Martha.

'I didn't run off! He *sold* me!' I said, starting to cry.

'Don't take on so, Ellen-Jane,' Luke said uncomfortably. 'He sold me too, didn't he – and Matthew and Mark.'

'Luke is doing so well now, and he comes to see me whenever he can. He earns a fortune in tips from the bereaved. He's very generous,' said Mary-Martha. 'Matthew is learning carpentry and doing well too – he carved Johnnie a lovely little wooden train. Ever so grand, isn't it, Johnnie pet?'

'And Mark?'

'Mark's a bad boy. He ran away from the fishmonger, says he couldn't stand it. Oh, Pa was so cross. But he's got a job in a department store now, just helping out with the stock, but they'll put him to serving customers soon.'

'And what about you, Mary-Martha?'

'Oh, I just keep home and look after Baby, and I do all the colour work too of course, for the tracts and the story books. I lead the same ordinary old life – but you, Ellen-Jane, you are famous! You are so brilliant. My heart was fit to burst with pride when I saw you. My own baby sister, such a little star! So it's all worked out for the best, hasn't it?' she said.

'I . . . suppose so,' I replied, ducking my head.

'You *are* happy, aren't you, Ellen-Jane?' Mary-

Martha swapped Johnnie to her other hip and seized my arm anxiously.

'Of course she's happy,' said Luke. 'She was always the little show-off, standing on her head and waggling her legs. She's doing the job she was born for. She's Diamond now. What was it that ringmaster girl called you? *She's* a caution too! You're Diamond the Acrobatic Child Wonder.'

'That girl is my friend Hetty. And yes, I am happy, very happy,' I said.

But that night I cried hard in my hammock because I wasn't part of my family any more.

Marvo saw my red eyes in the morning and asked what was wrong. I wouldn't tell him. I didn't even breathe a word to Madame Adeline when she gave me cocoa with cream for a breakfast treat, but as soon as I was alone with Hetty I burst out sobbing again.

'Tell me, Diamond,' she said, holding me close and rocking me.

So I told her that I didn't have a proper family any more, sobbing so much that I made her bodice wet.

'Try not to take it to heart,' she said softly.

'But I am so, so sad! I don't have a ma, and my pa don't want me, nor my brothers, and even Mary-Martha don't miss me very much,' I wailed.

'I don't have a ma now either, though she's always in my heart. I have a dear pa, but I dare say he don't miss me either. I have sisters and brothers – very dear brothers – but they aren't my family now.'

'So you haven't got a family either, Hetty?' I said, knuckling my eyes.

'Yes, I have. I've got *you*. And we've both got Madame Adeline. What more could we want?' she asked.

'Yes, that's true,' I said, cheering up instantly.

'And don't forget, you've always got your dear old Grandpappy Beppo,' said Hetty, which made me shriek with laughter.

Seeing Mary-Martha and Luke did unsettle me for weeks though. I looked for them in the audience long after the circus had moved on to other towns.

'Don't you ever wonder if any of your kin are watching you?' I asked Hetty.

'Well, I did hope I might see my friend Freda when we were at the seaside back in the summer, but I'd have definitely spotted her in the audience. Freda is a girl who can't help sticking out in a crowd,' she replied.

'But what about *your* brothers and sisters?'

'Oh Lord, *they'd* never come,' said Hetty.

My stomach tensed up. It was no use. I had to tell her.

'Your brother Jem came once,' I whispered.

'Yes, he came looking for me and marched me back home,' said Hetty.

'He came after that – in Gillford. I saw him in the audience,' I said, making a clean breast of it at last.

'Are you sure, Diamond?'

'Certain sure.'

'Then why didn't you tell me?'

'I didn't tell because . . . because I thought if you knew you might change your mind and go back to him, and I couldn't bear that because I wanted you to stay so much. Oh, Hetty, am I very wicked? Are you cross with me?'

'No, I'm not cross,' said Hetty, but she sounded very sad, and that made me feel even worse.

I watched her carefully the next few performances – and though she was word perfect, never missing a beat, her eyes swivelled round and round the ring as she spoke, and I knew she was checking, looking for Jem, even though we were in a different part of the country now. All through November we edged our way towards London, because we had a three-week Christmas show arranged on Clapham Common.

Mr Tanglefield wanted all the acts to have a festive theme, so Hetty worked day and night stitching away at new costumes. She made Mr Marvel's monkeys matching scarlet outfits edged with white fur. He found a big oval looking glass, put artificial grass around it so that it looked like a frozen pond, and set the monkeys 'skating' on it. The adult monkeys picked up their feet and swayed to and fro like real little skaters, but baby Mavis slid across the pretend pond on her behind and got an extra laugh.

Hetty made two really big red dresses for the female dancing bears, and they took turns to waltz around the ring with Bruno. Then the third bear lumbered into the ring dressed as Father Christmas, with a big sack of toys, which made all the children in the audience scream with excitement.

Mr Tanglefield even suggested Hetty make a simply vast Father Christmas costume for Elijah.

'How ridiculous can you get!' she said to Madame Adeline and me. 'The man's off his head!'

'I hope you didn't tell him that,' said Madame Adeline.

'No, no, I just sweet-talked him, telling him that his Father Christmas idea was wonderful but perhaps it might detract from Elijah's oriental allure if he was forced to plod around wearing a red tent and a vast false beard. I've suggested festooning him with holly and ivy instead, though I'll have to pad the holly leaves in some way so that the poor beast isn't prickled to death. And I'm making Old Tangletummy a grand new costume in festive red and green trimmed with gold.' Hetty paused. 'What about you, Madame Addie? Would you like a scarlet spangled dress?'

'I've done my best *not* to be called a scarlet woman

all my professional life,' said Madame Adeline. 'But I will wear one if you think it will look effective, Hetty.'

Hetty held the bright red silk up under Madame Adeline's chin. It made her face look very pale and tired.

'I think your lovely pink costume suits you much better,' said Hetty. 'Will you be altering your routine with Midnight at all?'

'Midnight and I are too old to learn new tricks,' said Madame Adeline.

'They couldn't be bettered,' Hetty insisted.

'What about me? Do I have to learn a new trick if I have a new outfit?' I asked. 'I don't have to do spring-board work, do I? I still don't think I'm brave enough.'

'I have a suggestion for your Mister Beppo,' said Hetty. 'Don't look so worried, Diamond. I won't suggest the springboard, I promise.'

'I wouldn't suggest anything to Beppo if I were you, Hetty,' Madame Adeline advised.

But Hetty was always a girl to throw caution to the wind. She squatted down beside Mister when he was smoking his pipe after tea and started whispering in his ear.

'Clear off, you little busybody. I don't want your suggestions, thank you very much,' he growled, but Hetty persisted. She went whisper, whisper, whisper, and I saw Mister's eyes gleam, even though his expression stayed surly.

'If you must, if you must! Now leave me in peace,' he said eventually.

'What have you suggested, Hetty?' I asked eagerly. Marvo, Julip and Tag were also full of questions.

'Oh, I just suggested that it might look better in the ring if you were properly matching – two boys and two girls,' said Hetty.

'But we're *three* boys, stupid,' said Tag.

'Don't you know that circus is all about *illusion*?' she asked. 'I'm going to fashion you a beautiful span-gled fairy frock with little wings, Tag, and until your own hair grows you can wear a curly wig.'

'*What?*' he spluttered.

'Tag a *fairy*?' Julip laughed.

'Hetty's teasing you,' said Marvo. He grinned and flexed his muscles. 'How about a fairy frock for me instead?'

Hetty was indeed joking, though it took a while for Tag to calm down and be convinced. She made me a new fairy dress instead, patiently sewing hundreds of sequins onto the bodice so that I sparkled in the ring, and she fashioned three forest-green velvet cloaks for the boys that covered them right down to their toes. Here and there she sewed little baubles on the velvet.

'How can we perform in *cloaks*?' said Tag.

'You won't wear them till the end of the act,' Hetty told him. 'When you perform the human column.'

We did not properly understand until the cloaks were all complete and the boys put them on. When Julip was standing on Marvo and Tag on Julip, their cloaks hung down, glittering with baubles. They looked for all the world like a Christmas tree. Then I clambered up, the fairy on the topmost branch.

It was a Christmas show to be proud of. We played to full houses. For Christmas week Mr Tanglefield even had us put on an extra morning show. We played Sundays too. The only time we had off was Christmas Day itself, and we were all so bone weary we slept a great deal of it. Mr Tanglefield organized a communal dinner in the big top itself, ordering a gaggle of great roast geese. We each had a huge plateful, with apple sauce and roast potatoes, with beer for the men and wine for the ladies.

No one felt like getting up the next morning, but Boxing Day was our biggest day of the year, with three sold-out performances. Hetty had a slight cold and a sore throat – Madame Adeline made her salt-water gargles and told her to whisper when she wasn't in the ring to rest her voice, but Hetty found that very difficult indeed. By the evening performance her voice was almost gone, and she was starting to panic, but Mr Tanglefield himself took her to his wagon and administered a medicinal cocktail of whisky and honey and lemon. I don't know which component did the trick.

Maybe it was just Hetty's own determination – but she was certainly in particularly fine form that evening.

'Ladies and gentlemen, boys and girls, children and babes in arms,' she cried out. 'Welcome to Tanglefield's Travelling Circus on this very splendid Boxing Day – and have we got a treat for you!'

We were playing to fine families from all over London. There were carriages lined up in a row at the edge of the common to take them home again. I loved looking at all the little girls in the audience, admiring their satin bows and party frocks and ermine jackets. They were all decked out so prettily, but none had such a splendid blue silk dress as me, none had silver spangles, none had fancy wings.

When we'd done the big farewell parade at the end, we were waylaid by the eager crowd. We were happy to linger, because they were plying us with all sorts of delicious tributes – chocolates and candy canes and crystallized fruits!

One solemn young lady in a fur-trimmed blue velvet mantle was staring hard at Hetty. She wore her hair tied back in a long fat pigtail like a bell rope, emphasizing her high forehead. She was gazing so intently, I could see a pulse twitching at her temple. She kept trying to press forward to get nearer to Hetty, but there was such an eager throng around her, this was proving impossible.

She looked around a little wildly, and saw me staring at her. She seized hold of my arm. 'Excuse me . . . I hope you don't mind my asking, but – but you must know that red-haired girl, the one who is the ringmaster,' she said.

'Yes, I do. She is my dear friend,' I said proudly.

'Could you – could you tell me her name?' asked the young lady.

'Her name is Emerald Star,' I said, because that was Hetty's professional name.

'Oh!' said the young lady, looking crestfallen.

'Don't you like the name? I think it is very beautiful. My name is Diamond. Diamonds and emeralds are both precious stones. They go together – and so do we,' I said, but I could see she'd stopped listening.

'I thought she was my Hetty . . .' she whispered to herself.

I blinked at her. 'Did you say *Hetty*?'

'Yes. Long ago I had the dearest friend in all the world – Hetty Feather. And when I saw your friend Emerald in the ring, I could scarcely believe my eyes. She is the exact spit of my own Hetty, and similarly gifted with words, and equally brave and bold and utterly splendid. It's hard to believe there could be two girls so alike, but I am obviously mistaken.'

'No, you're not! Emerald Star is her professional name but she is really your Hetty,' I said. *She is mine too*, I thought fiercely. *She is my own Hetty, not yours.*

But I could not deny Hetty this chance to see an old friend. I had felt so bad at having kept quiet about Jem.

'Hetty, Hetty,' I called loudly. 'Hetty, here is someone to meet you!'

Hetty heard me calling in spite of the hubbub. She elbowed her way cheerily through the crowds and stood before us. She peered at the young lady. For a moment she looked blank – and then her whole face crumpled.

'Polly! Oh, Polly, it's you!'

She flung her arms wide, and the two girls embraced as if they could never bear to let each other go.

'I *knew* it was you, Hetty! But what in the world are you doing here? I thought you'd be a servant now, like all the other hospital girls. Every day when I go for a walk I look down into all the basement kitchens and wonder if you're there, scrubbing and scouring.'

'I was a servant – a perfectly dreadful one! I wouldn't do as I was told.'

'Why does that not surprise me!' Polly said, laughing.

'And then I went up north and was a fisher girl.'

'Hetty!'

'And *then* I went back to the country to my foster family.'

'To your brother Jem?'

'Yes, but – but then the circus came, and I couldn't help myself. I ran away to join it!'

'Oh, Hetty, I *knew* you'd somehow do something exciting!'

'And what about you, Polly? Look at you, so grown up and ladylike! You have such lovely clothes.' Hetty stroked Polly's velvet mantle admiringly. 'Your family must be very rich!'

Polly went a little pink. 'Well, I suppose we are well-to-do,' she said awkwardly.

'And – and what do you do?'

'I still go to school. I would dearly love to stay on till I am eighteen and then study further at a ladies' college, but Papa does not want me to become a blue-stocking,' said Polly.

'Oh, you were always so clever!'

'And so were you! It's so wonderful to have found you, Hetty. I beg your pardon, Miss Emerald Star!'

'Well, we must keep in touch now and meet up as often as we can. We are here until the beginning of January so we can visit each other. Wait till you meet Madame Adeline, Polly! She has been almost like a second mother to me—'

'Lucy! Lucy, oh thank goodness! We thought we'd

lost you for ever in this wretched crowd. Come here, dearest!' A large, anxious lady came hurrying through the crowd, tears spilling down her plump cheeks.

'Lucy, my little Lucy!' She chided her as if she were a tiny girl, patting her with her soft white hands, rings and bracelets all a-jingle with agitation.

'Calm yourself, Mama,' said Polly.

'Lucy! Oh dear Heavens, we've found you!' This was clearly Papa now, as plump and pink as her other parent. 'Come, dear, we must find the carriage.' He pulled at Polly's arm.

Polly looked at her parents, then back at Hetty. Their hands were still clasped.

'Lucy! Say goodbye to – to the young person and come away at once,' said the papa.

'But – but this is Hetty,' Polly said bravely. 'My friend from when . . . when I was little.'

The woman gave a little gasp.

'Don't be ridiculous, dear,' said the father. 'Come away this instant. You're upsetting your mama.' He looked at Hetty coldly. 'Let her go!'

He turned Polly round and pulled her away. Hetty didn't try to hang onto her hand. Polly turned round once, looking desperate. Hetty smiled gaily and waved, even though there were tears in her eyes.

She watched until Polly and her parents were swallowed up by the crowd.

'Why did they call her Lucy?' I asked.

'Because she is their daughter now. They adopted her,' said Hetty. 'They changed her name. They changed everything.'

'But why won't they let you be friends with her?'

'Because we're very different sorts of girls now,' said Hetty. 'She is a young lady – and you and I are circus girls, Diamond. We should be pleased and proud. It's a very fine, rare thing to be a circus girl,' she said, but she was crying properly now.

The Christmas shows were a triumph, but from January all the way through to Easter we had no bookings at all.

'Don't look so downcast, chickies,' said Madame Adeline. 'We'll be going into winter quarters.'

'And what do we do there?' Hetty asked.

'We rest! And I for one will be heartily glad to do so.'

Madame Adeline certainly looked very tired and drained. The thrice-daily performances had been hard on her and she'd grown very gaunt. Her collarbones stuck out painfully when she wore her low-cut costume, and her fleshings wrinkled badly because her legs had become so spindly. When she was fully made up and wearing her long red wig, she still looked beautiful, but in the early morning, hobbling around, exhausted, she seemed like an old, old lady.

Hetty looked after her determinedly, doing most of the chores in the wagon, fetching water, making fires, even doing the cooking. She was remarkably defensive if anyone looked awry at poor Madame Adeline.

Tag once called her a doddery old woman – a relatively mild epithet compared to some of the names he'd called me! – but Hetty slapped his face hard and hissed at him to show a little respect.

Midnight needed a rest too. Some weeks ago he had stumbled on a stone while exercising on the common and had jarred his leg. He really needed to rest for a few days. Madame Adeline had gone to Mr Tanglefield and begged for him to have a little respite from the relentless performances over Christmas, but Mr Tanglefield had been adamant.

'If you and that nag wish to stay part of this show, then you'll perform. If you're too old or unfit, then you've no place here and you can get out today,' was his brutal response.

So Madame Adeline had been forced to put poor

lame Midnight through his paces at each performance, though it nearly broke her heart.

The winter quarters were in the grounds of a disused factory in a bleak suburban town. There was no grassy meadow for poor Midnight. When his leg was better, Madame Adeline led him to a distant park and rode him gently there, but he remained out of sorts and dispirited.

None of the animals seemed happy in their new cramped environment. It was particularly miserable for huge Elijah. He had very little exercise, tethered permanently in the dingy yard. He paced the three steps his ball and chain allowed, his trunk swinging this way and that, but he bore his captivity in stoic silence. The big cats and the dancing bears were noisier, roaring and growling a good deal of the time, only ceasing when they gnawed great lumps of meat at meal times.

Even the sea lions seemed to miss bobbing about on their rubber balls, and barked in a melancholy fashion whenever they stuck their sleek heads out of the water. Only Mr Marvel's monkeys seemed content, often staying in character and acting out their dancing and skating routines within the confines of their cage.

Mr Marvel clapped them solemnly and encouraged me to do so too. 'They like to be appreciated, Diamond,' he said. 'Performing's in their blood now. They're missing their show something chronic.'

'What about you, Mr Marvel?' I asked.

'Me? Oh, I've been ready to retire for years and years. I have a dear little cottage in the country. Mind you, I haven't been there in many a moon. It was my late brother's home. I think of it longingly sometimes. I could quite easily turn into a pipe-and-slippers gent, you know – but I can't let my babies down.' He smiled at his monkeys fondly and they chattered lovingly back, but this might have been because he was feeding them with peanuts through the bars of their cage. 'You miss performing too, don't you, little Diamond?' he said.

I didn't think I missed performing at all. For the first two or three days of winter quarters I slept a great deal of the time, falling into a heavy slumber the moment I curled up in my hammock. I slept everywhere in fact. I fell asleep on Madame Adeline's velvet sofa, on Hetty's lap, even halfway through my evening meal. It was because I was so bone weary after the relentless three performances each day for weeks.

Then I woke one day and realized that my head was clear, my bones didn't ache, I felt full of life – and there was no fear in the pit of my stomach. I still had to practise every day, but even Mister relaxed a bit and read a newspaper while he put us through our paces, nodding or tutting in a cursory manner.

It meant I had weeks and weeks and weeks of free time to be with Hetty, all day and every day. Seeing

Polly had stirred up many painful memories of her time at the Foundling Hospital. She started telling me all about it as we huddled together in a corner of Madame Adeline's wagon. I asked her a hundred questions. I was especially keen to hear about Hetty when she was my age.

'Would we have been friends then, if I'd been at the hospital too? Would you have liked me almost as much as Polly?' I asked.

'I'd have liked you *more*,' she said.

'Tell me the games you played together. And tell me about the fierce matrons. And tell me about what happened when you were really naughty,' I begged.

'Perhaps I'll simply read you little extracts from my memoirs.' Hetty went to her leather suitcase and opened it up carefully. I saw a bundle of letters tied up with blue ribbon. She cradled them gently in cupped hands.

'Who wrote the letters, Hetty?' I asked. 'Are they from a sweetheart?'

'They are from Mama. They're far more precious to me than any sweetheart's love letters.' She laid them carefully back in place and picked up a silver necklace.

'That's pretty,' I said.

Hetty held it up so that I could see it was a little sixpenny piece on a chain. 'This is from a sweetheart,' she said.

I was sure this was Jem.

'But you don't wear it?' I asked.

'No, because I'm not anyone's sweetheart now,' she said, a little sadly.

'And what's this?' I picked up a little black and white china dog. 'Oh, I like him!'

'Bertie won it for me at a fair,' said Hetty.

'Bertie? *Another* sweetheart?' I said, a little crossly.

Hetty laughed. 'I dare say you will have sweethearts of your own when you're a bit older,' she said. 'In fact I have a feeling young Tag is keen on you, Diamond.'

'*Tag?*' I exclaimed. 'He hates me! He's forever tormenting me.'

'He's just trying to get your attention,' said Hetty. 'He's not a bad boy really. You could do worse than him.'

'No I couldn't! He's the *worstest* worse,' I said with feeling.

I looked at the notebooks in the case. There were three thick volumes, one red, one blue, and one green, each page crisscrossed with Hetty's tiny scribbly writing. 'I can't read it all,' I said.

'I will read a few pages aloud,' said Hetty, flipping through the first volume. 'Now, where shall I start?'

'Start at the beginning,' I said.

So she did – and I wouldn't let her stop. She read to

me most of the day – and the next and the next. When she came to the first passage about Madame Adeline, I squeaked with excitement.

'You must read it to Madame Addie too, Hetty!'

'I think I am a little too candid about her at times,' said Hetty. 'I would not hurt her for the world.'

I was even more excited when she came to the last quarter of the third book – and met me!

'Are you going to be extra candid about me, Hetty? Are you going to write about this terrible, wretched girl who trails around after you and drives you mad?' I asked.

If Hetty had written any such thing, she didn't read it aloud. She said lovely things about me!

'Oh, you are such a special friend, Hetty! If I were ever clever enough to write a memoir, I'd fill page after page with all the things you say and do.'

'Well, I'll give you some more reading and writing lessons, and we'll buy you a notebook and get you started,' said Hetty.

She was as good as her word. She bought a new notebook from a stationer's in town, with a leather spine and edges, and a swirly violet pattern that reminded me a little uncomfortably of angels' wings.

'I haven't always been a very good girl,' I said. 'Must I write down all the bad things I have done?'

'You don't have to, but it makes it a more truthful account,' said Hetty.

'But won't I get into trouble and be punished?'

'No one will be reading your memoir, Diamond, except me – and if you've been bad, I'm sure I'll find it understandable, especially as I've been a very bad girl myself. I used to think folk might read *my* memoirs one day. I thought they might be good enough to be published as a special book, but I can see that was a ridiculous idea.' Hetty sighed wistfully. 'I don't know why I'm bothering to write so much. No one will ever want to read about a foundling girl – or a kitchen maid or a fisher girl, or even a circus girl for that matter. Can you see Polly's parents rushing to the bookseller's to buy their precious daughter such an account?'

'Yes!' I insisted, though I could see she had a point. Then I suddenly remembered one of the fairy stories I had coloured. There were two contrasting illustrations: one of a girl in a sooty apron and ragged dress, weeping in a kitchen before a meagre fire, and another of the same girl in a magnificent evening dress hurrying in her sparkly slippers from a grand ball as a clock struck twelve . . . a number I now dreaded.

'I know a story about a kitchen maid!' I said, and described the illustrations to Hetty. I remembered them well: I had laboured hard to get the right shade of pale gold for the heroine's hair and I'd patiently painted tiny jewels all over her Chinese-white ball dress. I'd talked to the girl all the while in my head, pretending that I was going to the ball too.

'I think that's the story of Cinderella,' said Hetty.

'Does it have a happy ending?' I asked.

'I suppose so. Cinderella marries a handsome prince.'

'Then you might marry a handsome prince too,' I said.

'No, thank you very much,' said Hetty. '*You* can have the handsome prince if he comes galloping up on his white horse.'

I thought about it. I'd never met a handsome prince, of course, but I'd known quite a few handsome boys – my three big brothers, and Marvo, Julip and Tag. 'I don't think I want one either,' I said.

'Then we'll be old maids together, and I dare say very happy ones too,' said Hetty. 'Here we are, Diamond. Here's your memoir book. Get writing. I'll help you with any hard words you don't know how to spell.'

I struggled hard for an hour or more, clutching my pen so tightly that it grew sticky with sweat. I had all the words in my head, but it took so long to get them out on the paper. Try as I might, my letters danced crazily up and down and were large and unwieldy, no matter how I struggled to keep them small and neat.

My nam is Dimon. I use to be caled Ellen-Jane Potts, I wrote, filling a whole page with this uninspiring sentence – and then I burst into tears because I was so ashamed.

I could not understand how I could paint so neatly when quite a little girl and yet could not even manage one proper sentence of writing now.

'Don't cry so, Diamond. You just need more practice, that's all,' said Hetty.

'I *hate* practising!' I wailed.

'Well, tell you what: why don't you tell me what you want to say and I'll write it all down for you,' Hetty suggested.

'But you have your own memoir to write.'

'I think maybe three great fat volumes are enough – for the moment, anyway. It is your turn now, Diamond.' She took the notebook away from me and sat, pen poised. 'Start talking!'

'From the very beginning, as far back as I can remember?'

'Yes!'

So I started – and Hetty wrote it all down for me. She wrote and wrote and wrote, and said I'd had a very full life for such a young person.

'So many things have happened, many of them dreadful,' I said. 'But now I have started a peaceful time where nothing much is happening at all, and that is quite heavenly. I wish we could stay in winter quarters for ever. Don't you, Hetty?'

'I don't! I guess I'm more of a showgirl than you, Diamond, for all you're so talented. I find I miss performing terribly. Don't you feel cooped up here? I long to be on the road again.'

Hetty was growing increasingly restless. She went on long walks every day, sometimes taking me with her, and carrying me piggyback when I couldn't keep up. She had a fancy to take me back to London to show me the sights. Reading her memoirs aloud had made her dwell on the past and she wanted to show me the Foundling Hospital.

'Will we go in it and see the fierce matrons?' I said anxiously.

'I should think *not*! They'd likely prod me with their rulers and prick me with their darning needles. I was their least favourite child by far. But I would like to see my little foster sister Eliza, who is still there, poor mite. I ran away when I was about her age. I should love to show you Hyde Park, Diamond, and the restaurant where I had lunch with Miss Smith and . . . Oh dear, she would be very shocked if she could see me now. I don't think the Religious Tract Society could possibly approve of circuses.' Hetty took a deep breath. 'Perhaps it's not wise to go back and try and revisit places or people. I think one should just go forwards. Yes, that's right, Diamond. Don't let either of us think about the past. Let's just think of our future and our family – you and me and dear Madame Adeline.'

'And Mr Marvel and Mavis and the rest of the monkeys,' I said, giggling.

We had no idea that everything was going to change. Mr Tanglefield shut himself up in his wagon for most of January, fussing with his accounts and poring over maps, plotting where we would be going when the new season started at Easter.

Then, in February, he started going on mysterious trips, sometimes staying away for three or four days at a time. Everyone relaxed at first, and there were several parties – but after a while folk grew uneasy.

'He's up to something,' said Mister, frowning. 'Why is he chasing off like this? Who is he seeing? I reckon he's on the lookout for a new act.'

'So do you think he wants to expand and make Tanglefield's a bigger circus?' asked Hetty.

'Nope, he's got to keep it tight. He'd need proper transport if he expanded too much – his own specially adapted train like the ones in America – and that ain't going to happen,' he replied.

'But you said he was looking for new acts.'

'*Replacement* acts,' said Mister. He nodded curtly at Hetty. 'Yes, you've a right to look shocked. I dare say he's looking for a brand-new ringmaster – or ringmistress, I should say. He's seen that having a female announce the show is something of a novelty that draws the crowds, but he'll be on the lookout for a glamorous young lady, saucy but sweet – not some shrill-voiced, whey-faced gingernob who knows nothing of circus tradition.'

He was trying to scare Hetty, but I knew she wasn't concerned about her own position. She was thinking anxiously about Madame Adeline.

Mr Tanglefield remained tight-lipped when he returned from his various mystery visits, but he started watching everyone closely while they practised. There was no show scheduled for weeks. We didn't even have a proper big top, just a large sawdust-strewn yard in the freezing cold – but suddenly everyone performed as if the old Queen and all her courtiers were sitting watching.

I found it so nerve-racking that I fluffed the easiest back-flip and landed on my behind. I didn't look where I was going and blundered straight into Tag, nearly making him topple too.

'You call her a little fairy? She's more like a fairy elephant today,' said Mr Tanglefield, laughing at me.

'Ha ha, poor darling. I don't think she's quite herself,' said Mister, but his own laughter was anything but jovial.

He managed to stay smiling at me until Mr Tanglefield strolled off to have his lunch. Then his face hardened. 'How dare you mess up such a simple routine?' he thundered.

'I'm sorry! I don't like it when he watches me. Please don't be cross,' I begged.

'You're there to be watched. You're a performer, aren't you? Well, you've got to sharpen up your act and no mistake. And it's time you learned something new, my little *fairy*.' He practically spat the word. 'You're going to have to spread those silly little wings.' He grasped me by the elbow and led me over to the springboard.

'Oh no! *Please* no! I can't do it. You know I can't!' I said, dissolving into tears.

'Can't – or *won't*,' said Mister. 'I don't want any of your hysterics, young missy. You'll learn. If the others can do it, so can you.'

'But it's so scary!' I protested feebly.

'Which is scarier, a simple little somersault or two, or a royal beating?' he asked. 'Now, line up with the others and concentrate hard. You're doing it, and there's an end to it. We've got to improve the act or we'll all be thrown on the scrapheap.'

Marvo ran to get soft mats and bedding and spread them out. 'There now! If you *do* fall, it won't hurt too much,' he whispered comfortingly.

'She'll try harder to do it right if we don't have the safety matting,' said Mister – but he let them stay in place.

I tried. I tried so hard. I didn't want to do it. I felt bile rise in my throat at the thought of the spring-board. Each time, I hurtled up and spun round and round, trying desperately to land on my feet – or indeed any part of me that wasn't my head. I was sick afterwards, whether I landed well or not. Even then Mister wouldn't let me off.

'Bring a bucket. She'll be fine,' he said heartlessly.

When Hetty saw what was happening, she marched up to Mister and stood right in front of him, chin up, arms folded.

'Stop torturing that poor child! You know perfectly well she's not old enough or strong enough to somer-sault through the air like that,' she said.

'Don't you tell me what to do! She's mine. I can do what I like with her,' he shouted.

'I'll – I'll report you!' said Hetty furiously.

'Oh yes? And who will you report me to, exactly?' said Mister.

'I could go and fetch a policeman and report you for being cruel to a child,' said Hetty, wavering a little.

'You fool,' he sneered. 'I'm her guardian now. I've taken her father's place. I can beat her black and blue if I care to. But just supposing you call a Peeler and he starts reading me the riot act, what do you think will happen to the little fairy here?'

'*I'll* look after her,' said Hetty.

'You're just a silly little girl yourself, not long out of that Foundling Hospital. As if they'd ever let you! No, they'd ship Diamond off to the workhouse, and I don't think even you would wish that on her.'

'Please don't put me in the workhouse!' I cried.

'It's all right, Diamond. Of course you're not going in the workhouse. Beppo's just trying to frighten both of us,' said Hetty, putting her arm round me.

He was succeeding too, because we were both trembling.

I had to continue my springboard work, and even Hetty could not help me. I gradually learned to control my body in the air and could just about do a double somersault and then land on the ground, but try as I might I couldn't manage to land on Tag's shoulders. I frequently hurtled into the three boys and sent them all sprawling – or if I did land accurately, I simply couldn't keep my balance and always took a tumble.

Then, one day that was no different from any other – I was just as tired, just as scared, just as despairing – I took off from the springboard, soared through the air, head tucked neatly between my knees, swivelled twice and landed lightly on Tag. I don't know how or why – it just happened! I stood there, keeping my balance, utterly astonished, wondering if I was actually dreaming, because most nights I dreamed of nothing else. But no, this was real, and it had actually worked. I had done the trick perfectly!

'Bravo!' Mister shouted. 'That's it! That's the way! Oh, what a crowd-pleaser! Again! Do it again before you forget how.'

So I tried again. We were all convinced it had been some magic fluke – me most of all. But I did it again, timing it perfectly, swooping up and up and up, then round and round again, and landing spot on, holding the position. I even managed to stretch out my arms to milk the applause.

'Good *girl*!' said Mister, and he actually clapped for all he was worth.

I expected Tag to be annoyed with me and give me a quick punch or a sly kick, but instead he thumped me on the back in congratulation. 'Not bad at all, Diamond,' he said.

'It was blooming brilliant,' said Marvo, tossing me in the air.

'Well done, Diamond. You truly *are* a little star now,' said Julip.

I couldn't wait to show Hetty my new trick, but she wouldn't watch properly. The moment I ran onto the springboard, she put her hands over her face and could not look until I'd landed safely.

'It's all right, Hetty! Look, I'm fine. I can do it now, see!' I shouted.

'But what if you slip?' Hetty asked.

'She won't slip. She's got it now,' said Mister.

'She *could* slip. She's springing up much too high. I can't bear to look,' she cried.

I couldn't reassure her, even though I did the trick perfectly again and again.

'I know it. It's in my head. I won't forget how to do it. It's like you riding Mister's penny-farthing. You kept falling off at first, but now you've mastered it you can ride it round and round every time.'

'But if I *do* fall I'm not likely to break my neck,' she pointed out.

'Try not to worry, dear,' I said, like a grown-up, because I wanted to reassure her. It made her burst out laughing, which wasn't quite the effect I'd hoped for.

'Anyway, Mister almost likes me now. He's stopped worrying about us being replaced,' I said.

'I don't think anyone's going to be replaced,' Hetty said firmly – but she was wrong.

During our last week in winter quarters there was a flurry of activity – folk painting their wagons, polishing up the horse brasses, testing equipment. Mr Tanglefield ordered everyone to have their wagons ready to be off at crack of dawn the next morning.

'And make more room in the yard,' he said. 'We have some new friends joining us today.'

'I knew it,' said Beppo.

'But we'll be all right now I've learned how to fly,' I said, taking hold of Marvo's big hand.

'I don't think Beppo's worried about *our* act,' Marvo whispered. 'Maybe he's anxious about his own.'

'But Beppo and Chino always make everyone laugh.'

'*Chino* does,' said Julip. 'But not Beppo. He's getting old. He looks all wrong when he gambols around the ring. You can see he's really stiff. No matter how comical his make-up, he never looks funny. He can't disguise his eyes.'

'Circus folk are supposed to look young and strong and spry, whatever kind of artiste they are,' said Tag.

'That's not true,' I said. 'Look at Mr Marvel. He's really, really old. It doesn't matter a jot.'

'I wouldn't be so sure of that,' said Tag. 'And I'd worry about your precious Madame Adeline – she's so long in the tooth she's been performing since Tanglefield's pa was in charge. I reckon she's for the chop.'

'I'll chop *you*!' I said, clenching my fists together and hitting him on the head.

I was so angry and struck Tag so hard, he actually ran away from me, which made Marvo and Julip laugh.

There was no laughing when the new folk arrived that afternoon. The whole company gathered silently, strained and tense. A blue and yellow wagon arrived first, the horse driven by a spry-looking man in his twenties.

'Do you think he's an acrobat?' asked Julip.

'No, he hasn't got the right physique,' said Marvo.

'He looks like a real showman. Maybe he's a new ringmaster!' said Mister, nodding his head at Hetty.

'Perhaps he's a clown,' she retorted.

'I doubt it – he's much too young,' said Marvo. He was meaning to be comforting, but Beppo quivered.

'Perhaps he's a trainer,' said Tag. 'He'll have an animal act. That horse pulling the wagon looks in good condition. Maybe he's an equestrian.'

Hetty and I both held our breath, though the horse was old and took a long time to pull the wagon neatly into place.

'That man's no horse-trainer. He can't even control that old nag,' said Mr Marvel. 'Besides, there's only one wagon. His animals won't tuck up in his bed at night, will they?'

Oh, poor dear Mr Marvel! When the man had unharnessed his horse and waved airily to the watching crowd, he opened the door of his wagon and two dark heads peeped out.

'Allow me to present Miss Daffodil and Mr Cornflower,' the man shouted.

Two strange, chunky creatures came ambling out, clapping their hands. At first glance I thought they were very swarthy, stocky children, for Daffodil wore a bright yellow frilled frock with matching stockings and black patent boots, while Cornflower sported a little blue sailor suit and wore a jaunty cap with an embroidered anchor on his head. But then I blinked and realized they were enormous monkeys, giant versions of Mr Marvel's tiny, spindly babies.

'Chimpanzees,' Mr Marvel whispered, and his face crumpled.

'They are very ugly and cumbersome – nowhere near as nice as *our* monkeys, Mr Marvel,' I said, taking hold of his hand. 'And I'm sure they can't perform such clever tricks.'

But the new man said loudly, 'Run and introduce yourselves to all these nice new folks, Daffodil and Cornflower.'

Daffodil held out her frilly yellow skirts and bobbed the most comical of curtsies, while Cornflower took off his sailor cap and bowed low. Then they hopped and skipped about the crowd on all fours, but stood up straight and offered a paw to anyone who took their fancy.

Daffodil offered her paw to *me*. I worried about hurting Mr Marvel's feelings, but I couldn't help grasping the strange big brown paw. Daffodil chattered happily in her own language, clearly saying she was pleased to be acquainted. She was equally polite to everyone.

Cornflower was far cheekier. He held out his hand, but always snatched it away before anyone could take hold of it, and then he cheeped with laughter, smacking his lips. He took especial liberties with Mr Tanglefield, running up to him and then punching him lightly in the stomach.

Mr Tanglefield was a slight man, but he had a pronounced pot belly. It was rumoured that he had to wear a tight corset to fit decently into his riding breeches. He was very self-conscious about his figure and struggled to hold his stomach in when he thought people were watching. It was therefore doubly comical for Cornflower to single out this part of his anatomy. We all spluttered, keeping our faces as straight as possible, because no one wanted to be seen openly laughing at Mr Tanglefield, particularly when he hadn't confirmed who was to accompany him on the new tour, and who was to be left behind. But Mr Tanglefield himself burst out laughing, in a high-pitched, squeaky voice.

'Very comical, Mr Benger. You have trained your monkeys well,' he said.

'Excuse me, sir, my two children are of the chimpanzee species, *not* commonplace little monkeys,' said their trainer.

Mr Marvel winced. His eyes were watering and he looked every one of his eighty or ninety years, but he stood as straight as he could, and said with simple dignity, 'I gather *my* services will therefore no longer be required, Mr Tanglefield.'

Everyone turned to Mr Tanglefield. He had the grace to look away uncomfortably.

'I think we both know you're a bit past it, Marvel.

Beats me how you've kept going all these years. But I think it's best to go now. Don't look so down-hearted. I'll make you an offer for those monkeys of yours. I dare say Benger can work them into his act. We'll give you a tidy little sum – it'll pay your rent for many months.'

Mr Marvel's fists clenched. 'You must be mad if you think I could ever sell my babies. I'd sooner sleep in the gutter so long as they could be there with me. But I won't need to resort to such desperate measures, thank you very much. I have a very snug little cottage in the country that's been waiting for me to occupy it for many a year. I'll be off first thing in the morning.'

'Oh, Mr Marvel!' I said, and I threw myself upon him. 'I can't bear it! I shall miss you so.'

'I will too, more than anything,' Hetty declared. She looked at Mr Tanglefield, quivering with emotion. 'How can you be so heartless? Why can't Mr Marvel and his monkeys keep their act? You can have *two* monkey acts! That would surely be a great novelty?'

'Great *liability*,' said Mr Tanglefield. 'We don't want old dodderers as part of the show. It sounds brutal, but it's business. Marvel's been past it for years. He can't even control his monkeys any more. Look at all the palaver when the little one escaped and held us all up for hours.'

'That was *my* fault, not Mr Marvel's!' I cried.

'Be silent, both of you!' he shouted. 'I don't run this show as a charity and I don't need shrill children to tell me how to do my work. All right, Marvel, I'll sort out the wages you've got owing by tonight, with a bonus for your long-term engagement. Then you can leave in the morning when we do. Now, don't just stand there, everyone. I'm sure you've got work to do.'

I hung onto Mr Marvel, starting to cry. He patted me gently on the head. He seemed very calm, but I could feel him trembling.

'I'll miss you so very much, Mr Marvel – and I'll miss my Mavis too, and all the other monkeys.'

'We'll all miss you, little Diamond bright. But don't grieve for me. I've had a long and happy life in the circus but I can't deny I'm getting old. Now it really is time for me to go.'

It was heart-breaking – but this wasn't the worst surprise on that dreadful day. Mr Tanglefield had insisted we leave a very large space beside his own wagon. We waited and waited to see who the new-comers were going to be. Then, just as folk were starting to cook their suppers, we heard the sound of a rumbling wagon and horses' hooves.

It was a very grand wagon, at least twice the usual size, drawn by four beautiful horses – three chestnuts and one grey.

Madame Adeline's head jerked and she stared at them, stricken.

'It's all right, Madame Adeline. I'm sure they're just pulling the wagon,' Hetty said hurriedly, though we could all see these were fine horses in the peak of condition.

We looked at the man holding the reins. He was tall and fit, and wore a strange broad-brimmed hat, a checked shirt, tightly cut trousers and astonishing studded boots.

'He's a cowboy!' said Julip, in awe. 'Like Wild Bill Hickok!'

'An equestrian,' said Madame Adeline, and closed her eyes.

'But he's a man – folk would far rather see a beautiful spangled lady on a horse,' said Hetty, putting an arm round her shoulders.

But then we saw the woman on another horse behind the big wagon. She was young and slim, with long blonde hair, wearing another broad-brimmed hat and a fantastic outfit – red with white fringing. She wore heeled red boots and rode a lovely chestnut mare with white socks, who trotted along with her head and tail up.

Hetty didn't say anything at all. Madame Adeline opened her eyes and then put her hand to her throat. We watched in open-mouthed silence as the man manoeuvred the wagon into place and unharnessed the four horses, while the woman swung herself down and went to open the door of their wagon.

Mr Tanglefield came running out to greet them, nodding his head, shaking hands, circling them eagerly, clearly thrilled to be welcoming them into the company.

'Dear Lord, he's behaving like a regular Uriah Heap, fawning all over them and acting humble,' said Hetty. 'How ridiculous! Who cares about a silly cowboy act? And that woman's showy scarlet boots aren't a patch on mine!'

Madame Adeline smiled at her wanly. She'd grown very pale. She couldn't take her eyes off the beautiful blonde woman. She watched as the door of the wagon was opened. There was a sudden wild howling, and three great black and tan creatures leaped out.

I remembered the fairy-story books. 'Wolves!' I cried, clutching Hetty.

'No, I'm sure they're dogs,' she said, but she pushed me behind her protectively.

They were joined by a little black and white dog, who jumped about ecstatically, chasing his three big friends.

'Behave!' the blonde lady shouted. All four dogs stopped in their tracks and sat obediently on their haunches, noses quivering. She gave them all a pat and a titbit. The black and white dog tried getting up on his hind legs and making a little whiny noise, clearing begging for more.

'Oh, I like the little one!' I exclaimed.

The lady heard me and smiled. 'This is Albie, our Brittany spaniel – he's our special little clown,' she said. 'Say hello to the little girl, Albie.'

Albie came and barked at me winsomely, rubbing against my legs. I tickled him behind his ears. The other three dogs all came bounding up too, and I took a step backwards.

'Don't worry, they're not wolves at all. They're German shepherd dogs and they wouldn't hurt a fly. This is our top dog, Sammy, though he's getting a bit wobbly on his legs now. This is our girl, Honey – now, you can't be frightened of her, she's the smallest German shepherd you'll ever see. Try stroking *her* ears and she'll fall in love with you. And this one's Joe – not the brightest of our boys, and he can't jump too high now, but he'll do anything for you if you offer him an orange for a big treat.'

'Then I'll be able to give him lots of treats!' I said excitedly – but then Hetty pulled me away, giving me a little shake. The lady was so smiley and friendly, but I realized I couldn't possibly like her *or* her animals if it meant Madame Adeline's act was threatened.

Hetty was openly scowling at the newcomers,

but Madame Adeline herself was bravely trying to smile.

'That's a beautiful mare,' she whispered, nodding at the blonde lady's chestnut horse.

'Nowhere near as splendid as Midnight,' said Hetty.

'Darling, it's pointless pretending,' said Madame Adeline. 'She's lovely, the prettiest, liveliest creature. And her rider is very pretty too.'

'You're prettier, Madame Addie!' I said.

'Much, much prettier,' added Hetty.

Madame Adeline put her arms round both of us. 'You're my dear sweet loyal girls,' she said. 'Oh dear goodness, I'm going to miss you so.'

'Don't say that! You're not going to go! You're the star of the show,' said Hetty.

But at that very moment Mr Tanglefield cleared his throat, rubbed his hands together excitedly and announced, his voice squeakier than ever with excitement: 'May I present the new stars of Tanglefield's Travelling Circus, engaged at great expense, but worth every single penny. They're fresh from their own Wild West Show at Earl's Court – Cowboy Jonny and his lovely lady, Lucky Heather, together with their show-stopping quality horses and their pack of prairie dogs . . . ta-daa!'

Cowboy Jonny took off his grand hat and waved it at the crowd. Lucky Heather swished her skirts and stood with her hands on her hips, her fingers resting on her pearl-studded gun holster.

The circus folk murmured and some clapped enthusiastically, though most glanced at poor dear Madame Adeline.

Mr Tanglefield was looking at her too. He cleared his throat. 'Your services will no longer be required, Addie,' he said, rocking backwards and forwards on his heels.

'For shame!' Hetty cried.

'Madame Addie's been part of the circus longer than anyone! She was the star act when I joined as a young girl,' said Flora, pink with emotion.

'Exactly,' said Mr Tanglefield. 'She's been here too long. Her time is over now.'

'Your own father employed her, Tanglefield. What would he say now?' said Chino.

'My father was a businessman. He understands that profit has to come before sentiment. Addie can't pull the crowds any more – she's an old woman,' said Mr Tanglefield ungallantly.

'How dare you insult her so publicly!' Hetty shouted.

'Hush, dear,' said Madame Adeline. She peered around at the circus artistes. 'Please do not trouble yourselves on my behalf. I know it's time for me to go.'

Cowboy Jonny and Lucky Heather looked stricken.

Lucky Heather walked over and put her hand gently on Madame Adeline's arm. When you saw them together, it was clear that she was young enough to be Addie's daughter – or even her grand-daughter.

'I am so sorry, Madame. Jonny and I didn't realize that our engagement would mean someone else's dismissal,' she said softly.

'Perhaps . . . perhaps there might be some way we could combine acts?' Jonny suggested.

'That is very gracious of you, sir, but I'm afraid it isn't practical,' said Madame Adeline.

'Yes it *is*!' Hetty insisted.

'Hush, child. No, Midnight and I are growing old and lame. Mr Tanglefield is quite right. I'm not needed here any more.'

'But *we* need you!' I cried.

'That's right! You can't just leave us. And where will you go, anyway?' asked Hetty.

'I'll manage perfectly, dears,' said Madame Adeline, though she looked grey with worry.

'But you don't have your own little cottage like Mr Marvel,' I wailed.

'Perhaps you would do me the great honour of sharing it with me, Addie?' said Mr Marvel, walking up to her.

She stared at him, clearly taken aback.

'Of course, it's not quite the sort of home you

deserve. And in case you think I'm being presumptuous, I must make it clear that there are two bedrooms, and you can live as my esteemed lodger, just until you find a more suitable home of your own – though if you were able to return my affection, then it would make me the happiest man in the world if you'd consent to be my wife.'

'Oh, Mr Marvel, how lovely of you!' I said. I ran to hug him, but Hetty held me back.

'Let Madame Adeline reply first!' she hissed.

Madame Addie seemed unable to say anything at all. Her face had suddenly flooded pink and her eyes were filled with tears.

'Oh dear, doesn't she *like* Mr Marvel?' I whispered. 'She's crying!'

'I think she likes him well enough. Perhaps she's crying because she's very touched by his proposal,' Hetty murmured.

Madame Adeline took hold of Mr Marvel's hands. 'Thank you. Thank you so much,' she said, tears rolling down her cheeks.

'There! Say you will actually marry him! Can Hetty and I be your bridesmaids? Oh, can we dress Mavis up as a little baby bridesmaid?' I burbled. 'And then can we come and live with you and be your daughters?'

'I've never heard such nonsense! You're *my*

daughter now!' said Mister. 'I paid good money for you and I have the certificate to prove it.'

'And you and I have a contract of employment, Hetty Feather,' added Mr Tanglefield.

'We can tear up these silly contracts and certificates,' Hetty muttered to me.

But Madame Adeline took hold of us and walked us over to her wagon.

'You mustn't protest too much, my darlings. You must stay here and continue your careers as artistes. You are both very talented and I'm very proud of you. I shall miss you terribly, but that can't be helped. I don't think I could take you both with me even if I thought it a good thing. I will have to depend on dear Mr Marvel. I doubt I have the ability now to earn my own keep, let alone the resources to feed and clothe two growing girls, much as I would love to.' She was crying now as she spoke. 'I'm not even sure I'll be able to keep Midnight.'

'Oh, Madame Addie, you *have* to keep Midnight. If you leave him here they might turn him into horsemeat!' I said, horrified.

'I joined the circus because of you, Madame Adeline,' Hetty declared passionately. 'I don't want to stay without you!'

'I've *never* wanted to stay!' I said.

'If I were younger, I'd take you with me, but I'm old

now, much too old,' said Madame Adeline. She took off her long red wig, and instantly she *became* a frail old lady, her own grey wispy hair flat and feathery, her scalp showing through in places, making her look extra vulnerable.

'You're still young to *us*,' said Hetty, throwing her arms round her. 'I can't be separated from you now. You're like a second mother to me – and I've already lost my first dear mama.' She burst into tears, loud terrifying sobs that scared me terribly. She was my big brave bold Hetty and I couldn't bear to see her crying like a baby.

'I could try and be a third mother to you, Hetty,' I said.

I was in earnest, but Hetty and Madame Adeline both started laughing, though the tears were pouring down their cheeks.

'Dear Heavens, look at the three of us!' said Madame Adeline. 'We're crying fit to rival Niagara Falls.' She fetched several handkerchiefs from her dressing table. 'There, girls, let us mop ourselves up. We've no call to be so sad. I am long past retiring age, as Tanglefield pointed out so unkindly. I am very lucky that dear Mr Marvel has made me such a generous offer.'

'But do you love him, Madame Adeline?' Hetty said doubtfully.

'No, I can't truthfully say I do, but perhaps I will grow to love him,' said Madame Adeline. 'He is a good kind man.'

'Yes, he is. He's been very good to me. I think *I* love him,' I said. 'And I know I love little Mavis. I will miss her so much as well.'

'Oh dear, I wish I was as keen. I don't really care for those ugly little monkeys. I hope Mr Marvel doesn't expect them to be *my* babies too,' said Madame Adeline. 'I will invite him to tea, but I don't really want the monkeys clambering over all my pretty things.'

'Yes, maybe that would be just as well. They can be very rude at times and they do little messes everywhere,' I said.

'One of them once used the top of my head as a water closet!' said Hetty, and we all laughed shakily.

Mr Marvel came to tea wearing his best suit, an outfit he'd clearly not worn for many years. He must have been a much bigger man at one time, because he could have buttoned two Mr Marvels and all four monkeys inside the voluminous jacket, and the trousers rivalled Beppo's clown costume, the hems trailing on the ground and totally obliterating his shoes. He had given himself such a fierce scrubbing that his face shone red and raw. His eyes were red too – perhaps he had had a private weep. But he presented Madame Adeline with a little posy of flowers and smiled at her radiantly. He gave me a kiss on my cheek and patted Hetty on the shoulder, but simply nodded shyly at Madame Adeline, clicking his heels together in salute.

I saw Hetty and Madame Adeline exchange glances, and for an awful moment I thought they were going to laugh at him, and that would have been quite dreadful – but Madame Adeline composed herself, exclaimed over the flowers, and sat Mr Marvel down in her best armchair.

She boiled a silver kettle on her spirit stove, made a large pot of tea and served her delightful pink and yellow cake, giving us all two big slices.

Mr Marvel drew a picture for her of his cottage and labelled each room: *our parlour*; *our kitchen*. He delicately omitted pronouns for the two small bedrooms.

'Perhaps you two little misses would like to come and stay with us next winter?' he suggested.

'Oh, yes please!' I said, clapping my hands.

'And if you will be kind enough to write down the exact address of this lovely cottage, Mr Marvel dear, I hope that you, Hetty, will write to me regularly to let me know how you both are,' said Madame Adeline.

'Oh, Hetty never writes letters,' I said without thinking.

I had paid close attention to her memoirs. I had begged to know more about Bertie the butcher's boy and Freda the Female Giant in particular, but she had never managed to stay in touch. She didn't even write to her own father, as far as I knew.

Hetty looked stricken now. 'I *will* write!' she said. 'I will write to you every week, Madame Adeline – and I will send you the schedule of our shows so that you will always know where to write back to me. You mean all the world to me, and I am going to keep in touch with you no matter what!'

etty was as good as her word. Every time we set up in a new field or meadow, she took her paper and pen and wrote at least two pages to Madame Adeline. She always left a little space at the end where I could scrawl *Love from Diamond*. At least I could spell my own name correctly now, though most long words still defeated me.

It was wonderful getting letters back from Madame Adeline. She said she was settling in splendidly, and found Mr Marvel a very pleasant companion.

'Does that mean she loves him now?' I asked Hetty.

'I'm not sure,' said Hetty. 'I think she's maybe making the best of things.'

Madame Adeline said the cottage had proved very damp and dirty at first, but she had spring-cleaned determinedly, and Mr Marvel had papered and painted every room. During most of the decoration he'd had to keep all the monkeys in their cage – after the first disastrous day when Marmaduke had snatched a brush and set about painting everything in sight, including himself, and little Mavis had gone for an ill-advised paddle in the bucket of wallpaper paste. But now the cottage was spick and span, and Madame Adeline had arranged all her pretty furniture and ornaments in her new parlour so that it looked almost like her wagon.

She had given *us* her old wagon so that Hetty and I could travel together, with Sugar Poke to pull us to each new venue. Mister was totally against such an idea – but surprisingly, Marvo and Julip and Tag stuck up for me.

'She's already getting too big for that tiny hammock and there's no room in our wagon for an extra bed,' said Marvo.

'She's not such a tiny girl any more. It's unseemly for her to share with us boys,' said Julip.

'Besides, she snores like a pig and keeps me awake half the night!' added Tag.

'I do *not* snore!' I hissed.

'I know, but I'm trying to help you get your own way, idiot,' said Tag.

It worked too! Maybe Mister knew that travelling together would be the only way to keep Hetty and me working hard at the circus, because we were missing Madame Adeline so sorely. He gave his permission for us to share the wagon – and for a while we were jubilant.

It wasn't quite such a splendid wagon without Madame Adeline's furniture and trinkets, but Hetty begged Mr Tanglefield for another advance on her wages, and we bought two small second-hand beds, a battered chest of drawers, and a big sagging armchair, large enough for us both to squeeze into at one go. It all looked very bare and shabby and ugly at first, but Hetty made a blue and white coverlet for both beds, and big cushions embroidered with bluebirds for the chair. She showed me how to make a rag rug, and I sat on the bare floor in between practices and performances, tatting away, Hetty beside me.

We also painted pictures for the walls. Hetty did the drawing part, but I came into my own when it came to applying watercolours. We did a portrait of dear Madame Adeline with her long red hair and her pink spangled dress. I was especially careful painting her face so that she looked beautiful, her eyes shaded blue,

265

her cheeks very pink, her mouth a smiling crimson. Hetty drew a second picture of Midnight, though she had to stare long and hard at the new horses to make the legs bend the right way.

I painted Midnight a glorious black, with streaks of white to emphasize his glossiness, and gave him lots of green grass to stand on, and a whole field behind him so that he could gallop around in carefree fashion whenever he fancied it.

Madame Adeline assured us in her letters that he was loving his new settled life in the country and was nowhere near as lame now that he didn't have to go through his paces three times a day. We hoped she was telling the truth and not just writing to reassure us.

Hetty was similarly tactful in her letters to Madame Adeline. She never told lies, but she was often economical with the truth. She wrote about our daily life of course, and always said we were well and quite happy – which we were *some* of the time. She didn't tell Madame Adeline that she was suffering from a series of sore throats, so that she had to gargle with salt water every day and gulp down Mr Tanglefield's medicinal whisky to manage any kind of speaking voice for the show. One day she was so bad she could scarcely croak, and Mr Tanglefield called in a local doctor. He made Hetty open her mouth wide and shook his head gravely.

'Her throat is very badly inflamed – she needs complete rest,' he said.

'She can't rest. She's a vital part of the show,' said Mr Tanglefield.

'That's *why* she's in such a state, shouting at the top of her voice twice daily,' the doctor told him. 'She should stay completely silent for at least two weeks. She has severely strained her vocal cords.'

'She's just got a sore throat! Can't you give her a cough syrup or soothing lozenges?' said Mr Tanglefield.

'Are you deaf, sir? The only cure is *rest*,' insisted the doctor.

'Very well,' said the ringmaster.

He resumed his role that evening, but he was out of practice and his own voice sounded squeakier than ever. The crowd fidgeted and talked through his announcements. He came out of the big top white and fuming.

'Ah, he's sorely rattled now!' said Mister gleefully. 'He knows he's not really up to the job himself. So if your little friend doesn't recover her shrew's tongue in a hurry, my guess is he'll find a replacement for her. There's many a pretty young girl who'd jump at the chance – *and* not try to throw her weight around and interfere.'

'Don't listen to him, Hetty. He's just trying to frighten you,' I said, though my own heart was beating fast.

But we all knew how ruthless Mr Tanglefield could be.

'If he dismisses me, who would look after you, Diamond?' Hetty whispered.

She went into town and bought her own syrup, her own lozenges, and doctored herself.

'I am able to perform now,' she whispered to Mr Tanglefield – and she just about managed it, though there was a permanent huskiness to her voice now and it was nowhere near its old strength.

I worried about Hetty's health and she worried about mine. I'd had a little growth spurt, and it made my arms and legs and back ache far more than usual. When Mister cricked me in the morning, I often felt as if my limbs would snap straight off. Although I was only an inch or so taller and maybe a few pounds heavier, I could not get to grips with my new, slightly sturdier body. I started misjudging simple somersaults and found using the springboard more of a nightmare than ever. I was terrified I'd lose the knack and fail to land with the pinpoint precision I needed. Each time, by some miracle, I managed it – but one day I was so scared, I couldn't get on the springboard at all, and the act finished without my flying finale.

Mister was waiting for me when we came out of the ring. Hetty was still busy announcing the other acts and couldn't protect me. He ripped my costume down to my waist and beat me on the back, where it would not show. It hurt terribly. I'm wincing now as I remember. When he was finished at last, I hobbled off to the wagon and hid underneath, shaking with sobs.

Marvo and Julip and Tag had been silently watching. Tag surprised me by wriggling under the wagon and lying beside me. He didn't say anything, but he took hold of my hand and squeezed it hard. We lay together on our stomachs, while I felt the blood trickling down my back. Tag squeezed even harder, his fingernails distracting me from the pain. He'd had his fair share of beatings in the past. He knew just how much it hurt.

I managed to get back into the ring for the grand parade, my costume sticking to my oozing back – and for many nights after that I undressed using my night-gown as a tent, pretending to Hetty that I'd suddenly become modestly bashful. I knew if she saw the stripes on my back, she'd challenge Mister – and then he might beat her too.

So both Hetty and I glossed over accounts of our own performances in our letters to Madame Adeline. We wrote comments on Flora, or Bruno and his bears, or the mighty Elijah – but we never mentioned Mr Benger or Daffodil or Cornflower in case Mr Marvel shared Madame Adeline's correspondence.

They were incredibly popular additions to the

company. The chimpanzees had the advantage of being much more visible in the ring. Mr Marvel's monkeys had been so small that folk up in the back seats could barely see them and failed to appreciate their tricks properly.

Daffodil and Cornflower made their presence felt, and interacted with the audience, scampering around the ring and suddenly snatching a cap here, a bonnet there. They tried them on themselves, preening ridiculously. When Mr Benger pretended to admonish them, they hung their heads and made little whimpering noises, and then rushed to return the headgear – only, of course, they generally put the gentlemen's caps and bowlers on the ladies' heads and saved the really elaborate old ladies' bonnets for likely young men.

They continued their fun and games with Mr Tanglefield, who always stood at the side watching each act. Cornflower gave him many more rabbit punches, and stuffed a cushion up inside his own sailor suit in glorious imitation.

I knew that all these seemingly spontaneous tricks were patiently taught day after day, the chimps generously rewarded with titbits. I don't think they knew *why* the audience laughed at their cheeky capers, but they certainly enjoyed their applause, and always stood and clapped themselves, grinning hugely.

We didn't write a single word to Madame Adeline about Cowboy Jonny and Lucky Heather either, though they were indeed the stars of the show now. They had a full twenty-minute slot right at the end. Cowboy Jonny always dressed in full Western regalia, his magnificent Stetson hat a permanent fixture on his head. In the ring he wore chaps too – fringed leather garments worn to protect his legs, which looked particularly dashing.

He rode Riley, a spirited chestnut who was extraordinarily agile. When Cowboy Jonny was on his back, he responded to the slightest pressure and pranced about the ring, in and out of a series of little fences, as if he were weaving intricate patterns, spinning round, even walking backwards.

Lucky Heather rode Sox – no, they *danced*, moving swiftly, gracefully and seemingly effortlessly to music. Sox's four white hooves were like elegant little kid boots. My eyes always watered watching them. I was so glad Madame Adeline couldn't see just how good they were.

Then the dogs bounded into the ring. Sammy, Joe and Honey jumped through hoops and over fences and stood up in a row together, all teetering on their hind legs, while little Albie deliberately knocked over each hoop and fence, and then hurtled into the three German shepherds, sending them flying.

'You're like Albie, Diamond,' said Tag, roaring with laughter.

'Yes, but who does the crowd love best?' said Julip, listening to them clap their hands sore at the little black and white spaniel's antics.

Then there was a wonderful riding interlude, with Cowboy Jonny and Lucky Heather leaping from one horse to another – not just Riley and Sox; they rode swift grey Rosie and dominant Ritzy and beautiful little Bella, all of them racing round and round the ring.

They finished their act with a wonderful Western set piece: Cowboy Jonny and Lucky Heather practised their sharp-shooting skills, firing loud blanks from their smoking guns and making everyone jump. It was such an exciting climax to the show that the grand parade of all the artistes and animals was almost over-shadowed.

Hetty was determined to hate them because they had taken Madame Adeline's place, albeit unwittingly. I found it difficult to resist the dogs, especially Albie – and of course the more I petted them, the more they wanted to be my friend. I saved all my orange tributes in the ring to give to them later as treats.

I was more wary of the horses, but one day, when I was watching Lucky Heather grooming Bella, she handed me a brush and said, 'Do you want to come and give me a hand, Diamond?'

I brushed my own hair every morning and felt indifferent about the whole process, but brushing Bella's mane and tail was another glorious matter altogether. She snuffled softly, obviously enjoying herself too. I rushed to groom her every day, and she always greeted me happily.

'She likes you, Diamond! Perhaps you could have a little ride on her back, if I hold you very steady?' said Lucky Heather.

'Oh, *please*!' I said. When I was straddling Bella's beautiful chestnut back, I was so full of pride that I had to shout at the top of my lungs, 'Look at me, Hetty, look at me!'

But Hetty would not look. Lucky Heather offered *her* a ride on any of the horses, but Hetty shook her head curtly. She wasn't a good horsewoman, so perhaps she wasn't tempted too much. It was another matter when Cowboy Jonny let Tag try on his Stetson and have a go at firing his gun. She couldn't help watching enviously.

'Would you like a go, Hetty?' asked Cowboy Jonny.

'No thank you,' said Hetty, with pinched nostrils.

'You're silly, Hetty,' I said as we got ready for that evening's performance. 'Cowboy Jonny and Lucky Heather are lovely. Why won't you be friends with them?'

'You know why,' said Hetty, pulling on her boots.

'Yes, but it's not really *their* fault that Madame Adeline had to leave,' I said.

'Yes it *is*,' said Hetty, and she tied her boot so fiercely that the lace broke, which made her curse. '*Now* look what you've made me do!'

'It wasn't *my* fault! Why do you always have to blame other people all the time?' I said.

'Don't you start lecturing me!' shouted Hetty. 'You're half my age.'

'But you know I'm right,' I said. 'Why don't you just calm down and try to make friends with folk like a sensible girl?'

She always laughed at me when I tried to talk like an adult. I hoped she'd do this now, and we'd stop this silly quarrel – but she lost her temper completely.

'Why don't you just keep your mouth shut, you priggish little fool!' she cried, and stormed out of the wagon.

I was left trembling with rage. Hetty really could be so difficult at times. I'd never really dared stand up to her before. I felt she was being very mean now. I knew she expected me to go running after her to apologize – but I wasn't one bit sorry. Hetty was being childish, not me.

'She's just jealous because I'm friends with Lucky Heather,' I said to my reflection in our looking glass. 'Well, silly her. *I* shan't say sorry. I shall wait until she says sorry to me . . .' Though I knew I might have to wait a long while.

I struggled to pin my own fairy wings on myself, but managed it somehow. I walked over to the big top to line up with Marvo, Julip and Tag. Hetty was there at the front, sucking lozenges for her throat. She didn't so much as glance in my direction, though she must have heard the silver boys greeting me.

So I turned my back on her too and started playing a rowdy push-and-shove game with Tag, wanting to show her I was having fun without her. I decided I didn't care in the slightest if Hetty and I weren't speaking – though I found I was still trembling.

'Are you cold, little one?' said Marvo, putting his big arm around me.

'I'm fine,' I said, trying to compose myself.

'She's just a little nervous,' said Julip. 'I know I always am.'

'Oh, you two!' jeered Tag. 'I don't know what's up with you. You're pathetic.'

'I'm not the slightest bit pathetic,' I said, and I pushed him hard.

I was trembling more than ever – and it didn't stop when we went running into the ring.

'Clap your hands together for the magnificent tumbling Silver Tumblers, together with little Diamond, the Acrobatic Child Wonder!' Hetty announced, sounding so enthusiastic I wondered if we were friends again after all, but she didn't smile at me or whisper good luck as I passed by.

I did my somersaults, forward and back, I did my flic-flacs, my cartwheels, my little prancing dance. I did not falter, I did not stumble. And then it was my turn on the springboard. Marvo and Julip and Tag had formed their human column.

I stepped onto the board, trembling more than ever. I suddenly felt terribly sick and wondered if I was going to vomit right there in the middle of the ring. I glanced at Mister. He was watching me intently, eyes steely grey. His hands were clenched, the knuckles white. I thought of the beating I would get if I refused.

So I sprang up in the air and hurtled forward – but the trembling seemed to take over, shaking me off course. I couldn't get quite high enough. I desperately tried to land on Tag's shoulders, but I was too low. My feet thumped into his chest, and he wobbled and lost his balance. He fell to the ground, bringing Julip with him – and I fell too, screaming.

Marvo ran forward frantically and caught hold of me just before I reached the ground. I still landed with a terrible thump, but he broke my fall. I lay there, utterly stunned. I stared upwards, my eyes dazzled by a very bright light. I remembered Ma's stories of Heaven, the shining land above the clouds. Had I died and arrived there already? I thought of all those avenging angels. I seemed to hear them rustling, beating their wings to get to me.

'Go away, angels!' I shouted in terror.

'Oh my Lord, she's talking of angels! Diamond! Oh, Diamond, you absolutely are *not* allowed to die!'

It was Hetty, kneeling beside me, clutching me desperately as if she were physically preventing me from ascending heavenwards. I blinked and realized that the brightness above me was simply the glare of the gaslight in the ring, the rustling the movement of the crowd as they stood up, gasping, wondering if I was dead.

Very gingerly, I tried to move. I was lying half on poor Marvo, half on the sawdust. My head hurt, and I felt blood trickling from my temple and a sharp pain in my wrist, but I still seemed to be breathing in and out, and I could certainly feel my heart beating in my chest.

'I – I don't *think* I'm going to die,' I mumbled. 'So don't be cross with me, Hetty.'

'Oh, Diamond, I'll never, ever be cross with you again! I feel so terrible. I'm sure you slipped because I'd upset you so much. I'm so, so sorry. I'll never forgive myself.'

'And I'll never forgive the pair of you, ruining the act,' Mister hissed. He pulled at me. 'Come on, get on your feet – don't just lie there like a broken doll. Show the audience you're fine!'

'She's *not* fine! She could have broken her neck! See how she's bleeding! Lie still, Diamond, until they've fetched a doctor,' Hetty commanded.

'Stand *up*, or I'll give you a royal beating,' Mister insisted, and so I struggled to my feet.

I swayed dizzily but managed to stay upright, clutching Hetty. Marvo stood up too, shaking his great head and flexing his huge arms.

'You caught me! Oh, Marvo, you were brilliant!' I said. 'Have I hurt you?'

'It would take more than a tiny pipsqueak like you to hurt me,' he said.

'And are *you* hurt, Julip? And Tag?' I asked anxiously.

They smiled and shook their heads at me, though they looked very shocked.

'Acknowledge the crowd! Stand up properly and take a bow!' said Mister.

'For pity's sake!' said Hetty, but Mister didn't have a penny's worth of pity for any of us.

We bowed, and the audience applauded furiously. I tried to wave at them, but I used my sore hand and my wrist jarred terribly. Hetty saw me wince and picked me up in her arms.

'Come, Diamond, I'm taking you to lie down in our wagon,' she said.

'Leave her be! You're staying here and getting on with your job!' said Mr Tanglefield. 'Come on, before the crowd gets restless. Announce the next act!'

'What's the matter with you men? How can you be so utterly heartless?' Hetty protested.

'You'll do as I say! You've signed a contract – you announce every act, whether you feel like it or not. We're professionals, circus artistes. All this fuss over one little tumble, and the child's not even badly hurt. You were the one who badgered me to employ you – so don't you dare look all reproachful and woebegone. I've had enough of your nonsense. You're employed by me, under my terms, and you do as I say, Miss High-and-Mighty Hetty Feather!'

'Please, Hetty, do as he says. I'm fine now – it was just a little bump,' I said quickly, not wanting to get her into further trouble.

'You'll get more than a little bump from me, my fairy,' Mister hissed in my ear – and when Marvo picked me up and carried me away, he followed.

They took me to our wagon. I hated letting Mister into our lovely little blue haven, but I couldn't stop him. Marvo laid me carefully on my bed and gently felt my limbs. I gave a cry when he got to my wrist, especially when he manipulated it.

'I'm so sorry, Diamond. I'm just trying to see if it's

broken. I *think* it's just a bad sprain. I'll send Tag for a doctor,' said Marvo.

'Nonsense! The child is fine, she says so herself. She don't need no doctor! What a pack of softies you are. I broke my wretched back and they didn't send for no doctor for me,' snapped Mister.

'Yes, and you've been in serious pain and crippled ever since,' Marvo pointed out. 'We don't want that to happen to Diamond, do we?'

'There's no "we" about it! *We* don't own her and *we* don't have a say in how she's looked after. *I* own her, and *I* decide what to do with her. Now clear out of the wagon. I need to have a private word with the little madam,' said Mister. 'I'm going to teach her a lesson or two.'

'Don't hurt her, Beppo. Look at the poor mite – she's terrified already and desperately sore. She's *learned* her lesson,' said Marvo.

'She needs to learn it again – and again and again, if necessary. It's the only way to teach her. I was even harder on you, and look at you now, rock solid.'

'I can take it. So can Tag. Even Julip. But look at Diamond properly, Beppo – *look* at her. You can't beat a little baby like her.'

'If I'd beaten her a bit harder, she'd concentrate better and not ruin the act,' said Mister.

'That's another thing – the crowd will be looking

out for her in the grand parade at the end. If you hurt her, they'll see – and they could turn ugly,' Marvo told him.

'Hmm . . .' Mister nodded curtly. 'I suppose that makes sense. Do you hear that, Diamond? Your big brother's saved your bacon. For today! Just you wait till tomorrow. Now wash that blood off your dirty face and comb your hair and stop that snivelling. We'll tie up your wrist and you'll be as good as new. I want you in that ring, smiling all over your face, at the end of the show, do you hear me?'

'I hear you, Mister,' I whispered.

He stomped off, and I threw my arms round Marvo's neck.

'Thank you for saving me twice over, Marvo,' I said fervently.

He helped clean me up and bound up my wrist with a big handkerchief. 'There! Is that better now?' he said.

I nodded, although I still hurt all over – and I knew that I'd be hurting far more tomorrow, after Beppo's lesson.

Marvo held my good hand as we walked back to the big top together. Julip and Tag looked at me worriedly.

'Are you really all right, Diamond?' Julip asked.

'I . . . think so,' I said.

'You should learn to roll up in a ball if you come a

cropper – then you don't hurt yourself, see,' said Tag. He put his hand very lightly on my back. 'Did Beppo beat you again?' he whispered.

I shook my head. 'No, but I think he will tomorrow,' I told him.

'I hate him,' Julip said, through clenched teeth.

'We all hate him,' said Tag. 'But he won't go on for ever, will he? Poor old Marvel and Madame Addie got pushed out. I reckon Beppo will be the next to go. Then we'll be free and able to manage ourselves.'

I wasn't sure I could wait that long. I thought of all the performances I still had to get through – all the springboard finales, all the beatings. When I went into the ring for the grand parade, I did as Mister said. I smiled and smiled, and waved my good hand and did a backward somersault and even managed a lopsided cartwheel – and I think the audience appreciated my recovery, because I could hear them clapping and shouting. I couldn't see them though, because my eyes were blurry with tears.

The moment we filed out of the big top, Hetty came running up, seizing hold of me anxiously. 'You poor little darling – you're being so *brave!*' she said.

But when I saw Mister, the trembling started again.

'There now, right as rain,' he said.

'Get away from her, you hateful old man!' Hetty shouted.

Mister stared at me meaningfully. 'Tomorrow, little fairy,' he said.

'What does he mean, *tomorrow*? Has he threatened you? *Tell* me, Diamond!' said Hetty, the moment we were back in our wagon.

I tried not to tell, but I was hurting so, and sick with terror. 'Oh, Hetty, he's going to beat me again!' I whimpered.

'*Again?*'

'He did that other time when I was too scared to do the springboard thing. I didn't dare tell you because I knew you'd be so angry,' I wept.

'Oh, Diamond.' Hetty put her arms tight round me and rocked me for a moment. She kissed the sore place on my head and very gently stroked my bad wrist. Then she led me to my bed.

'There now. Rest a while,' she said.

She reached under her own bed and brought out her suitcase. I watched as she pulled off her fleshings and coat and folded them carefully away into the suitcase, on top of her memoir books and treasures. My heart started beating so fast I could scarcely breathe.

'Oh, Hetty, are you running away?' I whispered.

Hetty nodded as she struggled into her grey print frock.

'But – but what about me?' I wailed.

'You're running away too, silly girl,' she said.

'But – but they won't let us!'

'They won't know. We'll wait until everyone's asleep – and then we'll sneak out.'

'Oh, Hetty!'

'You don't want to stay, do you?'

'No!'

'Then we'll go. We'll pack your fairy outfit, yes? And Maybelle. And you can wear your blue dress and your pinafore.'

'But what about all our things?' I said, looking around the wagon. 'They won't all fit in the suitcase!'

'We'll have to leave them. We'll just take what we can carry.' Hetty was looking in her purse. 'That Tanglefield owes me heaps of money, damn him. I wish there was some way I could break into his wagon and steal what's rightfully mine.'

'Don't! He'll catch you. What if he catches us anyway? What about your contract? And, oh Hetty, what about Mister? What will he say? He *bought* me!'

'You've given him more than five guineas worth. I'm not going to let you stay here a day longer and have him terrify you. I don't know what's the matter with me! I should have taken you away long before. But we're going now.'

'Really? This isn't pretend?'

'This is absolutely real.' Hetty stopped her packing and came and sat on the bed beside me. 'I know you've really hurt yourself and this is all horribly scary, but you're going to keep on being a really brave girl and we're going to do this together. We're running away tonight.'

'We're running away tonight . . .' I repeated, still scarcely able to take it all in. 'So I won't be here tomorrow when Mister comes for me?'

'No, we won't be here. We'll be far, far away.'

'And they won't catch us?'

'Of course they won't. Not if we're very, very quiet. We'll wait till everyone's fast asleep – one or even two o'clock. And then we'll creep out, you and me. I'll carry the case and I'll hold your hand – not your sore hand, the other one – and we'll run together, very swiftly, very silently, right across the meadow and away. Can you do that?'

'Yes, as long as you're with me. Oh, Hetty, I'm still a bit scared though. They'll be so angry if they *do* catch us.'

I had a hot, burning feeling in my head. I could hardly get my words out properly. I hung onto Hetty, following her round and round the wagon, unable to rest. I badly wanted to show her I was really brave, but I kept thinking of Mister and his cruel grey eyes and his beatings.

I rubbed my aching wrist, which Marvo had bound up so tenderly. 'Can I say goodbye to Marvo?' I asked.

'No! You mustn't say a word to anyone!'

I thought of dear Marvo. I knew I would miss him a great deal. And Julip. And perhaps I would even miss Tag. I thought of great Elijah and the dancing bears. I thought of Bella and the other horses. I thought of the three German shepherds and dear little Albie. I wished I could say goodbye properly to all of them – but I knew Hetty was right.

We were packed and ready now, but we had to wait hour after hour, because we could still hear men carousing and women singing as the circus folk relaxed after the show. I cuddled up close to Hetty, and although I tried hard to keep my eyes open, I found I kept drifting off into dreams. I thought I was back in the big top, jumping on the springboard and then tumbling through the air, missing the boys altogether, crashing down, down, down into the sawdust. I woke, crying, and Hetty always hushed me tenderly.

'Are we really still running away?' I asked.

'Yes, we really are, Diamond. We're going to start a whole new life for ourselves, you and me.'

'But who is going to look after us?'

'I'm going to look after you, silly. Even though I haven't made a very good job of it so far,' said Hetty.

'Yes you have.' I paused. 'And I'll look after you.'

'That's right: we'll look after each other.'

'Is it time yet? It's very late.'

'Not quite late enough. We've got to make sure every single person is fast asleep. If someone calls out, then we're done for. You go back to sleep for a little while.'

'But then it might get to be tomorrow before we realize it,' I said anxiously.

'I'm not going to sleep, I promise. I'm watching and listening and waiting. Hush now.' Hetty stroked my hair and very softly sang the *Twinkle, Twinkle, Little Star* song, over and over, touching me on the tip of my nose every time she sang the *diamond* part. I clung to her and fell asleep again, even though I struggled not to.

A while later Hetty shook me gently. 'Wake up, Diamond!'

'Is it time now?' I whispered.

'Yes, it's time.'

I shivered.

'Look, I'll tie my shawl tight round you – that will help to keep you warm. Now, we're going to have to creep very, very carefully, not making a sound – and it'll be very dark with the camp fires all out, but I'll hold your hand,' Hetty murmured. 'We mustn't whisper, we mustn't cough or sniff, we mustn't do anything at all. Just creep. We can do it, Diamond. We're going to go far away and you'll never, ever see Beppo again.'

I swallowed hard and squeezed Hetty's hand.

'Ready?'

'Ready!'

Hetty very slowly opened the door of our wagon, easing the latch up carefully so that it didn't make the slightest sound. The sudden chill night air cleared my head a little, but it all still seemed as if I might be dreaming. Hetty crept through the door, making sure that the suitcase didn't bang against anything and make a noise, and I followed, out into the darkness. We felt our way down the steps to the ground and then stood still, listening.

There was absolute eerie silence. Hetty waited a few seconds, and then gave me a little tug. We crept over the grass along the semicircle of wagons. I bit my lip, not even daring to breathe, as we passed Beppo's. Then we were by the silver boys' wagon, then Flora's, then Bruno's, then the new big fancy one belonging to Cowboy Jonny and Lucky Heather – and then there was a sudden snuffling.

Little Albie was lying under their wagon. He'd caught our scent and was yelping a joyous greeting.

'Shh, Albie! Quiet! Oh, please, don't make any more noise!' I begged.

But the three German shepherds were awake now too, and they started barking loudly.

'We'll have to run for it!' Hetty said, gripping my

hand tight and pulling me along. But the four dogs were leaping up in a circle around us, thinking this was a glorious new game – and now we heard wagon doors banging, people calling, Elijah trumpeting in the distance.

Mr Tanglefield came running out of his own wagon, a lamp in one hand, his whip in the other. 'Trespassers!' he cried.

'They're not trespassers!' said Mister, running too. 'What are you up to, you little varmints? Do you think you're getting away from me, little fairy? Wait till I get hold of you!' He was brandishing his stick at me.

'Run! Run, Diamond!' Hetty cried, tugging me desperately – but Mr Tanglefield cracked his whip in our direction, and she screamed as it caught her on the tip of the ear, making her double up, clutching her head.

'Stop that! You can't whip a *child*!' Cowboy Jonny shouted.

'Get him, Sammy, Honey, Joe!' cried Lucky Heather, snapping her fingers. The dogs all leaped up at Mr Tanglefield and knocked him backwards.

I pulled at Hetty and she managed to scramble up, still holding her case. We started running desperately into the dark, but there were footsteps behind us, and I heard the hard rasp of Mister's breath and the swish of that terrible stick. He was horribly light on his feet, and gaining on both of us. Suddenly I felt his hand on my shoulder and I yelled out in terror – but then he fell away, landing with a great thump on the ground.

I turned round and saw that someone had leaped on him and tumbled him over, someone else was clutching at him, and a third was trying to hold him down. My three silver brothers!

'Run, Diamond! This is your chance!'

So I ran and Hetty ran, both of us sobbing and gasping, but Mister was up again, screaming at us, and Mr Tanglefield too, and we knew they could both outrun us. But then Hetty darted sideways and started pulling at some large heavy object lying on its side by the big top. The penny-farthing!

'Quick, quick, Diamond! I'll get on the saddle and you scramble up and sit on my shoulders!' she gasped.

She wedged the case in front of her against the handlebars, and I clawed my way up until I was sitting on top of her, clutching her hair.

'You can balance, I know you can!' Hetty cried, and she started pedalling furiously.

The penny-farthing wavered and wobbled, and I thought we might fall straight off, but Hetty steered frantically, and suddenly we were off in a rush. I had to grip hard with my thighs and tuck my toes into her armpits, but my legs were as strong as steel from all my practising. I could cling to her easily – and she pedalled and pedalled and pedalled.

We raced along the path across the meadow, and although we could still hear furious shouts behind us, they were getting more and more distant. At the edge of the meadow we had a moment's terrible panic, because the gates were locked, but we jumped off and somehow hauled the great machine over the railings, and then shinned up ourselves and were over them too.

We struggled back onto the penny-farthing, and Hetty pedalled faster and faster along the smooth empty pavements, on and on and on, until we were right through the little town and out the other side. We still couldn't rest. We rode along country lanes and tiny byways until we reached the next town, miles away from the circus.

Then we did at last topple down from the penny-farthing. We lay spread-eagled on the dusty pavement, stretching our aching limbs.

'We've done it, Diamond! We've actually done it! We've run away!' Hetty cried. She gave a great whoop, her throat clearly better now.

'And my lovely silver brothers helped us – and Cowboy Jonny and Lucky Heather too!'

'I wonder if those dogs have eaten old Tanglefield!'

'I hope they go and give Mister a good bite too!'

We started giggling hysterically and found we couldn't stop. Hetty actually drummed her boots on the ground she was laughing so much. Then she rubbed her ear and yelped. 'I'm bleeding where that beast whipped me!' she said indignantly.

'I think I'm bleeding a bit too, from my sore head. And my wrist aches. And I'm very thirsty,' I said.

'Oh dear, we're in a right old state! Come on, then, let's try and find you a drink somewhere.'

There was a horse trough nearby, but Hetty wouldn't let me drink from that. We walked down the road to a little market square, Hetty pushing the cycle and lugging the suitcase.

'A drinking fountain!' she cried triumphantly, and we both had a great iron mugful of cold water.

There were stalls in the market, empty and covered with cloth, but Hetty searched in the gutters and found two bruised apples, a squashed tomato and several old carrots.

'There! Just think of this as a very early breakfast,' she said as we leaned against a hoarding and munched eagerly.

'Hetty – you know we've run away?' I said.

'Yes.'

'Well, where are we running *to*?' I asked.

Hetty went on chewing a carrot thoughtfully. 'I – I don't really know!' she said.

'Oh. Well . . . shall we try and make our way to Madame Adeline? I'm sure she would welcome us, and Mr Marvel wouldn't really mind, would he?'

'We *could* go there. We well might at some point – but perhaps it's not fair to expect them to look after us.'

'I don't think we can go back to *my* home, not unless Pa's changed his mind about me,' I said, a little sadly.

'No, of course we're not going there, Diamond. And I'm not going to drag us all the way up to Yorkshire and *my* pa, though I'd love you to meet him some time. Now, let me try and think of the best thing we can do.'

For several minutes Hetty was quiet. I tried to wait patiently, but I was getting anxious.

'I think I know where,' I said at last. 'We should go back to your country home. To your old sweetheart, Jem. He would be glad to see you, Hetty, and maybe he wouldn't mind me coming too.'

'He's not my sweetheart any more, Diamond. He might well be married to someone else by now. I know he would still welcome us both into his house – but I don't want to feel dependent on anyone else, not now. I want to stay an artiste, earning my own living.'

'Then must we join another circus?' I asked.

'No, I think we've both seen enough of circus life. But there must be some other way we could be performers, you and me. I know! I'll ask Mama!'

She said it as if her mama were standing right beside us. I couldn't help looking round, though I knew that Hetty's mama was dead.

Hetty put her hand to her heart and closed her eyes. She looked ghostly pale in the lamplight. I fidgeted nervously. I saw her lips move as if she were whispering, but I couldn't hear a sound.

Then she opened her eyes and smiled at me.

'Did she have a suggestion?' I asked.

'Oh, Mama was a little cryptic, as usual. She told me to look all about me,' said Hetty.

She whirled round and round, her head back, clearly looking. I looked too. I could only see the market place.

'Do you think she wants us to have a market stall?' I said.

'I don't think so,' said Hetty. 'Though I'd be quite good at selling things.'

She suddenly stopped and stared at the poster on the hoarding we'd been leaning against. It was an advertisement with lots of swirly writing, so fancy that I couldn't read any of it.

Hetty stabbed at it excitedly. 'Look, Diamond! It's an advertisement for the Cavalcade – I think it's a music hall. These are all the artistes: Lily Lark, the Sweetest Song Thrush, Peter Perkin and His Comical Capers, Sven, the Russian Sword-swallower, Araminta, the Exotic Acrobatic Dancer! They're all *performers*, Diamond, just like us! And . . . oh my goodness!' She was squinting at the smallest names right at the bottom of the bill. 'It *can't* be! Well I never!'

'*What*, Hetty?'

'There's a performer called Little Flirty Bertie. Could it be *my* Bertie, I wonder? He always said he wanted to do a music-hall turn, calling his act Flirty Bertie. Well, we shall find out! I know what we're going to do, little Diamond. We're going to take to the boards and be music-hall artistes!'

READ HETTY FEATHER'S
OTHER ADVENTURES!

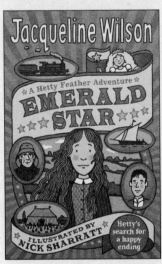

*When my mother named me, she must have
been thinking of a lucky four-leaved clover.
I'm sure Mother wanted me to be lucky.*

Turn over for a sneak peek!

1

'**W**HO'S COMING TO PLAY** then?' I yelled, running out of our house.

'Me!' said Megs, jumping up from the front step, where she'd been waiting for me patiently.

'Me!' shouted Jenny, Richie, Pete and Mary. Bert can't talk properly yet but he crowed.

'Me!' shouted Daft Mo from two doors down. He's a great gawky lad now, but he isn't right in the head and can't start work at the factory, so I let him play with us.

'Me!' shouted Jimmy Wheels, bowling up on his wooden trolley, the cobbles making it rattle violently.

Jimmy's my special friend. Some of the alley folk think he's as daft as Mo because he talks funny, but he's sharp as a tack.

'Now don't you encourage them kids, Clover Moon,' said Old Ma Robinson, leaning against the crumbling brick wall of her house and lighting her pipe. She puffs herself silly, Old Ma. Her face is turning as yellow as a smoked haddock. 'They're wild enough left to their own devices, but with you stirring them up they get up to all sorts.'

'Quit nagging her,' said Peg-leg Jack, stumping his way down the alley for his lunch-time pint of ale, his scrappy terrier trotting beside him. 'Clover's like a little mother to all the kids.'

'Better than a mother,' Megs muttered indistinctly, sucking her thumb.

Our own mother died when Megs was born. She can't remember her, naturally. I'm sure *I* can. Her name was Margaret. Megs is called after her. I wish I was, but my name is special too because Mother chose it.

She must have been thinking of a lucky four-leaved clover. I'm sure Mother wanted me to be lucky. And though I started off with blue eyes like all babies, they're now clover-green. Mother was sweet and soft and beautiful, with manners like a true lady, and she sat me on her lap every day and played with me. She still does so, in my dreams. Fat chance of Mildred ever doing that. She's Pa's second wife. She doesn't even cuddle her own children, never mind Megs and me. She shouts and she slaps and we try our best to keep out of her way.

Jenny and Richie and Pete and Mary and Bert are Mildred's children, our half-brothers and -sisters. Bert is the baby. I carry him even when I'm doing my chores. He howls whenever I set him down. He's fourteen months old so he should be toddling around, but his legs buckle whenever I put his funny fat feet on the floor. Pa's worried that there's something wrong with his legs and he'll end up like Jimmy Wheels, but I think Bert's just lazy.

Jimmy Wheels gets around all right on his trolley, even though he can't walk. Megs used to be frightened of him, especially when he came up close. She squealed like he was a mad dog about to bite her ankles. I had to give her a talking to – Jimmy Wheels is sensitive and I didn't want his feelings hurt. His dad makes it plain he's ashamed of having a crippled son, but Jimmy's got a lovely ma. He's lucky he doesn't have a stepmother like Mildred. Sometimes I think I'd sooner have spider's legs like Jimmy's so long as I didn't have Mildred.

She'd been nagging at me since six in the morning, when we'd lit the copper for the big wash. I hate

Mondays – all that soaking and scrubbing and boiling and rinsing and wringing until my hands are crimson and my arms ache and my dress is soaked right through and even little Bert tied on my back looks as if I've dropped him in a puddle.

But now the sheets and underwear and aprons were flapping on the line across the cobbles, and there were a dozen other lines all down the alley. Only half the folk bother to do a weekly wash. I don't think Old Ma Robinson ever washes her bedding, her clothes or herself. You can smell her coming before you see her.

'What do you want to play then?' I asked.

'Families!' cried little Mary, rolling up her pinafore to make a cloth baby.

'Murderers!' shouted Richie and Pete, pulling manic faces and curving their hands as if about to strangle someone.

'Grand ladies! And I'll be the grandest lady of them all,' said Jenny.

'Races!' said Daft Mo, who had the longest legs.

'Yes, races!' Jimmy Wheels pleaded, because he was the fastest of all, thumping his hands down on the cobbles and rattling along like a cannon ball. He could speed freely under the sheets, and didn't mind being dripped on either, but the rest of us would be slapped in the face by wet cotton as soon as we took a few strides. But the white sheets had given me an idea.

'We'll play sailing ships,' I said, seizing the bottom of a sheet and making it billow in the wind.

We'd never seen the sea and hadn't seen any sailing ships when we walked all the way to see the filthy Thames – just barges and tugs and rowing boats – but every child had peered at the tattered pages of the nursery-rhyme book I'd stolen off the second-hand stall in the market.

I was the only one who could read. Mr Dolly had taught me when I was six or so. I was already in charge of Megs and Jenny and Richie, who bawled non-stop when he was a baby. Mr Dolly was shocked that Mildred wouldn't let me go to school, but I was much more use at home being her skivvy and minding the little ones. Mr Dolly said it was a shame because I was a bright little thing, so he showed me all my letters and made me figure out a story about P-a-t the d-o-g and J-e-t the c-a-t, and before I knew it I could read any column in his newspaper, though I didn't have a clue what all the politics were about.

I loved my stolen nursery-rhyme book though. I learned the rhymes by heart and could see every detail of the coloured illustrations even when I closed my eyes. *I Saw Three Ships* was one of my favourites, especially the comic duck in Navy uniform peering through his tele-scope. Mr Dolly let me peer through his old telescope to see how it worked. He didn't need to explain the Navy to me though, because you can see Peg-leg Jack any day of the week down the Admiral's Arms public house.

So we played sailing ships. We each seized a sheet and shook it hard and jumped up and down, pretending we were sailing on a choppy sea. I let Jimmy Wheels have Mrs Watson's longest double sheet that nearly trailed on the ground when she hung it on the line. He seized hold of it, rearing his head up and singing his version of a sea shanty. His hard, calloused hands were filthy from propelling himself along the ground, so the bottom of the sheet suddenly had a new black palm-print pattern. I hoped Mrs Watson wouldn't notice when she came to take in her washing.

We shook our sheets, pretending to race each other, and then I seized hold of the big black apron Daft Mo's ma uses when she's out with the coal cart.

'Watch out, sailors, here's an enemy ship approaching!' I yelled, waving the apron.

'That's just a piddly little ship! *My* ship's much, much bigger,' said Richie scornfully.

'Yes, we're not scared of teeny tiny enemies,' said Pete. 'We'll push them overboard!'

'They're small all right, but they're deadly,' I said, waving the black sail. 'Can't you see the flag they're flying? It's a skull and crossbones. Oh Lordy, pirates!'

'Pirates!' the girls shrieked.

'Yes, pirates, and I can see their captain at the helm. He's small but he's burly, with a big black beard and bloodstains all down his pirate cloak and a peg leg,' I said.

'I'll bet it's just Peg-leg Jack that you can see and I ain't afraid of him,' said Pete.

'No, this is a real pirate captain, I'm telling you, and he's got a hook for a hand that'll rip the innards out of you, and a cutlass in his teeth that will take your head off at one blow,' I said, to make him squeal. He picks on my Megs sometimes, so he needs to be put in his place.

'He's not really there, is he?' little Mary quavered, hiding behind her own sheet.

I shook my head quickly to reassure her, but then shouted for everyone else's benefit, 'He's coming, he's coming, his ship is getting nearer! Any minute now he'll swing over on his special rope with all his pirate army and he'll have your guts for garters. Watch out, Pete – he always goes after boys like you first, to stop them telling tales.'

Pete waved his sheet violently. 'He's not going to get me. I'm sailing away, faster, faster. I'm leaving that silly, smelly old pirate far behind, see!' he yelled. He tugged his sheet so hard there was a sudden snap as the frayed washing line broke. All the sheets sailed to the ground and lay in a sodden heap.

'Oh Lord, better run for it!' I shouted – but we weren't quick enough.

Mrs Watson came charging out of her house, her blouse wide open because she'd been in the middle of feeding her baby when she heard our shouts.

'You wicked, pesky little varmints!' she bellowed. 'I spent all blimming morning washing them sheets. Who did it? Was it you, Clover Moon? You're always the ringleader in any mischief. You wait till I tell your mother!'

Pete stared at me, red in the face with fear and guilt, terrified that I'd say it was him. But I wasn't a pathetic little tell-tale.

'See if I care,' I said. 'And that woman's not my real mother anyway.'

I hitched Bert higher up my back and marched off. Megs ran after me, thumb in her mouth like a stopper.

'Oh, Clover,' she said indistinctly. 'Oh, Clover, now you're for it! She'll wallop you.'

'Then I'll turn round and wallop *her*,' I said, though we both knew that Mildred was much bigger than me, and far stronger too. Her arms were like great hams from heaving huge trays of bottles at the sauce factory before she married our pa. She walloped seriously, with all her strength, until her face was as pink and moist as ham too. 'Yes, I'll wallop Mildred – *whack-whack-whack* – and then I'll tip her in the coal hole and lock the door on her, and then you and me will run away together,' I declared. 'Perhaps Bert can come too. If he's good.'

'Will we really?' Megs asked, her eyes round.

'Of course we will!'

'But where will we go? And where will we live?'

'We'll run away to the seaside and we'll go sailing, just like we played. And we'll make a house in an old boat on the sands. We'll make it so cosy. We'll have one bed with lots of blankets and soft pillows, and we can squash up into one chair. It'll be such fun playing there.'

'What will we eat?' asked Megs.

'We'll eat fish of course. I'll go fishing every day and catch lots of fishes, and then we'll make a fire on the beach and cook them in a frying pan for our dinner, and we'll buy day-old bread and a pot of jam for our tea,' I said.

Behind me, Bert heard the word *jam* and started crowing and clapping, thinking he was about to get a spoonful. His cries became urgent.

'In a minute, Bert. Megs is going to take you home,' I told him.

'No! We're running away, the three of us,' said Megs.

'I wish we could. We will soon. But we need to save some pennies first,' I said. 'Now go back home, Megs. Don't worry about Mildred. You know she hardly ever wallops you. You can say you were looking for me but couldn't find me. And then say Bert started crying so you took him home. Go on now.'

'But what will you do?'

'I'll sneak off by myself for a few hours until I know Pa's home. She won't be so fierce with me then,' I said.

'Oh, Clover, I don't like to think of you by yourself. And I'm not good with Bert the way you are,' said Megs. 'I don't think he likes me much.'

'He absolutely loves you, Megs.' I loosened the ragged blanket tying Bert to me and eased him round to my front. 'There, Bertie – give your sister a big toothy grin. You love your Megs, don't you, darling? Pull a funny face at him, Megs, and tickle his tummy. That's it – make a big fuss of him.'

Megs tickled Bert and he hunched up, chuckling.

'There now! He's laughing at you. Look, he's holding out his hands. You want a cuddle with Megs, don't you, Bert?' I unravelled him and thrust him into Megs's arms.

'I can't suck my thumb now,' said Megs, struggling.

'Well, you can't in front of Mildred anyway, because she'll rub bitter aloes on it and then you won't be able to suck it for ages. Here, I'd better tie Bert to you, just in case he wriggles too much and you drop him. We don't want him ending up like poor Daft Mo, do we?' I said, busily binding him tightly to Megs's narrow chest. 'Don't wriggle so, Bert! Tuck your little arms in, there's a good boy.'

I got them sorted and then gave Megs a little pat on the shoulder. 'Off you go, lovey. I'll see you later.'

'You'll miss your tea.'

'Never mind. Maybe I'll go down the market and scrounge something. I'll be all right. Bye now.' I ran off quickly, knowing Megs couldn't run fast enough to catch me up, especially lugging Bert. I ran to the end of Cripps Alley, down Winding Lane, and then ducked into Jerrard's Buildings and hid halfway up their stairwell. It was pitch dark there, and you could hear if anyone was coming.

I hunched up, my head on my knees, and had a little private weep.

'Hard as nails,' Mildred always said, because no matter how hard she walloped I'd never cry in front of her. I'd clench my teeth and ball my fists and glare right back at her. One time she hit me so hard I fell over and whacked my head against the fender, but even then I didn't cry. Afterwards my shoulder bled so much I couldn't peel my frock off, and my forehead came up in a lump as big as a hen's egg, and I was so groggy I nearly fell down again when I was pulled up – but I *still* didn't cry because that would mean Mildred had won and I was never, ever going to let her.

I didn't cry doing the chores, not even when I burned my hand on the iron. I didn't cry when the big lads from the Buildings seized hold of me one Saturday night when Pa sent me out for a jug of ale. I didn't cry in front of anyone. Of course I cried in bed when the pinky-purple burn throbbed, of course I cried as I tried to scratch the feel of the lads' hands away when I was alone in the privy, of course I cried privately for my own mother when I saw Jimmy Wheels' ma watching out for him tenderly.

I wished Mother was with me now as I huddled on the stairs and wept. I imagined her putting her arm around me, rocking me gently, murmuring words of comfort. I tried smoothing my own hair, hugging my own shoulders, whispering softly to myself.

'*There now, Clover. Don't cry so. I know you were only trying to look after all the kids. You weren't making deliberate mischief. You just wanted to get them all playing so they could have a bit of fun. Don't fret – if Pa's home Mildred won't whack you too hard. And even if she does, you're strong, you can bear it, you're used to it,*' I mumbled. I slipped my hand down the back of my dress and felt the long raised scars on my shoulders. '*It won't hurt for long,*' I lied. '*Come on, you've had your weep. Dry your eyes and get cracking before someone stumbles over you in the dark.*'

I scrubbed at my face with the hem of my dress and then took a deep breath. It was a mistake because half the lads mistook the stairway for a urinal. I ran down the stairs for a gulp of fresher air and then set off down the road, head up, arms swinging, trying to look as if I didn't have a care in the world.

I got to the market and eyed up the fruit on the stalls, wondering if I dared snatch an apple or an orange and then run for it. Most of the stallholders knew all us kids from the alley and yelled at us to clear off if we came too near. I'd do better later, when they were packing up for the night. Old Jeff the Veg saw me sighing and offered me a carrot.

'Thanks, Jeff!' I said gratefully, taking a large bite. The carrot was old and woody, but it was better than a raw potato, which I'd sometimes eaten in desperation.

I wandered off and stood outside the bread shop, breathing in the warm smell of newly baked loaves, pretending the carrot in my mouth was delicious crust. Inside, Mrs Hugget saw me staring but turned away to serve a lady. She was good to Jimmy Wheels and Daft Mo and gave them free currant buns, but she'd never weaken when it came to the rest of us.

I so loved Mrs Hugget's buns. Once a gentleman gave me a shilling for handing him the wallet that had just fallen out of his pocket. I spent it all on a huge bag of buns, some with currants, some with icing, some with extra lard and spice. I shared them with all the children in our alley and we had a lovely feast, though I suffered for it when Mildred got wind of my sudden good fortune.

'You should have handed that money over to me, you useless spendthrift. I'm your mother!' she'd said, shaking me.

'You are *not* my mother, thank the Lord,' I'd said, so she shook me harder, flapping me like a dusty doormat. For two pins I think she'd have used a carpet beater on me.

Still, I was the winner that day. I'd bought the buns and shared them immediately because I knew that once she saw the money she'd want to get her hands on it. We all had our buns safely in our stomachs. In fact Megs had two because there'd been one left over and I insisted she have it because she's the skinniest.

I looked hopefully at passing gentlemen now, and any ladies with dangling reticules, but couldn't spot any fallen wallets or purses today. I walked on, chewing the last of my carrot, dodging in and out of the stalls, then skipping quickly down the length of the road to warm myself up. I didn't have a shawl, let alone a coat, and my feet were always cold because the soles of my boots were patched with newspaper.

I saw myself reflected in the shop windows and turned my head abruptly. That ragamuffin girl with tangled black hair and ugly rags wasn't *me*. I wasn't Clover Moon from Cripps Alley. I was little Miss Clover-Flower Moonshine from one of the big villas opposite the park, and I was on my way with my mama to choose a new doll for my birthday present.

I slowed down and walked more decorously because my imaginary mama told me it wasn't ladylike to skip in the street.

'*Watch your conduct, Clover-Flower,*' she said. '*You need to set an example to all the poor ragged children who play in the gutters.*'